MARRY *Me* TOMORROW

MARRY *Me* TOMORROW

JESS JEFFERIES

JUST ADD INK PUBLISHING

Marry Me Tomorrow

Copyright © 2025 by Jess Jefferies

All rights reserved.

Any references to historical events, real people, or real places are used fictitiously. Names, characters, and places are products of the author's imagination.

Paperback ISBN: 979-8-9873301-4-2

E-book ISBN: 979-8-9873301-5-9

First printing, 2025.

Library of Congress Control Number: 2025900196

Just Add Ink Publishing

Murfreesboro, TN

JustAddInkPublishing@gmail.com

Book Cover by Melody Jeffries

Interior design by Jess Jefferies

Also by Jess Jefferies
Unlucky In Love Series
Thirteen-Year Crush
Bumping into You
Marry Me Tomorrow

To anyone who has been hurt before, here's to finding your strength to keep going. You are worthy, you are seen, and you are stronger than you know.

And to those up against a wall, know that even the toughest walls crumble.

MARRY *Me* TOMORROW

Chapter 1
Trent

The lake glimmers under the morning sun as I walk down the marina dock. Golden light scatters on top of ripples that lap lazily against the dock posts. At the far end of the dock, a single fisherman sits and adjusts his line. His battered hat casts a shadow over a face weathered from time.

"Good morning," I call out, my voice breaking the stillness. "How's the fishing going?"

He looks up, the corners of his mouth lifting into a faint smile. "A few nibbles but not much else. The fish must be sleeping in today."

I chuckle, stopping a few feet away. "They have a habit of doing that. I'm Trent, by the way."

Straightening slightly, the man tips his hat in greeting. "Nice to meet you, Trent. I'm Henry. Henry Monroe. It's my first time back here in years, actually. Just moved into the senior home down the street."

"Chessie Valley Homes by the Lake?" I ask.

"That's the one," Henry replies with a nod. "Figured I'd take advantage of being so close to the water. Used to fish here all the time."

I gesture toward his fishing gear, noticing the careful arrangement of lures and a thermos close by. "Looks like you've still got the touch, even if the fish aren't cooperating."

He chuckles softly, a sound that seems to carry the weight of unspoken memories.

"What brings you down here, Trent?"

"I work here. I've actually been running the place for almost a year and a half now. I took over the marina for my parents, Edmund and Maureen Hughes. They are ready to retire."

"I know your parents, good people. Managing the marina is a big commitment to take on," Henry says, his tone equal parts curiosity and admiration.

"Doesn't feel that way to me," I say shrugging. "This marina has been a part of my life as long as I can remember. My parents ran this place since before I was born. I was raised here. I played on our double decker pontoon boats with my friends when we were kids, pretending to be pirates. I broke my leg climbing trees, testing out all the best ones as we created new trails for the hikers. As I grew, I started working here every summer, soaking up the rhythms of the lake. There isn't a corner of the marina I don't know or a task I can't handle. And when I went off to college, I studied business, dreaming of the day I'd take over the place."

"It's nice to have some place where you feel you belong," Henry says, his voice thick with something heavy. He glances at the water. "I want to try to get down here most mornings. Gives me something to look forward to. I need that these days."

I sit down on the edge of the dock, the wood warm beneath me. "You mentioned it's your first time back in years. If you don't mind me asking, what brought you back here after all this time? Other than moving into the senior home down the street."

Henry's smile wavers. He looks away, his eyes catching on the autumn trees lining the shore. Their leaves blaze in fiery reds and oranges reflected on the still surface of the lake. For a moment, he seems lost in the scene before him.

"I lost Cora, my wife," he says, his voice quieter now. "She passed away about fourteen months ago. After, I had medical bills piling up, and it was getting harder for me to live alone. My granddaughter came up to help. We did everything we could, but it wasn't enough. We needed more money." He pauses, swallowing hard. "And I didn't want that life for her, taking care of an old man. So, I told my granddaughter to sell my house and that I'd move into Chessie Valley Homes by the Lake. It was the right thing to do—but losing my wife and my home so close together . . ." His words trail off, carried away by the faint breeze making ripples in the water.

"I'm sorry to hear that," I say gently. "That's a lot to go through in such a short time."

Henry nods. His weathered hands adjust the fishing rod with practiced care. "It's been tough, but we've been able to use the money from the house sale to pay some of the bills and to cover my costs at the care center. I know things are still tight, but my granddaughter is helping me manage it all. She's doing her best for me. And this place? It's not so bad. Being near the water helps. Makes me feel close to my Cora again. She loved it here. We'd come all the time—picnics, fishing, just sitting together. You were a lot younger then." His eyes meet mine, sharp yet softened by memory and scanning my face as if seeing something familiar. "You remind me of myself when I was younger, you know. Full of life, full of hope."

The unexpected compliment leaves a pang in my chest of something I can't quite name. "Thanks. That means a lot. If you ever need company down here, just let me know. I'm always around the marina."

Henry's smile returns, tentative but genuine. "I might take you up on that, Trent. Nice to have someone to talk to."

"And maybe next time," I say, grinning, "we'll get those fish to cooperate."

He laughs, a low, warm sound that feels like the first hint of spring after a long winter. "Here's hoping."

The conversation I had with Henry lingers with me throughout the day. I can't shake the sadness that clung to Henry's words, the quiet grief woven through his story. The weight of it all still sits heavy in my chest.

He reminds me of my own grandfather Samson and how lost he was after his wife passed. Her absence shattered us all, but it was easy to see it hit Grandfather the hardest. I can still picture the way he'd sit in her favorite chair, staring out at the water like he was waiting for her to come back home. I don't know how he would have pulled through without our family rallying around him.

I think of Henry's love for his wife and their connection to the marina. It stirs something deep within me. The way he finds solace here, how just being near the water connects him to his late wife—it feels significant. I understand that pull, because my own soul is tethered to this marina.

If I ever lost the marina, I know I'd feel the same—a longing to return, to hold onto what it represents, onto what it means to me. It's not just a place; it's a lifeline. And somehow, that makes me feel inexplicably drawn to Henry, as though we share an unspoken understanding.

Then the thought strikes me, clear and certain. I grab my phone and quickly search for the number to Chessie Valley Homes by the Lake.

It only rings once before a cheerful voice answers. "Chessie Valley Homes by the Lake, this is Edna. How can I help you?"

"Hi," I say, my voice steady, determined. "I was wondering if it's possible to make payments toward a resident's monthly fees—anonymously, if that's okay. Maybe call it a discount they've earned or something, so they don't get suspicious. Would that work?"

The line goes quiet, and for a second, I wonder if I've lost Edna. "Are you still there?"

"Yes," Edna replies, her voice a little choked. "Yes, I'm here. And yes, that's absolutely possible. What a thoughtful gesture."

"It's for Henry," I say. "Henry Monroe."

"Oh, Mr. Monroe? That's wonderful. He's such a kind man. Thank you."

"I'd like to pay a thousand a month recurring for him."

"Oh dear, that is so generous. Thank you so much."

We finalize the details, and I hang up feeling lighter than I have all day. The thought that I might have eased even a fraction of Henry's burden fills me with quiet satisfaction. My day passes with a smile plastered to my face.

When I enter the marina office building, Greg, my best friend and the marina's marketing director, leans his head out of his office. "What if," he says, "we added trivia nights or karaoke nights and hosted them in the lodge starting in April or May?"

I stop walking and lean against the doorway to his office. "I think that sounds fun. Do we know anyone who could emcee something like that?"

Greg swivels in his chair, his pen tapping rhythmically against his desk. "There are a few businesses that go around to different places. I'm sure if we made it a regular thing, we could get a good deal."

"Alright, sounds good to me. I've really got to get someone in to help manage the marina shop, though." I step inside and sink into one of the chairs across from his desk. "Where are we on applicants?" The faint hum of Greg's computer fan fills the room, mingling with the muted sound of voices from the marina shop.

Greg's office is almost the same as mine—same desk, chairs and setup, just without the meeting table—but you can tell he is married. Holly, his wife, has her little touches all over the office. Framed photos of them, a plant by his window, they all show she cares. It makes my office look dull and a bit pathetic in comparison.

Greg types on his keyboard, his brow furrowed. "No one else has applied since that last guy from Middle Tennessee State University. But you didn't want him . . ."

"Because he wouldn't be able to work full-time." I run a hand through my hair, sighing. "I just don't understand how we can't find someone who isn't a college kid to take this job. It's decent benefits and good pay."

"I know, man. In the meantime, we can keep switching off and on shifts. Of course, your mom has offered to come back and help."

"You know I can't have her do that. She wants to enjoy her retirement, and I don't want them to think I can't handle the marina myself. You know?"

"Yeah, I get it. The right person will come along. We just have to be patient. It's not like you're going to just run into the perfect person out of the blue."

"No kidding. Wouldn't that be great?" I stand and stretch, the chair squeaking as I push it back. "I'm going to head to my office. I've got to try and make a dent in the paperwork that's been piling up."

Greg chuckles. "Good luck with that."

A Few Months Later . . .

Chapter 2

Jenny

"What do you mean I can't get a loan?" I say, frustration simmering in my voice as I face some finance guy in a crumpled suit. His tie is slightly askew, and he peers down his long, pointed nose at me, his glasses sliding down to the edge.

"It means, Miss Monroe, that you don't have any collateral, so we can't in good conscience loan you that sum of money," Mr. Finance Guy says, his tone dripping with condescension. He adjusts the papers in front of him, the faint rustle of them sounding overly loud in the sterile, overly bright office. "You said it yourself; you don't have a full-time job. How could we expect you to repay the loan?"

"My grandparents had their home loan through you all for over thirty years," I say, my voice straining. I will not cry in front of Mr. Finance Guy. "You know we're good for the money."

"Ah, yes," he replies with a smug smile that makes my stomach twist. "It's unfortunate that you sold the home. We could have taken out equity from the property to loan you the money."

"But we had to sell it," I say, the words spilling out quickly. My fingers curl into fists at my sides. "We need the money from the house to cover Grandma's medical bills and Grandpa's care center costs."

"I'm sorry, but my answer stands," he says curtly, not sounding sorry at all as he closes the file with an air of finality. The swish of the paper echoes ominously. "If your circumstances change, though, we'd be happy to reconsider."

I nod solemnly, swallowing the lump rising in my throat. I'm not sure how much longer I can afford a place to stay and covering Grandpa's retirement home payments and the never-ending medical bills. The money from selling the house will only last so long.

As I step out of the bank into the cold winter air, the world feels both too loud and eerily distant. The chatter of people on the street blends into the faint hum of passing cars, and the brisk air only amplifies the cold knot of uncertainty twisting in my chest.

I'll just have to figure out a solution. I've always been able to land on my feet, and this will be no different.

Still rifling through the papers from the bank as I enter the crosswalk, I hear someone yell, "Look out!"

Before I can process what's happening, I'm yanked back into a wall of arms and muscle. The force of the pull and the slick, icy sidewalk send me stumbling backward. I lose my balance and land with a thump on top of a stranger. A car horn blares behind me, sharp and jarring. The sound makes my heart pound as I realize how close I'd been to stepping into traffic.

I take a shaky breath, blinking rapidly, and find myself staring into the most startling blue eyes I've ever seen.

"You okay?" the stranger asks softly, his voice warm and steady.

I nod quickly, my cheeks burning as I scramble to find my voice. "Yes, thank you," I say, my words coming out a little breathless.

"My pleasure," he says with a crooked smile that's almost as dazzling as his eyes. "But, uh . . . if it's alright with you, do you mind if we stand? The cement and ice aren't the most comfortable, you know?" He gestures at the sidewalk.

My face flames even redder than my red Converse as I realize I'm still half-sprawled across him. "Oh my gosh, I'm so sorry!" I scramble to my feet. "Thank you," I say again, brushing at my jeans as if that will somehow erase the mortification. "I'm sorry. I wasn't paying attention . . . my mind's just been all over the place this morning."

"It's all cool. No sweat," he replies, standing and brushing a speck of dirt off his shirt. "I'm just glad you aren't a pancake in the street. That wouldn't have been a great start to anyone's day."

"No, I can't imagine it would." I freeze, staring up at him. He's tall—at least six-foot-three or four—with messy blond hair peeking out from under a cap that reads "Chessie Valley Lake Marina and Lodge." His tanned skin and relaxed demeanor make him look like someone who spends his days in the sun. But it's his eyes that hold me captive, shimmering like sunlight on water. They are the most stunning I-want-to-swim-in-those-sea-blue eyes I've ever seen. I blink at him, lost for words.

"Miss?" he says, waving a hand in front of my face. "Are you sure you didn't hit your head?"

"Oh. I'm—" I feel my brain short-circuiting. "Yes. I mean, no, I'm okay. I'm sorry, did you ask me something?"

He chuckles softly, the sound low and warm. "I asked what your name was and if you needed anything, but I think I know the answer to my own question."

"Oh?" I ask, tilting my head in confusion. How could he possibly know who I am or what I need?

"Yes, you need one of Holly's famous Sunrise Sin muffins." He gestures for me to follow him down the street. "Are you allergic to oranges?"

I nod my head, then quickly correct myself. "Err, no, I'm not. Allergic to oranges, that is."

"Great! You'll love For the Love of Sugar. We'll be there lickety-split."

Who is this man? And maybe I did bump my head, because no one is this cheerful after being knocked on their back by some crazy, scatterbrained stranger—not that I'm crazy but . . . well I sure am starting to feel like it.

We walk past a few storefronts, the scent of fresh bread and coffee wafting through the air. The faint hum of downtown Chessie Valley fills my ears, the buzz of conversation and the occasional laughter blending into the background. We pass a sign denoting this as Chessie Valley Square, the heart of downtown Chessie Valley.

"Here we are," he announces, opening a door with a sign that reads For the Love of Sugar. We step into a cozy bakery. The warm scent of vanilla and cinnamon envelops me.

"Holly!" he calls out cheerfully. "We need two Sunrise Sin muffins, stat!"

"Hold your horses, Trent," replies a petite brunette with a huge bun of hair atop her head. She must be Holly. She's busy filling an order for another customer, her smile kind and her hands moving with efficient precision.

Once the customer leaves, Holly turns to us, her expression shifting to one of concern. "Are you okay?" she asks me. "Trent, what did you do to her?" She swats the arm of the man that brought me here before coming around the counter to inspect me.

"You're bleeding!" she says. "Let me get my first aid kit." Her tone leaves no room for argument. I open my mouth to protest, but she's already darted away.

"Shoot!" Trent says. "You are."

I see the scrape on the palm of my hand. "I didn't notice," I say. I call after Holly, "Really, it's alright. It's just a little scratch."

"Nonsense," she replies, returning with a small kit in hand. "It'll only take a minute. Then I'll get you Sunrise Sin muffins and maybe a Butter Me Up bar too."

"Oh, I couldn't," I begin, but she cuts me off with a raised hand.

"It's on the house," she says. "Please, as a favor to me. I have to make up for whatever this oaf of a man did." She shoots Trent a glare.

"Dude!" Trent says. "I didn't do anything." He holds up his hands defensively. "Honest, I just saved . . ." He turns to me and whispers, "What's your name?"

"Jenny," I whisper back.

"Right, I just saved Jenny here from being flattened like a pancake by a car in the street. I'm a hero. Don't I deserve a little recognition for my heroic acts?"

Holly rolls her eyes but smiles as she tends to my scrape. "Probably your fault in the first place," she mutters.

"You two are the funniest siblings," I say with a hesitant laugh, hoping to lighten the mood.

Both of them freeze, wide-eyed, before bursting into laughter. "Dude," Trent says, "Greg would die if he heard that!"

"Oh, no, Jenny," Holly says, still chuckling. "We're not siblings. We've just been friends since childhood. I'm happily married to his best friend, Greg." She holds out her hand to show off a simple but elegant wedding band.

After cleaning up my scrape, Holly hands me two orange-cinnamon muffins and a vanilla-coconut bar. "These are my Sunrise Sin muffins and a Butter Me Up bar."

Trent grabs one of the muffins, stuffs the whole thing in his mouth, and turns to leave. "I've got to head back to the marina," he says. "The place won't run itself."

"I'm sorry," I say, "I didn't mean to keep you."

He swallows, then waves off my apology with a grin. "No need for that. I was happy to help. I hope this turns your day around. Just keep your head up when walking near the street, okay?"

I nod, watching as he jaunts out the door, his easy stride radiating confidence. Once he's gone, I settle into a chair and pull out my sketchpad. I don't normally sketch people, but there's something about Trent—that mix of warmth and energy—that I need to capture. My pencil moves across the page, sketching his bright smile and those lake-blue eyes.

An hour later, my food is untouched, but the sketch is finished. It's not perfect. I normally go for the more abstract and landscape drawings, but it captures the essence of the man who saved me.

"Wow." Holly's voice startles me. "That's amazing," she says, her eyes wide with admiration. I snap the sketchpad closed, embarrassed. I'd been so lost in my art that I'd forgotten where I was.

"I'm sorry," she says. "Just normally people finish my baked goods quickly, and when you didn't, I thought something was wrong. Plus you'd been so focused, I just wanted to check and make sure everything was okay." She looks at me a moment. "Is it? Okay, that is?" she asks gently. The question, paired with the morning's events, makes my throat tighten.

"Yes . . . no . . . I don't know, honestly," I sniffle a little as the morning at the bank and nearly getting hit by a car comes crashing back to me. "Any chance you're hiring?" I said softly, almost jokingly.

A sad but contemplative look crosses Holly's eyes, her gaze momentarily distant. "Unfortunately, I'm not," she says, her voice tinged with regret. But then, as if struck by an idea, her expression brightens. "But I know who is. And I happen to be good friends with him."

Before I can respond, she glances toward the counter, calling back to another baker bustling behind the glass display case. "I'm taking a break!" she announces, wiping her hands on her apron. With a bright smile, she pulls out the chair across from me and sits down, her enthusiasm evident in the way she leans forward slightly, her elbows resting on the table.

She shares everything there is to know about the Chessie Valley Lake Marina and Lodge. Her words flow with the ease of someone who not only knows the place intimately but holds genuine affection for it. As she speaks, I can almost picture it—rustic wooden docks, shimmering water, the hum of activity mixed with the calm of the lake. The artist in me itches to paint it, and I haven't even seen it yet.

"That place sounds wonderful," I say, my heart lifting as hope stirs in my chest. "And from what you're saying, it's an assistant-type position."

"That's right."

"I could definitely handle that."

Holly's lips twitch, suppressing a smile, as she says, "There's one more thing I haven't mentioned yet, and I hope it doesn't sway you from interviewing."

"Oh no," I reply, a knot forming in my stomach. "What is it?" The hope that had been bubbling up inside me threatens to evaporate just as quickly.

She hesitates, then finally says, "Trent, the one who brought you in here . . ."

I nod slowly, encouraging her to continue.

"Well," she says, "he runs the marina, so you'd be interviewing with him."

Relief washes over me as I laugh lightly. "Oh, that doesn't sound bad at all! You made it seem like there was going to be some awful catch. Trent was so kind to me today. It shouldn't be a problem to work with him." That tiny flicker of hope starts to settle more comfortably in my chest.

Holly waves a hand as though brushing away her earlier hesitation. "He is kind. I just wasn't sure . . ." She trails off, her lips twitching again before shaking her head. "You know what? Never mind. I'm in love with this idea, and think you'd be perfect for the position." Her enthusiasm is infectious as she adds, "I'll talk to my husband Greg—you remember I told you he handles the marina's marketing—and I'll make sure you have an interview first thing tomorrow."

"You're heaven-sent," I say, the weight in my chest easing for the first time in days. Then, a thought occurs to me. "Do you also happen to know of a place to stay?"

Her brows lift, and she tilts her head slightly, studying me as though piecing something together. "Did you just come to town?"

"No," I say, shaking my head. "I've been staying in a motel. I was living with my grandpa, but we just sold his house and moved him to an assisted living home, so now I'm looking for a place to stay—one that's on the cheaper side."

"That's awful," she says genuinely. "Rentals are so hard to come by here." She pauses for a moment, clearly searching her mental filing cabinet. "Unfortunately, I don't know of anywhere right now," she says, her tone apologetic. "But I'll keep my ears open for you and let you know the moment I hear something!"

Chapter 3
Trent

"Good morning, Henry," I call as I make my way down the dock, the crisp pre-spring air carrying the faint scent of the last of the frost melting away. "How's my favorite regular this morning?"

"Trent, my friend!" Henry's face lights up. "It's good to see you. I'm thrilled the weather's warming up early this year. Winter's not much for fishing—or being outdoors."

I glance at Henry's hands now, steady on the rod. The calluses on his fingers tell stories of years spent working as a woodworker that shaped his quiet, thoughtful demeanor. He's the kind of man I hope to be one day—someone who's lived a life full of love and family, who feels their absence so deeply it hurts. The kind of man who can still find solace in a quiet morning on the water.

The sun is warm on my back, a stark contrast to the cold breeze hitting my face as I sit down beside him, the bench creaking under my weight. The faint splash of a fish breaking the surface interrupts the stillness, and a dragonfly flits by, hovering just above the water.

"Well, it looks like a great day for fishing," I say, stretching my legs out in front of me. "It's early in the season, but it shouldn't hurt the potential catch."

"Nope, even in January. There are plenty of fish in the lake." Henry casts his line out again with a smooth flick of his wrist. The lure makes a soft plop as it hits the water. "Shouldn't be hard for an old man like me to catch one. What about you, though? Have any fish caught your eye lately?"

I laugh at his not-so-subtle mention of my dating life. "The marina keeps me plenty busy," I say, leaning back and resting my arms along the back of the bench. The wood feels rough in some places under my fingers but worn smooth in other places from years of use.

Henry shakes his head, a small smile tugging at the corners of his mouth. "Well, don't let it take over your life. You ought to have someone you can share that kind heart with. Other than us old fishermen who bother you and those guests you always have coming and going."

"You're no bother," I reply, patting him lightly on the shoulder. "But you best be careful, or you'll start sounding like my mom."

"I've always liked Maureen, nice lady. You ought to listen to her," he says, chuckling softly. His laughter is like the creak of a rocking chair, warm and familiar.

I laugh too, standing and brushing the dust off my jeans. "Alright, enough of that. You've got fish to catch, and I've got a marina to run. See you around, Henry."

As I walk away, I glance back to see him adjusting his hat, his gaze fixed on the water. The rhythmic click of his reel follows me down the dock. The cool breeze stirs the leaves in the trees lining the shore, carrying with it the faint scent of pine.

What is it with everyone trying to marry me off? Lately, my parents and even grandfather have been grilling me about my dating life. And now Henry too. What is everyone so worried about? I'm a happy bachelor living my best life. So what if my life is consumed by this marina? It's been working out so far, right?

And yeah, someday I want that right person for me. But someday can wait a bit longer, in my opinion.

"Good morning," Greg calls out, his voice cutting through the soft hum of the AC unit as he strides into the office. His tone carries an unusual energy.

"Good morning to you too," I say. "Someone seems extra chipper this morning." I barely glance up as I scan the rentals scheduled for today. The faint smell of paper and ink mixes with the lingering scent of lake water from my morning rounds. Two groups are coming in for pontoon rentals, and a few regulars will pick up fishing boats—a steady start to the day, though the to-do list is already long.

Greg's boots thud across the wooden floor, the sound slightly muffled by the worn area rug, as he approaches my desk. He sets down a paper bag with a triumphant grin. "I bring good news," he announces, his voice carrying the same excitement as a kid on Christmas morning.

A rich, sugary aroma wafts up from the bag, immediately triggering a low growl from my stomach. It's a smell I'd recognize anywhere: Holly's Sunrise Sin muffins. My mouth waters just thinking about the warm, gooey center of oranges and the flakey cinnamon-sugar topping.

"Dude, did you bring my favorites?" I rub my hands together like I'm about to dig into a treasure trove. Food might as well be my sixth love language, and Holly's baked goods? They're practically legendary. It's a good thing I have this marina to look after because if not, I'd easily gain a hundred pounds.

"Yep," Greg replies, his smile growing. "And good news. Did you hear that part?"

I'm already unwrapping a muffin, the wax paper crinkling under my fingers. "Sorry, got distracted by the muffins. What's this good news you bring me this fine morning?"

Greg shakes his head, amused, and leans casually against the corner of my desk. "I found you a manager for the marina shop."

I'm so caught off guard that I inhale my muffin too quickly, choking on the cinnamon sugar crumbs. "You what?" I croak between coughs, my eyes watering as I fumble for the water bottle on my desk.

"I found you a manager," Greg repeats, clearly amused by my reaction. "You know, for the position you've had me post on the website for months now? I found someone to fill it."

"Without me interviewing them?" I rasp, still recovering my breath.

Greg chuckles, crossing his arms. "No, I'm not that crazy. But this person comes highly recommended." He takes a bite of his own muffin, crumbs spilling onto his shirt.

I look at my half-eaten muffin, then narrow my eyes, suspicion creeping into my tone. "Let me guess. Holly recommended this person, didn't she? Is that why she sent in muffins this morning?"

Greg grins, brushing crumbs from his shirt and looking entirely too pleased with himself. "Man, you know Holly has a knack for this kind of thing. Holly told me about the girl she's recommending last night, and I have to say, from what Holly says, you should definitely give this girl a chance. I think she will be just what you need."

I rock back in my chair and glance around at the organized chaos of my office. Stacks of papers threaten to topple over, unsorted orders clutter the desk, and unopened stock boxes are piled haphazardly in the corner. It's not exactly inspiring confidence in my ability to manage it all. I could use some help.

I sigh, rubbing the back of my neck. "I guess I could interview her. She's not a kid, though, right? I don't have time for someone who's going to bail after a month. As we both know, I need some help managing a bit of everything since my parents have stepped back fully."

Though I wish they would help me convince Grandfather to pass ownership to me. Having to go to him for big things takes so much more time than it should.

"Nope, not a kid," Greg says, licking muffin crumbs off his fingers. "She's about our age, from what Holly said."

"Fine," I concede reluctantly. "Let her know I can interview her tomorrow." Greg's sheepish expression stops me in my tracks. "What now?" I ask.

"Well," he says, scratching the back of his head, "Holly might have told her to come by today . . . and that you'd be more than happy to interview her. And I kind of told Holly that would be fine."

"Dude, do you see this place?" I gesture at the mess surrounding me. "I don't even know where I put the job listing."

Pulling off my baseball cap, I rake a hand through my hair before jamming it back on. "And I'm not even dressed for an interview."

Greg waves a hand dismissively. "This is what you wear every day. Nobody's expecting a suit and tie. Besides, I can print a copy of the job listing for you. Give me two minutes."

He darts out the door and across the hall, his footsteps fading quickly. I take a moment to tear into the muffin again, savoring the burst of warm orange-cinnamon filling as it melts in my mouth. Less than two minutes later, Greg's back, waving a freshly printed sheet still warm from the printer like a victory banner.

"Thanks, I guess," I say. "Do you at least know when this mystery girl will—" My question is interrupted by the soft chime of the front door as someone walks into the marina store.

"That's probably her," Greg says, slipping out of the room. "I'll bring her back here. Straighten up a bit while you've got the chance."

"Naw, I'll just interview her outside," I call after him. "I'll walk her around the marina so she gets a feel for the layout."

"Sounds good, man. Good luck." Greg says before heading out the door and back to his office.

I shake my head, eyeing the piles of papers and unfinished projects. But before I can do much more than stack a few papers, I hear a soft, tentative voice call out from the shop.

"Hello? Holly said you'd be here. Is this a bad time?"

The voice is gentle, uncertain, yet strangely familiar.

"Just a moment," I call out, tucking the job listing under my arm and adjusting my hat. My shoes scuff against the floor as I stride toward the door, mentally preparing myself to meet this Holly-approved candidate.

My steps falter the second I see her.

Jenny.

Chapter 4
Jenny

I can do this. I will rock this interview for this job. This job I desperately need. My artwork isn't selling because I haven't been able to do any shows recently after moving back to town to help my grandpa. And I can't keep living in a motel because the cost is just too much. I need somewhere that I can work and make money while I figure everything out. Hopefully this job will be just the thing.

Holly mentioned Trent will be doing the interview. He seemed nice when I met him yesterday. Hopefully, he is in the same good mood today.

"I should have guessed," says Trent with a big grin on his face as he walks forward, stopping in front of me.

"I'm sorry, what do you mean?" I ask, shifting slightly as my bag strap digs into my shoulder.

Trent just shakes his head, then removes his baseball cap, revealing messy hair that looks like it has seen one too many days under that cap. Running his hands through it, he says, "I should have guessed it would be you that Holly sent to me."

"Is there something wrong with me?" I ask. My pulse quickens as my thoughts spiral. I need this job. This interview has to go well, and right now, it's not seeming like it will. Although,

Trent is still smiling, and his eyes twinkle with something that feels more like amusement than judgment.

"No," says Trent, "it's just a very Holly thing to do." He gestures to the front door. "So, let's walk and talk. I'm not your typical boss, and this isn't a typical job. I thought we could walk around the marina and lodge as we talk."

I nod as he holds the door open for me, the soft chime of the bell above the door ringing out as we step into the crisp morning air. The faint scent of lake water and pine greets me, mingling with the lingering aroma of coffee from the shop counter.

"Why do you want this job, Jenny?" he asks, his voice cutting through the soft murmur of distant boat engines.

"Well," I say, my fingers playing with the strap of my bag. I guess I should just be completely honest. "It's not that I necessarily want this job, but I need it."

"Oh?"

"Yeah, I just moved back here from Atlanta. I was raised here but have been working in Atlanta since I graduated from college there. My grandmother recently passed away and because of that, I had to pack up and move here to help my grandpa. I am trying to take care of my grandparents' medical bills and retirement home costs. We sold their house, but the money from the sale is only going to cover so much. That's why I was so distracted yesterday and stepped into traffic without looking, because I'd just left the bank. I was trying to get a loan, but with no collateral to my name and no full-time job . . . well, I was unsuccessful." I pause my long rambling, glancing over at Trent.

His expression is unreadable, but then something in his eyes softens, like a ripple in calm water.

"I'm not looking for a handout," I say. "I am a hard worker. That's how my grandparents raised me to be. And I've held just about any job over the years, so I should be able to handle a marina store."

Trent holds up his hand to pause me, and I stop mid-step, the gravel crunching under my Converse. "You say you've had a variety of jobs, but what is it you did in Atlanta?"

"Oh, that. I'm an artist. Or at least I was trying to be. I had the occasional art show at galleries in Atlanta and did fairly well, but the uncertainty of that won't cover my grandpa's costs."

"I see," Trent says, stopping in front of a gazebo that looks out over the water. A light breeze rustles the nearby trees, carrying the faint scent of the lake as we stand in silence for a moment.

I wish with everything in me that I could read minds. How is it fair that superheroes can do that but I can't? I mean come on, give a girl a break already.

"Let me tell you a bit about the job," says Trent, "so you can see if it's something you'd actually want to do full-time. It requires more than just running the store."

I nod. "Okay."

"What I would need is someone who could run the shop, including restocking, doing inventory, running the register, managing the reservations, and prepping the rentals for the next day. I also need someone to do administrative stuff for me, billing, filing, registering guests, stuff like that. You wouldn't be required to do anything with the boats. I manage all of that." He motions us to walk toward the docks and boats.

The wooden planks of the docks creak slightly as we walk. There are about six docks lined up along the side of the lake, their edges glinting faintly in the sunlight where the water laps against them. Each dock has spots for about ten boats, probably for people who rent out spaces for their boats. Further back, a cluster of fishing and pontoon boats is corralled in a separate dock area, likely holding the rentals. We walk near these as Trent explains more about some of the boat owners and regular rental people.

The way he speaks about each patron, with genuine warmth and a hint of pride, I can tell how much he cares about them and his job. I could tell the first time I met him that he's a people person. This must be the perfect job for that.

"I would be responsible for maintaining the boats," Trent says, "refueling, cleaning, moving them in preparation for the next day, and receiving them from people returning them at the end of the day."

The smell of the lake mixed with the faint chemical sweetness of gasoline from the docked boats lingers in the air, and I nod, taking in the ripples glistening on the water's surface. Somewhere in the distance, the rhythmic hum of an engine drones, fading in and out like a heartbeat for the marina.

"That sounds doable," I say with a smile, brushing a strand of hair away as the breeze plays with it.

"It would also include helping to clean and reset the cabins once we open those in a couple weeks." His tone is casual and his eyes steady, searching mine for any sign of hesitation.

"I can handle that," I say, my voice firm. "I worked part-time as a hotel maid when I was just starting up my art, so I'm not opposed to housekeeping." Memories of scrubbing grout and folding corners of crisp white sheets flicker briefly in my mind.

"Good. Of course, just like with the boats, you wouldn't have to do any maintenance on the cabins. When they open up, you would just manage check-in and checkout and prep for the next guest." His fingers brush absently against a railing as we walk.

"Nothing you're telling me sounds like something I can't handle. And I plan to be around for a long time. I don't want to move away from my grandpa now that he is all alone."

"Understandable," Trent says, nodding as his gaze drifts over the water. "When would you be able to start?"

"What?" I ask, caught off guard. Is he really offering me the job? "You don't want to check references or interview other candidates?" I ask, my tone tinged with incredulity.

"Jenny, I've had this posting up for a few months now, and the only people who have interviewed are college kids who can't work full-time. I need someone who can and is capable, and you fit both categories. Plus, you come highly recommended from someone whose opinion I value more than most."

"But she only just met me," I argue, the warmth of the sunlight on my face doing little to calm my racing thoughts.

"Are you saying you don't want the job?" Trent asks, his eyes bunching in confusion.

"Yes, I mean no, of course I want the job, but that just seemed too easy. And nothing these past few weeks has been easy. Either way, you offered and I accept." I straighten my shoulders and hold out my hand to shake his.

He stares at me a bit before a big smile stretches across his face, the kind that reaches his eyes. He takes my hand in his. His hand is warm in mine and envelops it completely. A shiver runs through me as we shake in agreement.

"So you can start today?" Trent's tone is filled with an eager energy that is almost contagious.

"Yes, if you want to show me the ropes." What else am I going to do? I can't paint in my motel room, and I don't want to just sit there twiddling my thumbs. Plus, it's too early for visiting hours at the retirement home.

"Sounds grreeaat!" he grins, drawing out the word and sounding just like that tiger from the cereal commercials. His dorky enthusiasm makes me chuckle, breaking the last of my tension.

I laugh at his impression as his eyes catch at something over my shoulder. His grin widens. "Henry!" he calls out, waving energetically.

I turn around to see my grandpa heading to one of the docks with his tackle box and fishing pole. Grandpa's face lights up when he spots me.

"Grandpa," I say, rushing over to give him a hug. "What are you doing out here? And so early?" The faint scent of his aftershave and the familiarity of his embrace makes me smile.

"That's your grandpa?" asks Trent, following behind me, his steps echoing lightly on the dock's planks.

"Yes, why?" I respond, glancing between the two of them.

"Because," my grandpa says, "Trent and I are best pals."

I stare at the two of them, dumbstruck, as they share a brief but warm hug.

"Good to see you, young man," my grandpa says to Trent.

"Good to see you Henry," Trent says, grabbing the tackle box and fishing pole from my grandpa. "You ready to catch some fish today?"

Grandpa beams up at him, his grin as wide as I'd seen in weeks. "You betcha. Jenny, I didn't think I'd see you here. What brings you to the marina?"

Trent looks over at me, grinning, "You're going to be seeing her around the marina a lot more now."

"Oh? Why is that?" my grandpa asks.

"I'm going to be working here," I say.

"Remember that office position I was trying to fill?" Trent says.

"Not my Jenny?" Grandpa's voice carries a playful warmth that makes my cheeks heat up. "You mean I'll get to see her pretty face every morning when I come fishing?"

"Of course, Grandpa. I'll be here every morning for the foreseeable future."

"Well, ain't that some great news." He embraces me in another hug. "Will you be commuting from the motel every day?"

"That's the plan," I say.

"Hopefully with this new job," my grandpa says, "you can get out of that motel and get a place nearby soon. I wish I could do more to help you."

My face flushes as Trent glances at me with a raised eyebrow.

"It's fine, Grandpa. I'm sure I won't be there too much longer. I'm sure a rental will open up around here soon. And

as soon as I have a steady paycheck, I'll be able to afford it."
I hope my answer eases some of his worry. But in all truth,
it may be a long time before I can afford a place. I've looked
at rentals around here, and the prices are ridiculous. I may
be in a small town, but it's still close enough to Nashville
that rental prices are high.

Once Trent and I get Grandpa set up on the dock with
his pole, we say our goodbyes. Trent is quiet as we walk back
past the gazebo and head into the store.

We stop behind the front desk where the register is, and
Trent, still quiet, pulls out a book with what looks to be
cabin rental reservations. The quiet rustling of the pages
fills the air, adding to the awkward silence.

When I am just about to fill the silence with my random
thoughts, Trent speaks up, "What if you stayed in one of
the cabins here?"

"What do you mean?" I ask.

"Like, move out of the motel and live in one of the cabins
here."

"I couldn't afford it," I wave him off, shaking my head.

"It would be at no cost," he says.

"What?" I ask, unable to believe I have heard him cor-
rectly.

"What if you stayed in one of the cabins here?" he repeats, his expression earnest.

I shake my head, "No, I heard you, but I can't believe it.
Why would you do that for me?"

"Well, Henry is probably one of my most favorite people
in the world, and I like to help out."

"I don't need charity," I say flatly, crossing my arms.

"Don't think of it as charity. Think of it as you are my store manager, and it's the manager's cabin. It comes with the job."

"Does it really though?"

"Well, I'm the boss, so it does if I say it does."

"What about the profit you'll lose because you won't be renting it out?"

He nods for a minute, looking at the reservation book, his fingers tapping lightly against the counter. "Well, there is one cabin that isn't rented often. It's farther away from the recreational part of the marina and closer to the boat rental location, so people don't like renting it as much. Honestly, it's vacant a good portion of the year. So really, you'd be doing me a favor by living there and upkeeping it."

"I see," I say. What is this guy thinking? He only just met me and offers me a job and now a place to stay . . . FOR FREE? Who is this guy? I debate with myself for a bit, but ultimately, I'd be stupid to pass up this opportunity. Smiling, I hold up one finger, "Well, if I am going to do you this favor, I have one condition."

"Name it," he says, smiling back at me, a glint of amusement in his eyes.

"I can do my painting in the cabin." I say, and then hurry to add. "Of course, I'll use a tarp. I always do when I paint, and if I get anything on the wood, I will sand it and restain it for you when I move out."

"Jenny, stop, it's okay." Trent holds his hand out to me. "I accept your condition."

I take his hand in mine, and we shake in agreement for the second time. That tingle jolts through me again, making me shiver slightly as I pull my hand back.

"Now," I say, "tell me how to run this place. I am going to be the best store manager-assistant this marina has ever seen!" I grin wide enough to match Trent's earlier enthusiasm.

Chapter 5
Trent

Why does my mother always insist on Sunday dinners?

The thought crosses my mind for the tenth time as I navigate the familiar winding road to my parents' house. The gray sky above matches my mood—clouded, heavy, and threatening rain. I'm not looking forward to this dinner because I know the inevitable topic of conversation.

My relationship status. Or rather, my non-existent relationship status.

While running the marina has been easier with Jenny's assistance at the lodge the past two and a half months, I still haven't had time to make any headway on my relationship status.

I step into my parents' house, greeted by the faint scent of roasted garlic and slow-cooked meat. The kitchen, warm and buzzing with activity, looks like something out of a Norman Rockwell painting. My mom, as always, is deftly working over a roast with potatoes, onions, and carrots—our family favorite.

"Hi, Mom."

She turns, wiping her hands on her well-worn apron before pulling me into a hug that smells like rosemary and dish soap. "Hi, Trenton. I'm so happy you could make it," she says, her smile as wide as ever.

"I always make it to Sunday dinners, Mom." My tone is dry, lacking the warmth she probably hoped for.

"Right, of course you do. It's just that lately . . ." Her voice trails off, and I'm silently grateful it does because I know exactly where she was heading.

We work in companionable silence, setting the table and bringing out steaming platters of food. My dad greets me with a nod from his chair, newspaper folded neatly on the side. Dinner begins with an awkward silence I've come to expect over the past couple months. The only sounds are the soft clinks of forks on plates and the low hum of the ceiling fan.

I glance up from my plate and catch my parents exchanging one of those looks. My stomach tightens, knowing what's coming next.

"Just say it." I stab a piece of carrot with my fork. I chew mechanically, the roast suddenly losing its appeal.

"Well," my mom starts cautiously, setting down her fork, "it's just that your father and I have been talking . . ."

"And?" I say, trying not to snap.

My dad clears his throat, his deep voice filling the space. "Son, your grandfather called us earlier this week. It seems like there's been some words exchanged with some of the extended family about the . . . stipulation in the contract for the marina."

Ah, the clause. The one that's been hanging over my head like an anvil. The words, etched in my memory, echo in my mind like a judge's gavel.

The transfer of ownership of the marina to New Owner is contingent upon the New Owner being married at the time of the transfer. This condition is intended to preserve the family-oriented nature of the business. If the New Owner is not married at

*the time of the transfer, they shall forfeit their right to ownership
of the marina, and the business shall instead be passed on to
the next eligible married family member, as determined by the
current owner or their estate.*

My parents never owned the marina. They just ran it while my grandfather retained ownership rights. However, with my parents' retirement and my grandfather not getting any younger, he is ready to pass over the ownership. Of course, since I grew up at the marina and have now managed it for a year and a half on my own, plus all the years of co-running it with my parents, my grandfather would like to transfer ownership to me.

With one catch: I have to be married first.

All of which seems ridiculous to me. What does being married have to do with running a marina? I've proven with my work over the years and with my degree how serious I am about owning and managing the marina and helping it grow and thrive. My relationship status shouldn't have any impact in this. It's frustrating to have this hanging over my head. How am I supposed to fall in love and get married when my life is all about the marina? It just doesn't make sense.

"What do you mean, words were exchanged?" I ask.

My mom shifts uncomfortably. "Well, your Aunt Ida called to tell me her daughter is getting married in the fall and that she'd be happy to take over the marina if you . . . weren't able to."

"Aunt Ida didn't . . ." The words die on my tongue, replaced by stunned disbelief.

"And she wasn't the only one," my dad adds. "We've had several calls this week. When your grandfather called to let us know the family has been expressing interest to him in taking over ownership also, we thought it best to let you know how serious this is getting."

"The extended family," my mom says, "is, well, you know . . ."

"Getting worried," my dad continues. "My father isn't going to be around for too many more years, and he and the rest of the family would like to get the ownership of the marina squared away before he does pass and it gets a lot messier."

"We know how much the marina means to you, Trenton," my mom says. "And we don't want you to lose it."

Dad cuts into his roast. "I don't know how long my siblings are going to be okay with the marina sitting in limbo. You've done a wonderful job managing it, but someone needs to own it—and soon. Your mother and I have put our hearts and souls into this place, but we're tired and ready to see it passed on to the next generation. However, my siblings wouldn't be opposed to taking it over either. As you know, Aunt Ida and Uncle Bert grew up here. And they raised their kids here most summers too. They're all familiar with the marina and would love to own it and perhaps manage it too."

"But Grandfather," my mom says, "agrees the marina is running smoother than it has in years with you managing it, and he wants to pass it on to you."

"But you're not married," Dad says.

My appetite vanishes entirely as I slump back in my chair. "Why can't Grandfather just remove the clause? Why do I have to choose between owning the marina and being married or letting some other family member own it and staying single? I'm not even sure I'm ready for a relationship yet."

"You know," my mom says gently, "he is determined to honor your grandmother's memory. The marina was her pride and joy, and he wants to ensure it stays family-run."

"I know," I murmur, the weight of their words settling heavily on my shoulders. "But that doesn't mean I have to like the clause. This marina is my home, my life. I don't want to lose it."

The next morning, I drag myself into the lodge, my head pounding from the restless night I'd spent replaying the conversation from Sunday dinner. The smell of coffee and pine greets me as I step into the back office, a small comfort amidst the chaos in my mind.

Jenny is at the front desk, her cheerful "Good morning!" bouncing through the space. I wave halfheartedly, too preoccupied to muster a reply.

Jenny has been nothing but a surprise. She picked up everything better than I could have ever imagined, and the last two and a half months have been a blur. Jenny has stepped into my life and put her stamp on everything. The regulars love her like she's everyone's granddaughter, not just Henry's. I never would have thought that my favorite regular would have been Jenny's family.

Henry has gone through so much with the loss of his wife and now losing his home. Not too long ago, I told Jenny, "It was so kind of you to put your dreams on hold to help your grandfather."

"Well," she said, wiping down the glass of a display case, "it was the least I could do, to be there for him. He gave up his retirement to help raise me after my parents left me on my grandparents' doorstep and never looked back."

"I had no idea he raised you," I said. "I'm so sorry your parents did that to you."

Jenny had nodded. "I wouldn't be who I am today without my grandpa Henry's and grandma Cora's love and support. They are everything to me."

Her voice had been so resolute, so full of love and gratitude. The memory stirs something in me, momentarily cutting through the fog in my brain. Now, I look around at how this place has changed over the past few months. Where previously there were bills and mail piled up, there are now neat stacks of organized papers with little pink post-it notes, reminding me when something is due or what I need to focus on.

A faint, citrusy scent of a cleaner lingers in the air, a stark contrast to the usual musty smell of the office. The boxes of extra supplies that once threatened to topple over are gone, neatly stored in the reorganized supply closet. Though it's still not showroom tidy, Jenny has created her own system. If you asked her for a Tanago hook or seven J-hooks, she'd flash you a confident grin and have them in your hands before you could finish asking.

Not only has my office received an overhaul, but the entire store practically sparkles. The items in the store have been moved into new locations and the customers are commenting on how much easier it is to find things.

I sit down at my desk and lean back. It's the first time in a long while that I've felt like I wasn't drowning in paperwork. I can finally enjoy my work without the administrative chaos hanging over me.

Well, except for the bigger anchor pulling me down. That clause may just be the death of me.

A soft knock on the door snaps me back to the present. Jenny stands in the doorway, her blonde ponytail slightly askew, concern flickering in her sapphire eyes. "Hey, boss. You okay? You didn't seem yourself this morning."

I want to brush her off, but the genuine worry in her voice gives me pause. "I'm fine," I say.

She raises an eyebrow. "You sure?"

I hesitate, then sigh. "No. Not really."

Jenny steps inside my office, sinking into the chair opposite me. "Alright, spill. What's got you so grumpy?"

"It's complicated," I admit. "You ever have a problem that you couldn't solve but you keep trying to think of a way to make it work? But then you remember that, oh yeah, you're super busy and don't have time to worry about things like that so you put it off. Only to be reminded that you still have a problem you need to solve?" Taking off my baseball cap, I run a hand through my hair before putting it back on.

"Every day," Jenny says. "But I like solving problems. Why don't you tell me, and maybe I can help?"

I laugh. "Yeah, I doubt that."

Her posture stiffens slightly, and I curse my thoughtlessness. "Not because you couldn't help," I clarify quickly. "It's just . . . delicate."

Jenny's gaze softens. "Well, Grandma Cora always said that keeping things in would darken your perspective on life and letting things out could open up a rainbow of opportunities. So just try me. For now, I'm not your employee—I'm your friend."

I nod, a subtle wave of weariness washing over me. She sounds just like Henry sometimes—calm, steady, and always knowing how to coax a confession out of me. There's an odd comfort in that, a familiarity that loosens the knot in my chest just enough to make talking feel possible.

Jenny sits across from me, her hands resting lightly on the arms of the chair, fingers tapping softly in a rhythmic, absent-minded way. She tilts her head slightly, her ponytail swaying as she waits patiently. There's no pressure in her gaze, just quiet encouragement, like she's saying: It's okay. Take your time, because I'm here for you.

"Well," I begin hesitantly, my voice carrying the weight of too many sleepless nights. "I love this marina. You know that."

She nods, her expression open, her eyes steady on mine.

"And I had hoped that one day the marina ownership could pass on to me from my grandfather," I continue, my words tinged with both pride and resignation.

Jenny's brows knit together slightly. "I thought your parents owned the marina?"

"No." I shake my head, the familiar frustration bubbling to the surface. "My grandfather owns it. But now he's ready to pass the ownership on to me."

Her confusion deepens as she leans forward slightly, resting her elbows on her knees. "I see. And this is . . . a bad thing?" Her genuine curiosity is almost enough to make me smile.

"No," I say quickly, exhaling a sharp breath. "It's what's in the ownership contract that's the problem." I pause, rubbing the back of my neck as the words form, heavy on my tongue. "There is a marriage clause. It says the new owner has to be married when the ownership is transferred. If they're not, they forfeit the right to own the marina, and it opens up to married family members that are interested in owning it."

Jenny's lips part in surprise, her eyes widening as she processes the information. "And marriage isn't a possibility for you?" she asks. "I mean in the near future?"

"Not really," I say.

"So, no girlfriend?" she asks.

I can't help the laugh that escapes me, sharp and bitter. "Nope. Not unless you count the marina. I've given my whole life to this place. I don't want to lose it, but this clause is . . ." I trail off, shaking my head as words fail me. "It's causing me so many issues."

"I see how that could be a problem," she says softly. There's no judgment in her tone, only understanding, and the compassion in her gaze feels like a lifeline I hadn't known I needed.

"Yeah," I mutter, running a hand down my face. "And apparently my relatives are now vying for the ownership rights. My grandfather wants to hold out as long as he can, but his health hasn't been great lately. He needs to pass on the marina sooner rather than later. And between him and my parents constantly asking about my relationship status and my extended family wanting to take over the marina, it's been a lot." I sigh heavily, the weight in my chest pressing down harder. "Anyway," I say, my voice quieter now, "thank you for listening.

Your grandma was right. I feel a little better now that I've let some of this frustration out."

Jenny's smile is warm, softening the edges of her features. "Well, I'm happy I could help, even just a little. I know this is a lot to carry, but don't let it weigh you down completely. Things always have a way of working out in the end."

Her words linger in the air like a soothing balm, and for a moment, I let myself believe her. "Thank you, Jenny," I say sincerely, watching as she stands and heads toward the door.

She glances back, her ponytail swinging with the motion. "Anytime," she says, her voice light but steady, as if to remind me that she means it.

As the door closes behind her, the room feels quieter, heavier somehow. I lean back in my chair, my fingers brushing absentmindedly over the edge of the desk. If only she could solve the one problem I can't seem to fix.

The following week, I sit in my office, not feeling much better about my predicament. Jenny's voice carries from the front desk. "I'll be right with you," she says. Her voice is warm and melodic, tinged with a professional politeness that somehow still feels genuine.

I get up from my desk chair and head out to see if I can help. She's at the counter, the cabin reservation book open in front of her. The pencil in her mouth bobs slightly as she jots something down with another pen she's retrieved from her ponytail. A small streak of graphite marks her cheek. She glances up as I approach, mouthing a quick "thank you," her sapphire-blue eyes sparkling.

Jenny truly fits in here.

My feet falter as I spot my mother standing in front of the newly displayed painting on the wall. Jenny finished it last week, a tranquil depiction of the lake at dawn with ducks gliding through a thin veil of mist. I insisted she hang it up, and the customers have already been complimenting it endlessly.

"Hey, Mom," I say, stepping toward her. "Anything I can help you with this morning?"

"What? A mother can't come and see her son for no reason at all?" She raises an eyebrow, her tone light but her expression lined with concern.

"She can, as long as she doesn't ask about my relationship status again. It hasn't been that long since we talked about it at Sunday dinner."

"Well, yes," she says, "but your father is worried, and so is your grandfather . . ." She trails off, the familiar worry creeping into her voice.

"Mom, I told you I'd get back to you as soon as I have something figured out."

"But, Trenton, you know we need to have something to tell the extended family. Soon."

"I'm aware, Mom," I say, my gaze wandering to where Jenny is now organizing fishing lures with practiced efficiency. Her blonde hair bounces lightly as she moves, catching the morning light streaming through the windows.

"Trenton, are you even listening to me?" Mom asks, a harried look on her face.

"Sorry, Mom. I got distracted by—"

"Mrs. Hughes!" Jenny's cheerful voice cuts in as she seamlessly materializes beside me. "It's so wonderful of you to stop in today! How are your spinach plants coming along?"

"They . . . they . . ." My mom's voice falters at the abrupt change in conversation. "They are doing better than I expected actually, I've got more than I know what to do with."

"If you have some to spare," Jenny continues, "I'd love to take some off your hands. I have the perfect spinach dip recipe, and as you know, I've been learning how to bake bread with Holly. Pairing the two would be so delicious."

"Well then," my mom says, a smile spreading across her face, "I will pick some and bring them by for you the next time I'm heading over."

"That sounds wonderful. Thank you, Mrs. Hughes, I'll be sure to make you a batch," Jenny says. Then she leans into me and loops her arm through mine as though it's the most natural thing in the world.

Shock flickers across my mother's face, and I'm so stunned myself that I can't even muster a laugh at her expression.

"Trent," Jenny says, turning her bright eyes on me and stopping my thoughts mid-track. "I know we were going to wait until Sunday dinner next week, but I got so excited when your mom popped in that I figured, what the heck, why don't we tell her now?"

"W-why don't we tell her . . ." I echo dumbly, trying to piece together what's happening. What is Jenny getting at?

"Yes, Trenton?" My mom says, her eyes gleaming with curiosity. "You have something to tell me?"

"Oh, er . . .yeah . . ." I look down at Jenny, and she shifts her hands around my arm. "We . . . wanted to wait . . ."

"Wait for what, dear?" My mom asks, her lips curving into an eager smile as she looks at Jenny nestled into my side.

"To tell you . . ."

"We're engaged!" Jenny announces brightly. She rests her head on my arm, sending an electric jolt through me.

My mother's eyes widen before she breaks into a grin that could rival the sun. "Trenton! How dare you not even tell me you were dating someone! And now you're engaged to boot! Oh, I can't wait to tell your father. He'll be over the moon! Your grandfather too. And here you had me thinking that there was no hope for you taking over the marina."

"Surprise," I say weakly, forcing a grin. I'm trying to piece together everything that is happening, but my brain is currently working slower than molasses.

Well, if you can't beat them, better join them. I plaster a grin on my face and press a kiss to the top of Jenny's head for good measure. Her hair is warm under my lips, smelling faintly of lavender and sunshine. My mom nearly swoons, her hand fluttering to her chest like she's just watched the most romantic scene in a movie.

"Oh, Trenton," my mom exclaims. "I always knew you'd find someone! I can't believe you kept this from me, you little rascal! Even with my pestering—it was all for naught!" She embraces Jenny and me. "You're engaged," she says excitedly, then glances at Jenny's hand. "Well, let me see it."

"See what?" I ask, still trying to fully catch up.

"The ring, obviously," my mom says, placing her hands on her hips.

"Um . . ." I start, but Jenny effortlessly cuts in.

"Oh, I'm so sorry, Mrs. Hughes, we had to get it resized. Trent didn't want to spoil the proposal by asking for my ring size, so he guessed. He ended up getting a size too big."

My mom pulls Jenny out of my arms and into a hug that's as tight as a fisherman's line when he's reeling in his biggest catch. The moment Jenny is pulled away, I feel an odd pang of loss, as though some invisible tether has been momentarily severed.

Strange. Wonder what that's about?

"Oh, don't worry about it at all!" Mom says. "Getting the wrong size happens all the time. Oh! Jenny, dear, you must come for Sunday dinner. I'll invite our friends, and we'll make an engagement party out of the whole thing!"

Jenny pulls back slightly, her cheeks faintly pink, though my mom still has her hands clasped tightly. "That sounds wonderful, Mrs. Hughes," Jenny says, her voice warm and genuine.

"This is the best news!" Mom exclaims, her smile widening. "I've always wanted a daughter. Not that Trenton isn't the perfect son, but there's something special between a mom and her daughter, don't you think?"

Jenny hesitates, her gaze dropping to where my mom's hands hold hers. "Oh, um, my parents weren't around much when I was little, so I wouldn't know much about the mother-daughter relationship."

"Well," my mom says, "don't worry about that. We'll start here with the two of us." My mom wraps her in another hug, swaying slightly. Jenny stiffens for a fraction of a second before melting into it, her arms circling Mom's back.

"No worries, Jenny," Mom says, her voice tinged with emotion. "We'll be two peas in a pod, the two of us!"

From where I stand, I catch the glimmer of unshed tears in Jenny's eyes before she quickly brushes them away with a blink and a bright smile. Jenny shifts her gaze to the register. "Oh! Mr. Newman is here for his bait. I'd better go help him." She releases my mom and heads back toward the shop. "I'm looking forward to Sunday!" she calls out.

Jenny waves to both of us before hurrying behind the counter, her ponytail bouncing as she scoops up a big bucket of worms for Mr. Newman. The older man tips his hat to her, a pleased grin spreading across his weathered face as she chats easily with him. The sight of her smile is like sunlight breaking through a cloudy sky, and for a moment, I forget the chaos swirling around me.

"Trenton, dear," Mom says, pulling my focus back. "I can't believe you're engaged. I need to know all the details." Her face is alight with maternal curiosity and uncontainable joy.

I glance at my watch, thankful for the steady flow of regulars keeping me busy. "Sorry, Mom, it'll have to wait for Sunday dinner. I have to go help out the guys. We don't want a bunch of cranky fishermen who can't get out on the water."

Mom, having worked at the marina for decades, understands and waves me off. "Of course not! But we have a lot of talking to do—and a wedding to plan!"

"Sure thing, Mom." I lean in to kiss her cheek, her familiar floral perfume tickling my nose. "See you Sunday!"

With a wave, I grab my key ring off the board and head out to the docks. The air is crisp and smells faintly of lake water and freshly cut wood. The gentle lap of waves against the boats fills the silence as I take a deep breath, trying to steady my thoughts.

I don't know what just happened. What was Jenny thinking telling my mom we're engaged? She has no idea what she's just gotten herself into. Because now that Mom has the thought of marriage in her head, there's little that can be done to get it out. And now I'll have to come up with some way to explain that it was all a joke. And if Jenny wasn't trying to be comical, then why did she say we were engaged?

My brain whirls as I move from one boat to another, helping each person with their rentals. The usual banter with the regulars goes right over my head. My words are automatic, my thoughts elsewhere.

The weight of the morning presses down on me, and just as I'm about to attempt sorting through it, my phone buzzes in my pocket. I pull it out to see a message flash across the screen.

> Greg: Man, have I got a story for you. You'll never guess what I heard.

Another ping.

> Gwen: You're engaged? When did this happen? Why didn't you tell us?

And another.

> Niall: Hey mate, seems like someone's been holding out at game nights. Let's all get together tonight and you can fill us in on your fiancée.

And another.

> Holly: Do you already have a baker for the wedding? If not, I'm doing your cake on the house. Just say the word.

Ping after ping lights up my phone, a relentless flurry of messages from friends and family. I swipe to silence it, but then turn it off entirely. Yep, Mom's already telling everyone about my supposed engagement.

I really need to talk to Jenny.

Chapter 6

Jenny

I avoid Trent for the rest of the day. My nerves are jangling like loose change in a dryer. I linger with customers longer than necessary, listening to all kinds of stories or chatting about the weather as though it were the most interesting topic in the world. When Trent comes into the shop, I dart out with a forced smile and a flimsy excuse.

"Just checking on this cabin," I say, my voice an octave higher than usual.

I don't know what came over me this morning, blurting out that Trent and I were engaged. This isn't how I wanted that conversation to go. And I really hope I still have a job—and a place to live—after all this. Oh, Jenny, what in the world got into you?

The sun dips below the horizon, painting the marina in hues of gold and lavender. The store is quiet now, the buzz of the day fading into the stillness of evening. I finish wiping down the counter after closing up, the sharp, citrusy scent of lemon cleaner clinging to the air. The cool dampness of the cloth soothes my overworked hands as I hum to myself, trying to focus on the simple task and not on what my mouth said this morning.

I turn to check the aisles, making sure everything is in its place for tomorrow morning, but come to an abrupt halt. Trent stands in my path, his arms crossed over his chest. His face is unreadable, but the steady rise and fall of his shoulders as he breathes hints at his calm resolve.

"We need to talk," he says, his voice steady but firm, each word cutting through the quiet like a blade.

I gulp, twisting the damp rag in my hands until water seeps between my fingers. "Well, I still need to do one last check on the aisles before I'm done for the night," I say, my voice wobbling.

"That can wait—fiancée."

"Right, about that . . ."

Trent's expression remains neutral. "Is the lodge door locked?"

"Oh, um, yes," I stammer, my heart thudding in my chest.

"Okay. Let's go talk in my office." He turns without waiting for a response, and his footsteps are firm and deliberate on the wooden floor, each one echoing in my ears like a drumbeat of inevitability.

Right, I guess that solves this mystery. I'm totally fired.

I follow him, my pulse quickening with every step. His office is neat but lived-in, with a faint scent of cedar and paper. The soft glow of a desk lamp illuminates scattered papers and two wingback chairs across from a desk and a well-worn leather chair.

He sits in one of the wingback chairs, its dark leather inviting, and gestures for me to join him. I hesitate, but his patient gaze nudges me forward. Sinking into the chair, I feel the cool leather press against my arms.

Before I can stop myself, words spill out in a rush, my voice tumbling over itself. "I'm sorry. I don't know what came over me this morning. I just heard your mom talking—well, I wasn't trying to listen in, but I did, so I'm sorry about that too. I shouldn't have told her we were engaged, when clearly, we aren't. It's just that what you told me about the marina and needing to be married had been on my mind, and when I heard her, I just—"

"Jenny," Trent says, holding up a hand, "take a breath and stop." His voice is calm, but there's a flicker of amusement in his eyes that surprises me. "I know you weren't serious about the engagement. It's maybe not the funniest joke to play on my mom, and she has already started spreading the rumor that we're engaged. So we're going to need to come up with a plan to explain all of this."

"So . . . you're not firing me?" I ask.

"What?" Trent pauses, then shakes his head. "No, I'm not firing you. It took me months to fill your position. And the regulars love you. There's no way I'm letting you go."

I breathe a sigh of relief. I'm so grateful I still have a job and a place to live. And now that I know I'll be at the marina for the foreseeable future, I have to tell Trent the truth. "Thank you, Trent, for letting me keep this job, but I do have to tell you that when I told your mom we were engaged, I wasn't joking. I was being serious."

"Serious?" Trent looks at me like I have two heads. "What are you talking about, Jenny? We are not engaged."

"I know. I know. I shouldn't have told your mom without talking to you first."

"Talking to me first? You mean telling me"—Trent gestures between us—"that we're engaged? Do you know how this is sounding?"

"Not good," I admit. "But just listen. After we talked the other day, I was thinking about what you said. And I think we could help each other out."

"By being engaged?" Trent says, his face full of confusion.

"Yes."

Trent's eyes widen slightly. "You can't be serious, Jenny."

"I am serious. As serious as a fisherman is about his gear."

"Well, what you are offering is definitely a solution to my problem," Trent says, his tone cautious. "It's one that you know has been weighing on me. But why are you doing this? There's nothing in it for you."

His blue eyes meet mine, steady and searching. I shift under his gaze, feeling the weight of the moment pressing down on me. Rising slowly, I walk over to the window and place my hand on the clear pane. The glass is cool under my fingertips as I look out at the marina.

"Trent," I say softly, still looking out at the boats gently swaying on the water. "There is a lot in it for me." I turn back to face him and lean against the windowsill, the edge pressing into my spine. A lump forms in my throat as I think about everything that brought me here. "This isn't just about you, okay? It's about what this place means to me."

His brow furrows in confusion. "What do you mean?"

I take a deep breath, gathering my thoughts. "When I was a kid, my parents moved around constantly. I never stayed in one place long enough to make friends or feel like I belonged any-where. They made it pretty clear I wasn't part of their plans, you know? I was an 'unexpected burden' to them, something they had to deal with, someone who just got in the way."

Trent's face tightens. "They actually said that?"

"Not in so many words," I admit, forcing a small smile. "But I could tell. Then, as you know, one summer, when I was in middle school, we went to visit my grandparents. And my parents left me there. They left without even saying goodbye."

His eyes widen. "Jenny, that's awful."

"It was. At first, anyway. I didn't understand why they didn't want me, why they'd just leave me like that. But what they didn't realize was that leaving me with my grandparents was the best thing they ever did for me. Henry and Cora welcomed me with open arms, made me feel like I finally belonged somewhere. Their house became my home. For the first time in my life, I felt safe, loved . . . stable."

Trent leans forward, his elbows resting on his knees. "Your grandparents sound like they were amazing people, even back then."

"They were. And Grandpa Henry still is. He's the reason I came back here, Trent. Leaving for college and venturing out on my own in the world has been wonderful, but leaving my grandparents is also the hardest thing I've ever done. I'd always longed to return to Chessie Valley. I wanted to be close to them, but I wasn't sure how to make it work with my job. Then Grandma passed, and fate forced my hand. And I'm here now. I'm making it work. That little cabin by the marina? It's not just a place to live—it's my sanctuary. It's where I have the freedom to paint, where I feel like I can breathe. This job? It's given me not only that cabin, but more importantly, it's given me a way to stay close to Grandpa and this community. It's given me stability. A home."

Trent nods slowly, his expression softening. "I guess I didn't realize how much this place means to you."

"It means everything," I say, my voice steady and sure. "The marina, the regulars like Mr. Newman, my cabin, it's all part of the life I've started to build here. And I don't want to lose it. I want to be near my grandpa as long as he's alive, and I want to stay in Chessie Valley, the only place I've really felt at home."

Trent looks at me, his gaze searching.

"So," I continue, "if we do get married, I'm guaranteed this job and this home."

"True," Trent says. "The rumor mill would be unhinged if I fired not only my best employee but also my wife."

"And if we do go through with a wedding, you'd be guaranteed ownership of the marina."

Trent nods, then looks into my eyes. "But marrying me . . . that's a huge step, Jenny. You're talking about tying yourself to someone you barely know. It's crazy."

I laugh softly. "Oh, it's definitely crazy. But I don't think it's as crazy as letting this place slip away from us. And Grandpa Henry likes you, Trent. He's got a knack for knowing when someone's a good person, so I trust his judgment."

"Yeah," Trent says, a small smile tugging at his lips. "He's called me a good egg once or twice."

"Exactly." I take one last look at the lake, the setting sun casting it in molten gold, and inhale deeply before I push off the windowsill and take a step closer to Trent. "Look, I know this isn't how either of us pictured our lives going. But I also know you've worked too hard to let this marina slip through your fingers. And I've worked too hard to leave my grandpa and Chessie Valley again. So, yeah, I want to get married. Not only because I want to help you but because I understand what it feels like to lose everything."

Trent's shoulders relax, and he runs a hand through his hair. "You're . . . something else, Jenny. I don't know what to say."

"Say you'll stop second-guessing my seriousness about this arrangement," I reply, a teasing edge to my voice. "If you need a wife to meet the requirements your grandpa set in place, then I'm your lady."

"Are you sure? You barely know me or my family," he asks, though his tone lacks the weight of genuine doubt it had previously.

I cross my arms and give him a pointed look. "I feel like I know you and your mom just fine, thank you. My grandparents raised me to do the right thing, and my gut is telling me to do this."

Trent leans back, crossing one leg over the other, and studies me for a moment. "Okay, well, if we're doing this, there are some things we would need to agree on first. Ground rules."

"Such as?" I ask, sinking back into the wingback chair.

"Well, living situation, physical affection, how long we would stay married—things like that."

I nod, already running through possible scenarios in my head. "Okay. What are you thinking?"

"I have a house walking distance from the marina," Trent says, his tone practical. "After we're married, you could live there with me."

"Logical," I agree. "We'd need to keep up appearances anyway."

"Exactly. And I figure we'd only need to live together for a year," Trent continues.

"Why a year?"

"Well, my thought was that if we're living together for at least that long, people will believe that we genuinely gave this marriage a go. So when we separate, no one will suspect that this marriage was all pretend. Plus, once I officially become the owner, I can change the contract to remove the marriage clause. After that, we wouldn't need to keep up the charade anymore."

"That makes sense," I say, nodding "And we wouldn't actually get divorced until I am ready to leave the marina, so I don't have to worry about a job or place to live after the year is up."

"That sounds reasonable."

"And for the last part?" I ask, hesitantly.

Trent takes off his baseball cap and runs a hand through his hair. "And . . . for the physical aspect, I think we should keep things simple. People will expect at least one kiss on the wedding day. But other than that, we keep everything else friendly, like holding hands and small gestures and stuff like that."

My brain stalls at the word kiss. My cheeks heat as I picture kissing Trent. Is Trent attractive? Absolutely. Have I wondered what kissing him might be like? Yep, and definitely more than once. But hearing him say it out loud sends my thoughts spiraling.

"So," Trent says, his voice pulling me back to reality. "Are you still in?"

I take a deep breath, steadying myself. "You won't get rid of me that easily," I reply with a small smile. "But I have one question."

"Hit me with it," Trent says, leaning forward, curiosity flickering in his eyes.

"When's the wedding? And how big or small is it going to be?"

Trent bursts into laughter, the sound filling the room and making me smile despite myself. His laugh is warm and contagious, a glimpse of the carefree side he so rarely gets to show lately.

And in that moment, I know the hardest part of this arrangement isn't going to be pretending to be married. It's going to be trying not to fall for him.

"Well," Trent says, "if my mom has anything to do with it, it'll be the event of the season. But since you are doing me such a big favor, we can do it any way you want."

"Remember, it's not a favor. We're both getting something out of this."

He chuckles. "Fair enough."

"I'm more worried about the financial aspect of it," I say, then look at the ground. "At the moment, I barely have enough money to get by, let alone put any toward a wedding."

"Don't worry about that," Trent says. "My parents will cover it. My mom is more than ready for me to be married. She's practically been preparing for my wedding since I was born."

"Are you sure?" I ask.

"I'm sure," Trent says. "And seriously, thank you for doing this."

For a moment, neither of us speaks, the significance of our agreement hanging heavy between us. Somehow, this crazy plan feels a little less overwhelming than it should—and a little more like the right decision.

Chapter 7

Trent

It shouldn't, I know, but thinking of marrying Jenny sends a shiver of excitement through me, a spark lighting somewhere deep inside.

Sitting across from her in my office discussing the details of our marriage has my heart beating hard in my chest, a reminder of how real this moment is.

Jenny looks up at me, her eyes shining with something I can't read. The warmth of her presence draws me closer.

"How about we go on a date tonight?" I ask, my voice steady though my pulse races. "We need to start acting like a couple."

"That sounds good," she says. "People need to start seeing us together." Her smile is soft and genuine, like sunlight breaking through clouds after a storm, and relief suddenly floods me.

I can't hold back—I stand and scoop her up in a big hug. The feel of her laughter against my chest, light and musical, makes me want to marry her tomorrow.

"So," Holly's teasing voice cuts through the air, "we're giving teddy-bear hugs now?" She startles us both as she walks in with Greg.

How had I missed the sound of them coming in? Setting Jenny down gently, I turn to face them, Jenny's warmth still lingering in my arms.

"So it's true?" Greg says. "You two are engaged."

Jenny and I glance at each other, an unspoken agreement passing between us before we nod in sync. "As true as a fish loving water," I say, grinning despite the nerves crawling up my spine.

"I knew there was a reason Jenny was supposed to work here," Holly squeals.

"Why didn't you tell us you all were dating?" Greg asks.

"Oh, leave them be!" Holly says, swatting Greg's arm. "It's none of our business, and it doesn't matter. Obviously they're head over heels for each other." She gestures toward us, then looks back at Greg. "Right, babe?"

Greg nods sheepishly. "Yeah, they look great together."

"Oh my gosh!" Holly squeals. "I'm so excited!" She throws her arms around me in a quick hug before abandoning me to pull Jenny into an embrace. "Oh, this night just got so much better! I can't wait to celebrate! Let's have a little engagement party tonight."

"You two up for that?" asks Greg, his tone easygoing.

"Well," I say, "we were planning a date—"

"Sure!" Jenny says quickly, her enthusiasm bubbling over. "I think it would be so much fun to hang out."

Holly and Greg exchange glances, their expressions shifting between confusion and amusement.

I smile, giving in. "Whatever the fiancée wants is what happens."

"I love that word, fiancée!" Holly says. "Do you have a baker for the wedding? Please let me do it! It will be my gift to you. I'm just so excited." Holly's words spill out so fast no one has a chance to respond. Finally, Holly turns to Greg. "Do Gwen and Niall know Jenny and Trent are engaged yet? They're coming out with us tonight, right? Text and make sure. No, I'll do it." She is already pulling out her phone, her fingers flying over the screen.

"Well," Greg says, "I guess congrats are in order, man." Greg reaches over, pulling me into a quick hug and clapping me firmly on the back. "And welcome to the family, Jenny," he adds warmly.

"Thank you!" Jenny says, "You all have been so wonderful since I came back into town, and so welcoming. I don't know why I ever left, to be honest," Jenny says, her voice filled with warmth and sincerity.

"I heard you lived here," Greg says. "But I wasn't sure when. Did you live here long?"

"Middle school and high school, then I left for college in Georgia," Jenny replies, her tone soft, as if lost in the memory.

"We probably went to school together," says Holly, her head tilting thoughtfully.

"Only my freshman year," Jenny says, "I was three years behind you all in school. But I do remember watching the football games and seeing Trent and Greg play." Jenny's cheeks flush pink as our eyes meet.

"Well," I say, puffing out my chest, "we were a pretty big deal back then, weren't we, Greg?"

"Sure were," Greg says, a nostalgic grin spreading across his face. "Those were the days, for sure."

"Gwen and Niall are confirmed," Holly says, looking up from her phone. "You all can reminisce about high school another day. Right now, we have an engagement to celebrate!" Holly links arms with Jenny and leads her out my office door.

As the girls walk ahead, I can't help but watch Jenny's profile. The way her hair catches the sunlight and the glow on her face makes my chest tighten.

I couldn't have picked a better fiancée if I'd tried.

"Hey, man." Greg elbows me lightly. "What's got you all emotional?"

Laughing, I shake my head. "Nothing really, dude. I think it just hit me that I'm actually getting married."

"Well," Greg says, "if you picked as good of one as I did, then marriage will be a breeze. And from what I know about Jenny so far, you'll be just fine." Greg claps me on the shoulder before following the girls out.

Jenny glances back at me, her eyes catching the golden light of the setting sun. My heart skips a beat. That's my future wife. I will do everything to make sure she is happy, even if this is just a temporary situation.

I hold the door open for Jenny as we walk into the Lunar Lounge. The familiar chime of the bell above the door blends with the low hum of conversation and the faint notes of a song drifting from the speakers. For as long as we've been old enough to go to a bar, we've always come here to celebrate. Big milestones or small victories, this place has seen it all. So, it's only fitting that Holly wants to come here to celebrate Jenny and my engagement, even if she and everyone else doesn't know the whole truth behind it.

"You been here before?" I ask Jenny, glancing at her as we step inside. The warmth of the room envelops us, and the mingled scents of citrusy cocktails, polished wood, and faint traces of bar food make the place feel alive.

"I haven't actually. By the time I was old enough for a place like this to be my scene, I had moved to Atlanta." Jenny's voice is tinged with curiosity as her gaze roams the room. Her eyes widen, taking in the eclectic chaos that is the Lunar Lounge.

The restaurant is not like your typical place. The walls are a vibrant masterpiece, painted with sprawling murals that pay homage to legendary singers from every genre imaginable. Elvis, Aretha Franklin, Freddie Mercury, and even Madonna seem to come alive under the glow of dim, colored lights. They're connected by swirls of music notes, gleaming instruments, and an explosion of vivid colors that make the walls feel as though they're in constant motion.

Above us, a dormant disco ball hangs like a sleeping star. Its mirrored surface catches faint glints of light, a hint of the magic it brings when it spins during special events. Sally, the owner, told us once that it only lights up for the most important celebrations.

The bar at the back of the room gleams under warm lighting, its polished surface reflecting a kaleidoscope of bottles behind it. Rows of liquors in every hue imaginable line the shelves, from deep ambers to electric blues. It's the kind of setup that promises any drink you can dream of. I catch a whiff of freshly cut limes as a bartender slices fruit for a cocktail.

"Wow," Jenny breathes, still taking it all in. "This place is incredible."

I grin. "Wait until the music really gets going. That's when it feels like home."

This restaurant has always been more than a hangout spot. It's been our refuge. Whether belting out an off-key tune on their Funky Friday Karaoke nights or laughing over shared memories, this place has always been a second home. For me, it's as comforting as the marina—the one other place where I feel completely myself.

As we weave through the tables, the hum of voices and the clinking of glasses create a backdrop to our conversation. We head toward one of the U-shaped booths nestled along the wall and big enough for our group. Gwen and Niall are already there, waving as they spot us.

"You dance, Jenny?"

"No," she says, "never been much for getting up in front of people to make a fool of myself, especially in big crowds."

"What about your art shows?" I ask as we walk. "Don't you have to stand in front of a bunch of people for that?"

"Yeah, I guess you're right," Jenny admits, brushing a strand of hair behind her ear. "But it doesn't feel the same as getting out in front of people I don't know and dancing, which I'm not good at. I created my art pieces and know them inside and out. Talking about them to people is like talking about your kid or your pet. You know?"

"I suppose that makes sense," I reply, nodding thoughtfully. "But I'd argue that dancing with someone you know can be like that too. You get to share your love of the song with everyone else who loves to dance and listen to the band sing."

Jenny swats me lightly on the arm, her laugh bubbling out. "You like being right, don't you?"

I smile broadly, my chest swelling with a playful kind of pride, and nod.

"I guess," Jenny says, "that means you're not going to let me just sit here and watch you all dance, then, are you?"

Pausing, I turn serious and take her hand gently in mine. Her skin is soft, and her fingers instinctively curl slightly against my palm. "I would never force you to do anything you don't want to do. I mean that, both in this scenario and in our future as husband and wife. You can always guarantee, with one hundred percent certainty, that I will do everything in my power to make sure you are well cared for and happy. You will never need to be scared of me or what I might think. I am committed to you and will uphold my title as your husband with everything I am, even if it is just a temporary thing."

Her smile softens as she looks up at me. Letting go of my hand, she reaches around me for a hug. The embrace is warm and grounding, her cheek pressing lightly against my shoulder. "Trent, you are the sweetest, most perfect arranged fiancé I have ever known," she says in a hushed tone.

"Hopefully I'm the only arranged fiancé you've ever had. Or do you have something else you need to tell me?" I say, crossing my arms with exaggerated offense.

Jenny giggles, the sound like the soft chime of bells. "You're such a dork. You know that, right?"

"I don't know if I should be offended by that or not," I reply, grinning despite myself.

She shakes her head, still smiling, before turning and continuing toward the booth where not only Gwen and Niall but also Holly and Greg sit waiting for us.

Chapter 8

Jenny

"Well, I was wondering when you two would make your way over here," says Holly, her voice warm and inviting as she scoots over in the booth to make room. The soft murmur of the restaurant around us is punctuated by laughter and the occasional clinking of plates and glasses.

"It's not like they could get lost in here," laughs Gwen, leaning casually on the table. Her bright smile reflects the colorful murals on the walls. "By the way, Trent, I hear you have some big news to share with us?"

Trent nods. "I do. I know you and Niall have talked with Jenny a handful of times at the marina, but let me officially introduce her as my fiancée."

"Congratulations, mate!" Niall says, his smile as big as the sun.

"So," Gwen says, folding her arms and narrowing her eyes like she's solving a crime in one of her books, "I might be the only one brave enough to say it, but this engagement caught us all by surprise. I mean, you two have only known each other a few months, right? We didn't even know you were seeing each other and then wham! engaged."

A beat of silence follows. A few exchanged glances. Greg lets out a low whistle.

"She's not wrong," says Greg, his brows raised like he's waiting for an explanation. "I mean, I work with you both and didn't know."

"Of course I'm not wrong," replies Gwen. "So why all the secrecy? We didn't even know you were dating."

Trent shifts beside me, clearing his throat. I see the flicker of panic in his eyes

"Well," Trent starts, "we just—"

The tension coils in my stomach. If I don't jump in, he might fumble this.

"Didn't want anyone to know," I cut in quickly. "I mean, wouldn't that look bad? I step in to manage the marina and then end up dating my boss? We didn't want anyone to know in case things didn't work out."

Where that lie came from, I'll never know. But Trent's shoulders dropping in relief tells me I made the right call.

"She's not wrong," says Niall.

"That's true," Gwen says, her suspicious gaze bouncing between the two of us like she's scanning for cracks in our story.

I force a smile, hoping she doesn't dig deeper. "We kind of hit it off from the get-go. And with Trent saving my life the first time we met, it wasn't hard for me to fall for him." I tuck my hair behind my ear, my pulse picking up.

Holly gasps, smacking Greg on the arm. "I knew that would happen! I knew it. I saw a spark of something between them that first day."

"Well, with how much easier my life became when Jenny started at the marina, it didn't take much for me to grow fond of her," Trent says, finally leaning back, his usual confidence returning.

The tension breaks. Greg lets out a chuckle. Niall shakes his head. Gwen, however, is still watching us, her lips pursed like she's debating whether to push further.

"How about you stop blocking the booth so we can all sit down and get some food ordered?" Trent adds smoothly.

"Of course you'd be thinking about the food, Trent," Niall says, shaking his head.

"In any case," Gwen says, stepping aside, "I would love to offer my event planning services to you."

"Oh wow," I say, "that's so nice. You really don't have to—"

Gwen stops me with a raise of her hand. "Nonsense. Trent has always been like a brother to me, and I would be honored to help you plan the event."

"You might have to get in line," chuckles Trent, sliding into the booth beside me. His shoulder brushes mine as he leans back, a faint scent of his cologne mingling with the spicy aroma of appetizers being carried to nearby tables. "I could see the wheels turning in my mom's head the moment she heard the news."

"Good point," Gwen replies with a knowing smirk, pulling out her phone. "Let me text her now so she doesn't go and get Emily Emerson to plan the event. Emily is always trying to swoop in and take my business. Give me one second, guys. This is for the good of Trent and Jenny's wedding. I've seen Emily's work, and while she's good, she's not me." She taps rapidly on her phone, her fingers flying over the screen.

Our server arrives, and we all place our orders, along with a selection of appetizers for the table. The smell of frying cheese and tangy buffalo sauce wafts through the air as another table nearby receives their food.

As the others dive into a spirited discussion about song requests for the band to play, I quietly observe, watching them input their selections into the small device on the table. Their laughter and animated chatter fill the space, and I can't help but smile at their easy camaraderie.

These are Trent's closest friends, and while I've met and interacted a bit with each of them during my time at the marina, seeing them like this—so relaxed, so tightly knit—stirs something inside me. A pang of sadness washes over me, heavy and familiar.

They are like family to each other. And alright, I know that Greg and Gwen are actual family, but there's a bond between them all that I've never truly experienced. The sadness sits hard in my stomach, its weight like a stone.

What am I doing? Am I invading this lovely friend group by inserting myself into the picture? Would Trent have found a wife who might fit in better with these people than I can?

A strong, warm hand folds over mine. My heart skips, and when I glance over, Trent is watching me, his brow furrowed with quiet concern. I smile faintly, adjusting my position in the booth to hide my moment of vulnerability.

"So, what music do you like to dance to?" I ask him, flipping my hand over and lacing my fingers through his.

"I like most of the songs they do," Trent says, gesturing to everyone in the booth, "but I don't think I'll request one tonight. Figured I'd sit back and enjoy what others select."

Niall, who's been half-listening, glances over with confusion etched across his face. "What? You're not dancing?"

Trent shrugs, rubbing his thumb over the back of my hand. The gentle motion sends a ripple of warmth through me. "I mean, I'd rather sit here with my fiancée."

"You not a dancer?" Niall asks me.

"Not really," I say.

"Too bad," Niall says. "You'll be missing out with Trent here then."

"He is quite the dancer," Greg adds.

"Is he?" I ask. I can't help but grin at Trent, who shimmies playfully.

"He is," Holly says. "Dancing and karaoke I have to say are some of his best talents."

"I had no idea," I say. "Trent, you've been holding out on me. What's your favorite karaoke song?"

Gwen leans in with a mischievous grin. "Oh, that's easy. Journey's 'Don't Stop Believing' is for sure his number one go-to song. Though he usually sings it with Margot, Holly's sister." Her phone buzzes, and she glances down. "Looks like your mom and I are in sync, Trent. She's on board with me being the wedding planner."

"Glad you could convince her," Trent says.

"Like it was hard?" Gwen says.

Trent holds up his hands in mock defense.

"We're meeting tomorrow," says Gwen, "to start planning. Does that work for you all?"

"So soon?" Trent asks.

"I like to get the ball rolling," says Gwen.

Trent looks at me for confirmation.

"Tomorrow sounds good to me," I say. I don't care when the wedding planning takes place, I'm just relieved that I won't have to handle the details of the wedding alone. I've never been one for the logistics, not even for my art shows—I prefer to focus on creating and let others handle the rest. I actually wonder if Mrs. Hughes and Gwen would mind taking full rein over most of the details. With this being a wedding that I've thought of for less than twenty-four hours, I don't have many ideas.

"If you have it at the marina," Trent says in a joking tone, "I could probably pop in for a few minutes." He winks at me.

"Hilarious, Trent," Gwen says. "But I could make that work."

The appetizers arrive, and the table erupts into motion. Plates are passed, and the sharp tang of marinara sauce mingles with the creamy richness of spinach dip. I sip my Dr Pepper, savoring the fizzy sweetness as I take in the lively atmosphere. The whimsical murals on the walls seem almost alive under the warm glow of the lights, each character frozen mid-performance.

I'm so absorbed in the details of the paintings that I don't notice the other couples have left the booth until I see them out on the dance floor. Holly and Greg get into the rhythm of the song as they dance, and Gwen and Niall are alight with playful energy.

"They're so perfect together," I whisper to Trent, my eyes glued to the dance floor.

"Which ones?" Trent asks.

"Both of them."

"They really are," Trent says.

"Have Gwen and Niall been together long? They're engaged, right?"

"Yeah," Trent says with a genuine smile. "They met on the cruise for Holly and Greg's wedding last summer. They had chemistry from the start."

As the song ends, I clap enthusiastically, inspired by their joy. "Let's dance one together," I blurt out, surprising even myself.

Trent turns to me, his expression serious. "Are you sure? I don't want you to feel pressured."

"I'm positive," I reply, my confidence growing. "And I think I have the perfect song for us."

Trent grabs the device to request songs and hands it to me with a grin. "Let's do it then! I'm always down for a good time."

Smiling, I type in a song that feels almost too fitting. As I confirm the selection, a tingle of nervous excitement courses through me.

Gwen and Niall return to the table, glowing from their dance. Holly and Greg stay out on the dance floor as a new song, "Islands in the Stream," begins. It's so perfectly them—effortlessly charming and full of heart.

I watch them dance, reflecting on how Holly's kindness has completely reshaped my life. Without her and her insistence that I was the perfect person to interview at the marina, I wouldn't have a job, a place to live, or the chance to see Grandpa every day.

Thankfully Trent agreed with her, and now I have a fiancé.

OMG, I have a fiancé.

It's not what I expected—I thought marriage would come from love, not a mutually beneficial agreement. But as I glance at Trent, I can't help but think how lucky I am that he's the one standing by my side. I feel like I'm getting more out of this arrangement than him, even if he is getting the marina.

I guess I couldn't have asked for a better person to arrange a marriage of convenience with.

Chapter 9
Trent

The device on the table pings, alerting us that our song choice is coming up next.

"What song did you pick?" I ask Jenny as we slide out of the booth. The leather squeaks slightly under the movement, and the buzz of the room feels louder now that we're standing.

"You think I'm just going to tell you?" she jokes, a playful glint in her eyes. She tucks a strand of hair behind her ear and smooths her shirt. She is clearly more nervous than she is letting on.

I glance back to see Greg and Niall each giving us an enthusiastic thumbs-up. Niall mouths something I can't catch over the din of the bar, but his grin is unmistakable. My stomach flutters with butterflies—not because I'm nervous about dancing with Jenny, but because I haven't had this much physical contact with her before.

As we step onto the dance floor, bathed in the warm glow of the lights, Jenny's smile beams. She looks radiant, her cheeks flushed.

"You ready?" she asks, her voice carrying a mixture of excitement and challenge.

Nodding, I respond with a grin, "You bet your bass, I am! Of course, I'm ready!"

The opening notes of the song fill the room, the familiar melody sending a jolt of recognition through me. I break out into a huge grin—I couldn't have picked a more perfect song if I'd tried.

Jenny steps forward as I take her hand in mine, and we start dancing to Bruno Mars' "Marry You." She is timid at first, barely moving as the music begins. The playful yet heartfelt lyrics are made even sweeter by the genuine look on Jenny's face as she meets my eyes.

My heart swells. The two of us dancing to a song about doing something impulsive and wonderful like getting married feels almost too perfect. If there were ever a song to sum us up, this would be it.

"Is it that look in her eyes, or this dancing tune," I paraphrase as I sing to her as we dance together, my voice smooth and confident. The room blurs around us, Jenny quietly joins in at the chorus, our voices blending effortlessly. Jenny's eyes light up as I pull her into a gentle twirl. I know our relationship is just starting and everything we're doing together is new for us, but something about all of it feels right.

She lets out a quiet laugh against my shoulder. "Fitting, don't you think?"

My hand tightens slightly at her waist. "Almost too fitting." The irony isn't lost on either of us. We aren't dancing like love-struck fools swept up in the moment. This is a deal, a logical arrangement—one that makes perfect sense on paper.

The dance floor lights reflect off her hair while she spins, and I catch the faint scent of her floral perfume as she steps back against me. Spurred on by the energy of the moment, our dance movements turn instinctive and unrehearsed. "Careful,

Jenny. Keep looking at me like that, and people might think this is real."

She rolls her eyes but doesn't step away. "Wouldn't want that."

Holding her close, I feel her warmth, and as I spin her again, her laughter rings out lightly and melodically. The flush on her cheeks deepens, and the smile on her face radiates pure joy. Her eyes meet mine, shining with a mix of surprise and something deeper.

If I didn't know any better, I'd almost believe our engagement was real.

It feels real.

It feels like this isn't just a marriage of convenience—it feels like there could be something more. Something genuine.

As the song slows, I pull her close for a gentle sway. Her hands rest lightly on my shoulders, and my arms encircle her as I guide her into a slow dance. The world narrows to just the two of us, the lyrics fading into the background as I dip her slightly at the end of the song.

The music dies out, and for a brief moment, there's silence. Then, a smattering of applause erupts from the crowd, and I don't need to look to know that the loudest applause is coming from our booth.

"Hi," I say softly as Jenny stands upright, the warmth of her hand still lingering against mine. Her eyes sparkle under the lights, and I notice her chest rising and falling as she catches her breath.

"Hi," she replies, her voice a mix of exhilaration and shyness. She leans in, her lips brushing my cheek in a quick, featherlight kiss. Her breath is warm against my skin as she whispers, "I think I want to marry you."

At her perfect use of the lyrics from the song, a laugh bursts out of me, light and full of joy, as I sweep her into a hug. Her arms wrap around my shoulders, and I lift her off the ground, spinning her in a full circle. Her laughter bubbles out, clear and bright, mingling with the distant hum of applause still lingering in the room. "Well, it's a good thing we're getting married then," I say.

When I set her down, her cheeks are flushed, and her hair is slightly out of place. I lean in and tuck a stray hair behind her ear, my fingers grazing her soft skin. She lightly leans into my touch, her breath escaping in a quiet exhale. I can't help but smile as I take her hand, threading my fingers through hers, and guide her off the dance floor. The faint vibrations of the wooden floor beneath our feet and the muted clink of glasses from the bar fill the space as the performers prepare for the next song in their set.

We weave through the crowd back to our table. The air around us feels warmer, the energy buzzing as if the entire room had been lifted along with our emotions.

When we reach our friends, their faces are glowing with excitement.

"I know you two are getting married soon," Holly says, her voice thick with emotion as she dabs at a tear sliding down her cheek, "but that was the sweetest thing I've ever seen."

"That should be your first dance song," Gwen says, giving us a half-smile. "I'll add it to the wedding notes."

"Mate," says Niall, his grin stretching ear to ear, "that was bloody brilliant. You two have real chemistry on the dance floor." He gives a dramatic nod toward Gwen. "Almost tops Gwen and me singing together for the first time. Almost, but not quite."

"Right," I say, rolling my eyes, "I think we were a hundred times better with our dancing, but I may be a bit biased."

Jenny snickers and smacks me lightly on the arm. "Oh, you," she says, her lips curving into a grin as she shakes her head.

I wake up the next day a little earlier than normal, and even though we were out late last night, there's a renewed energy coursing through me. The air feels crisp and cool as I stretch, and a sense of calm replaces the weight that's been pressing on me for months. Managing the marina, worrying about its future—everything suddenly feels like it's going to work out.

Last night, when Jenny and I got back to the marina, we said good night under the glow of the dock lights. She headed back to her cabin, and I returned to my house, the echo of her laughter still lingering in the quiet night air.

Now, lying in bed, I can't help but think about the changes ahead: planning a wedding, getting a ring, marrying Jenny, living together. Dude, I'm going to have a wife soon. The realization hits me like a wave, both thrilling and surreal.

That thought pulls me out of bed. Padding barefoot across the cool wooden floor, I head down the hall and peak into one of the spare bedrooms. It smells faintly of cedar and salt, like the rest of the cabin, but the space feels impersonal. Sunlight filters through the slats of the blinds, illuminating the neutral walls and simple furniture. It's been a guest room for years, functional but uninspired. I look over the rest of my home, the loft, living area, and kitchen, and a thought hits me. This house looks just like my office, lacking a woman's touch. But I guess that's all about to change. I can't wait to see how Jenny makes this house a home.

After getting ready for the day, I head toward the office. The crisp morning air greets me as I step outside, carrying the faint scent of seawater and freshly cut grass.

As I push open the store door, a familiar voice calls out, "Good morning!"

I glance up to see Jenny, radiant as ever, standing behind the counter. She waves, her smile bright and easy, and I feel a warmth that has nothing to do with the morning sun. She's wearing jean shorts and a flowy white top, her hair pulled up in a slightly messy bun with loose strands framing her face. The urge to reach out and tuck those strands behind her ears is almost irresistible. Last night while we were dancing, there was a palpable physical connection, but I don't want to scare her away by coming on too strong. So I resist the desire to touch her hair.

"Good morning," I reply, my voice lighter than usual as I walk to the counter. "You're in earlier than expected."

"Mm-hmm," she says, before continuing a song she was humming, her eyes twinkling. "I woke up at three this morning and couldn't go back to sleep. I had an idea for a painting and had to get started. I made a lot of progress and figured I should freshen up before meeting with your mom and Gwen. It wouldn't do for the future bride to be covered in paint."

She beams up at me, the image of her covered in paint making me smile. I imagine her in her element, focused and glowing, and my stomach flips at the thought. If she's this captivating talking to customers and selling bait, I can only imagine how radiant she must be when she's painting.

"I got up a little early myself," I say, leaning casually on the counter.

"Really?" Jenny asks.

"Yes, I want to get a few things done at the marina before my mom and Gwen get here. That way, I can make sure to have some extra time for the wedding planning."

"Oh, good!" Jenny says, her tone a mix of relief and excitement. "I don't know the first thing about weddings and didn't really grow up dreaming about my perfect wedding." She raises her hand as more words spill out. "Not that this has to be my dream wedding or anything, not that I'd even know what that was . . . What I mean is . . ."

Smiling, I step closer and gently take her hand. "Jenny, it's okay. Even if this marriage isn't forever, you can still have the wedding you want. Start thinking about what's important to you, because, trust me, my mom is going to go all out—me being her only kid and all."

"Oh no," she says, her voice dropping with worry. "Won't it break her heart when we get divorced?"

"We'll worry about that later," I say, releasing her hand as she tucks a stray hair behind her ear. "And, Jenny, trust me. You're doing my mom and me both a favor. I don't know if I'd have ever gotten married otherwise. The marina has been my sole focus for years—there hasn't been much time for dating, let alone finding a wife. My mom always said the marina was like my family. And I guess now it actually gets to be, with you here and all."

She pauses, considering my words, before nodding slowly. "I guess that's kind of true, huh? Especially with us both living at the marina."

As she turns to input something into the computer, I feel a nervous energy rise in me.

"So . . . I was thinking," I start, then clear my throat. "You know how you'll be moving in with me when we're married?"

"Yes," Jenny says.

"Well, I was thinking about my house and how soon it will be our house. And I wanted to let you know that I want it to feel like your home too. You're welcome to do anything you want to it."

Jenny spins around, her eyes wide with surprise. "Thanks, Trent, that means a lot."

"Of course," I say. "So whenever you want to come by and look at it, let me know. You can start planning what you want to add or change before you officially move in. I'm open to about anything. Changing the living area, kitchen, the bedroom." My cheeks burn, and I know they must be red. "I mean bedrooms," I add quickly. "I'm not assuming we'll share a room or anything like that."

I rub the back of my neck, struggling to explain myself. Why is this so hard? "What I'm trying to say is, there's the room I stay in, obviously, but I have two extra rooms. You can pick from either one and make it your own. And I've thought about your painting too. I want you to keep the cabin you're in now as an art studio. If you'd like."

By now, my face is on fire, so I shut up and stick my hands in my back pockets, slowly backing away. Her expression softens, and unshed tears shimmer in her eyes.

"Wait," she says softly, stopping me before I can retreat. "You don't have to go. And thank you—that's such a sweet offer. I've always dreamed of having my own art studio, somewhere I can just create without having to clean up every time. I appreciate it."

"I want you to feel happy here, Jenny."

She smiles at me. "I think I will be."

"Want to drop by my house tonight? After the marina closes?"

"That sounds great," she says.

I grin at her. "Well, now that that's settled, I need to get going on work at the marina before Mom and Gwen get here. Bye."

I hightail it out of there as calmly as I can, feeling like my face might still be on fire. Once I'm outside, I round the corner and lean against the wall of the building, letting out a long breath. In less than twenty-four hours, I've acquired a fiancée, and now we're making plans for when she will move in with me. What more can this day bring?

Chapter 10
Jenny

Trent scurries out the door, his ears pink from embarrassment. A soft smile spreads across my face as I glance back at the counter where the morning sunlight streams through the windows, casting a warm glow across the worn wood.

I don't know what I've done in life to deserve a guy as sweet as Trent. Not that he's mine, per se, but at least he's mine for now. That counts for something, right? Bonus: I get my very own art studio.

He likely doesn't realize it, but when he'd offered me that space, I could've swooned right then and there. It's like a book lover being handed a library, complete with a comfy chair and one of those rolling ladders. My mind buzzes with possibilities as I picture how I'd rearrange my cabin once I move into Trent's house—easels by the windows for natural light, shelves for paints and brushes, maybe even a little table for sketching.

The thought keeps me buoyant as I finish my morning tasks. The familiar buzz of the shop surrounds me: the soft creak of the door opening, the clink of bait buckets against the counter, and the murmur of customers chatting. Before I know it, the steady rhythm of work carries me into late morning, until a pair of determined figures stride in.

Mrs. Hughes and Gwen arrive looking ready for battle, binders tucked under their arms. They look striking in their professional attire—Mrs. Hughes in a pencil skirt and a flowing yellow and white blouse, Gwen in a tailored black pantsuit with a vibrant purple button-down. The faint scent of citrusy perfume drifts through the air as they pass by the counter, their heels clicking against the floor. These are women who get things done, and the energy they exude is equal parts inspiring and intimidating.

"Hi, Gwen. Hi, Mrs. Hughes," I call out, grabbing a bait bucket for Carlton, one of our regulars. "I'll be right over." The faint, salty scent of fresh bait fills the air.

"Have a great day, Carlton," I say as I hand him his bait bucket. "And good luck out there! I hope you catch something big."

"Thanks, Jenny," he says. "Looks like you've got a busy day ahead of yourself." He nods toward the office door where Mrs. Hughes and Gwen have disappeared.

"A busy day for sure. I've got a wedding to plan."

"Ah, yes, I did hear that through the grapevine. Seems like it just took a great gal like yourself to get ol' Trent to finally settle down."

I laugh and wave Carlton off, cheeks warming. Stopping by Greg's desk, I tell him, "I'm stepping away from the shop for a bit. I'll be in the back with Gwen and Mrs. Hughes. Let me know if anyone gives you any trouble."

"Trouble?" he teases, leaning back in his chair. "You act like I wasn't handling things just fine before you started here."

"Sure," I say with a playful smile, "but the customers like me better than you."

Greg waves me off good-naturedly as Trent walks in, Trent's hair slightly mussed and cheeks flushed from the brisk marina air.

"I saw Mom and Gwen pull up," Trent says, "and tried to hurry over as fast as I could without skipping the safety rundown for the pontoon rental."

"No worries," I say. "I just finished with Carlton and let Greg know I wouldn't be in the shop. We're good to go."

"Great. Let me wash my hands, and we'll dive into the wedding planning," Trent says, heading toward the sink. His sleeves are rolled up, revealing forearms dusted with faint streaks of grease—proof of his earlier work on the marina's boats.

"As long as you don't get cold feet, I think we can manage waiting for you to wash up," I tease, earning a laugh as he disappears into the back.

When I step into the office, the sheer volume of materials on the table freezes me in place. Magazines, fabric swatches, and floral arrangement books are strewn across every available inch, and the faint scent of freshly printed paper mingles with the citrus notes from earlier.

Footsteps behind me make me glance back as Trent joins me, his hands still holding a towel after a quick rinse. "Looks like they've got the works for us today," he says.

"Yeah." My voice comes out smaller than I intended. Trent sets the towel down on a nearby table, then he turns to study me.

"Don't tell me you're getting cold feet now?"

"What? No! Especially not after you just promised me my own art studio," I say. As we step forward to claim out seats in front of the table, I shake off some of my nerves.

Mrs. Hughes doesn't waste a moment. "Alright, now that you're both here, let's start with the most important question," she says, clasping her hands together.

Trent leans back in his chair, a grin tugging at his lips. "She already agreed to marry me. Isn't that the most important question?"

"Of course not," Gwen interjects, her tone light but firm. "We need to set a date."

"Oh, that." Trent says sheepishly.

"Yes, that," replies Mrs. Hughes sweetly.

My stomach drops. A date! How did we not settle on a timeline for the wedding when we were planning for this fake marriage?

Gwen fills the silence easily, pulling out some pictures of weddings with reds, oranges, and yellows. "How about a nice fall wedding? In the background, you could have the leaves changing colors, and we could transform the barn to an elegant yet rustic vibe to add to the fall theme."

"Well," I say timidly, "we aren't looking for a long engagement." I glance at Trent for confirmation.

"Definitely not," he agrees quickly.

Gwen and Mrs. Hughes exchange looks. "Is there some other news you want to tell us?" Mrs. Hughes asks.

Realizing how our eagerness to get married so soon might come across, Trent's ears turn red and my face flushes. "No, nothing like that!" I say.

"What we mean," Trent says, "is we're already working together and living so close. Why drag it out?"

"How about the beginning of April?" I suggest hesitantly.

All three sets of eyes turn to me, each of them looking slightly shocked. The silence stretches for a beat too long before Mrs. Hughes says, "But it's mid-March now. That's only two or so weeks away."

"You're right," I say. "I see how that could be not ideal for everyone."

"No," Trent says, his ears still tinged red. "That could work. Like I said, we do want to get married sooner rather than later. As long as it's not April Fools' Day, I'm game."

"A spring wedding would be beautiful," Mrs. Hughes admits. "And the cherry blossoms will be in bloom then too, but that's much too soon! I'm not sure we could get everything ready in time." Mrs. Hughes looks at Gwen.

"I really am okay with a simple wedding," I say.

Gwen shakes her head. "I don't do simple." Then she looks through her planner and adds, "It would be really tight, but I if we push it back a week, I can pull this off. Would Saturday April twelfth work for you all?"

I nod, then look at Trent.

"Looks like we have a date," Trent says, his grin softening as he glances my way. "Now that we have that settled, everything else should be easy peasy, right?"

We all laugh, though Gwen's and Mrs. Hughes's laughs sound strained. Even I know full well the mountain of decisions still ahead. But in that moment, surrounded by the buzz of plans and the warmth of shared excitement, it all feels doable, at least to me.

"Okay," Mrs. Hughes says, "so now that the date is settled, and you're sure you don't want the beautiful fall wedding Gwen was showing . . ." She looks at Trent and me, giving us time to respond. When I shake my head, she says, "No, okay, well then we'll need to get save-the-dates out as soon as possible." Her pen poised over a notepad, she says, "Let's decide on a pattern for the invitations, and I'll come over tomorrow so we can start working on addressing the envelopes."

I nod, my thoughts already swirling with color palettes and fonts.

"And," Gwen cuts in smoothly, flipping through her meticulous planner, "if we can decide on a cake design today, I can get you both in for a cake tasting with Holly first thing in the morning. Do you have a preference for flavors?"

The thought of cake perks me up. "I love lemon cake, and it might be nice to have something fresh and bright for a spring wedding," I say, imagining the tangy sweetness melting on my tongue.

"Great idea!" Mrs. Hughes beams at me. "Lemon feels perfect for spring. What do you think, Trent?"

"I'm down for anything Holly makes," Trent says, "but if her Sunrise Sin muffins can be turned into a cake, it'd be out of this world."

Gwen's pen moves swiftly across the page as she nods. "Noted. I'll check with Holly as soon as I leave the marina. As for catering," Gwen continues, her voice firm and efficient, "I have an excellent caterer I use for many events. Hopefully we can get them with this soon of a date. I'll try to pull as many strings as I can."

Mrs. Hughes turns to Gwen. "Are you referring to the caterer that you used at our Christmas event last year?"

"That's the one," Gwen confirms with a small smile.

"Excellent!" Mrs. Hughes says, clapping her hands together. "They were simply divine. Going along with Jenny's suggestion of a fresh cake, I think we should ask the caterers to create a light and refreshing menu. I'm thinking salads, fruits, maybe chicken. Gwen, could you coordinate that?"

"Will do." Gwen adjusts her glasses and jots down another note. "We'll schedule a tasting in the next day or two. I just need to go over a few options with the caterers first. For now, I'm thinking we stick with this light and fresh theme—maybe incorporate fresh flowers? A wedding outdoors at the marina? For the bridesmaids, pink and yellow are great spring colors. For the men, tan and white suits, with a pop of pink or yellow in the ties. What do you think?"

The rapid-fire suggestions take a second to sink in. I blink, then smile. "I love that. Maybe a soft pink to accent the cherry blossoms?"

Gwen pauses, her head tilting thoughtfully, then nods in agreement. "Jenny, I will get you in for a dress fitting as quickly as I can. Bridesmaids and groomsmen fittings following that. And then, of course, the parents of the bride and groom. When can we expect your parents to come in for that?"

I hesitate a moment before saying, "They won't be."

"Oh?" Mrs. Hughes asks.

"They're not really involved in my life," I say.

Trent takes my hand and gives it an assuring squeeze. "But her grandpa Henry will be there, and he'll need a suit."

I nod. "Yes, he'll walk me down the aisle."

Gwen and Mrs. Hughes nod solemnly. "We can do that, dear," Mrs. Hughes says.

"Of course," Gwen adds.

"Anyway," Trent says, quickly changing the subject, his tone warm and calm. "If you're all set on having the wedding at the marina, I know just the spot for the ceremony. Once we wrap up here, I'll show you all."

The meeting rolls on, the table turning into a battlefield of papers, fabric swatches, and scribbled notes. Discussions about flowers, centerpieces, and timing blur together as my energy wanes. Even the vibrant descriptions of daisies and peonies start to lose their luster.

Sensing my growing fatigue, Trent pushes back from the table with a stretch, his fingers lacing together above his head. "I think we've made some great progress," he says. "Speaking for both Jenny and me, I'd say we're officially wedding-planned out. How about we take a stroll to the spot I mentioned and talk about the ceremony and reception there?"

Grateful, I give him a small smile as I push back my chair. My legs feel stiff as I stand. "That sounds perfect. I can't wait to see the spot."

Turning to Gwen and Mrs. Hughes, Trent gestures to the table. "Feel free to leave everything here until we get back."

They nod, their focus already shifting back to their binders and notes, and we follow Trent out of the office.

"Be right back," I call to Greg as we pass the front counter. "We're checking out a location really quick, and then I'll swap back with you."

Greg waves us off with an easy smile. "Take your time. I've got things under control."

As we step outside, the crisp scent of the marina greets us, mingling with the faint brine of the water and the occasional whiff of diesel from the docked boats. The sunlight warms my skin as we walk, the rhythmic lap of water against the docks calming my overworked brain. Beside me, Trent walks with an easy confidence, his hands stuffed in his pockets and a small, thoughtful smile on his lips. For the first time all morning, I let myself relax, ready to see where this next step will take us.

Chapter 11
Trent

After being cooped up for so long in my office talking wedding plans, the fresh air feels like a gift. Now, I'm hoping I didn't build this location up too much in my head. Jenny, Gwen, and my mom follow me across the marina grounds. The crunch of gravel underfoot mixes with the distant hum of boat motors.

This marina holds so many memories for me. When Mom and Dad ran the marina and I was just a kid, I spent hours exploring these grounds. I'd climb trees and scramble over rocks, making up games as I wandered through the woods. I can still picture the perfect tree that I always dreamed of turning into a treehouse. And since I haven't gotten around to that, I figure I'll build it for my kids someday. Not that this wedding is going to bring about kids or anything. This is just a marriage of convenience—she's helping me, and I'm helping her. That's it.

"So where are you taking us?" Jenny asks, stepping up beside me. Her voice pulls me back to the present, and I glance down at her.

"Well, there's this spot I loved when I was younger," I say, gesturing to the path ahead. "Last summer, I finally got around to making a walking path that leads to it. It's hard to describe, but it's kind of . . . perfect."

"You haven't added it to the marina maps yet?" she asks, brushing a strand of hair out of her face as a breeze flutters through the trees.

"Nope," I reply with a grin. "Haven't found the right name for it yet. Maybe you can help me with that?"

We take the final turn down the path, where sunlight filters through the trees and dapples the ground with golden spots. The gentle rustling of leaves overhead and the faint chirp of birds create a peaceful soundtrack.

When we reach the clearing, everyone stops in their tracks. The path opens into a circular field surrounded by cherry blossoms about to bloom, their pink petals bright against the blue sky. The scent of flowers mingles with the crisp breeze coming off the water. Small patches of wildflowers peek out of the grass.

To the left, an opening reveals a view of the lake below. It's elevated just enough to give the perfect vantage point, and on windy days like today, you can hear the waves crashing against the rocks.

Simply put, the view is breathtaking.

I'd originally thought that this location could be a spot for picnickers to come and have a nice outing. I also thought it could be a location for events, I guess like weddings, but I never thought it would be for my wedding.

I shift awkwardly, suddenly unsure. What if what I see as perfection feels underwhelming to them? Seconds stretch into what feels like minutes, and the silence starts to claw at my nerves.

"So . . ." I venture hesitantly, rubbing the back of my neck. "Would this work?"

"Would this work?" Gwen says, her eyebrows shooting up. "Did you just ask me if this would work?"

"Uh, yeah," I say, pulling off my hat and running a hand through my hair. My palms feel clammy now. This was definitely a bad idea.

"It's perfect," my mom whispers, her voice thick with emotion. She dabs at her eyes with a tissue.

"Trent," Jenny says softly, her voice trembling slightly as she looks at me, "this place is incredible." Her eyes glisten, and she reaches out to take my hand.

"It's more than perfect," Gwen declares, breaking her silence as she strides forward, her heels digging into the grass. She looks around like she's cataloging every detail. "Trent, you and I are going to have a talk. This could be the wedding location for spring. Do you know how many people in Nashville would want to be married here?"

"Umm . . . a lot?" I ask, still processing her reaction.

"Exactly," Gwen says, her tone decisive. "This could open a whole new revenue stream for the marina. With the cabins for overnight stays, this field for ceremonies, and the barn you have for events, you could corner the market for weddings. Especially for couples who want to get out of the city but stay close."

"Oh wow," I say, my mind spinning.

"Do you really think so?" Jenny asks, her voice tinged with excitement.

"Absolutely!" Gwen says. "There are a few minor adjustments we'd need to make, but nothing too invasive." She flips open her notebook and jots something down. "I think we will have time for what is needed, but we're going to be pushing it.

You all sure you don't want a fall wedding? This place would be just as gorgeous in the fall."

We both shake our head in unison.

"What would need to be done to it?" I ask, frowning slightly. "I don't want to ruin the beauty of this place."

"Well, for starters," she says gesturing toward the edge, "we'd need a fence to block off the drop to the lake. But a small white picket fence would do the trick—simple yet effective."

I nod as she continues, "We'd also need an arch for the ceremony. Nothing permanent, just something that can be stored and set up to match each wedding."

"That seems reasonable," I agree.

"It would be adorable with tree-stump seats," Jenny chimes in, her eyes lighting up. "Not just for weddings, but schools could use it for field trips or outdoor classes."

"The chairs could be dual-purpose," Mom says. "They'd work for weddings and educational programs alike. I think it's a brilliant idea, Jenny."

I glance back out over the field, picturing the stump seats scattered around the clearing. The idea starts to take root, and I already know where I can source the wood and preserve the seats so they stay nice.

"That all sounds very doable. I'm in," I say finally.

"Great!" Gwen claps her hands together. "Now, for your wedding. We won't have the chairs in time, but I'll arrange for some to be brought in. What do you think about setting the arch here?" She points toward the opening, where the lake serves as a stunning backdrop with the cherry blossoms framing it.

"Yes!" my mom says enthusiastically. "And the chairs could fan out like this." She gestures with her hands, walking around the field to map out an imaginary setup. "Jenny could make her entrance from the path we just came down."

"That sounds lovely," Jenny says, giving my hand a gentle squeeze. The small gesture pulls me back to the moment, reminding me that we're in this together—for better or worse.

Later that evening, after locking up, I scan the marina grounds for Jenny. I'd planned to walk her to my house so she could get a feel for it and figure out what she wants to change, but she must have already left. With only two weeks until the wedding, there's still so much to do.

I glance toward her cabin and see a soft glow through the window. The light's on, so I head over, the crunch of gravel under my boots the only sound in the still evening air.

About ten feet from the cabin, I catch sight of Jenny painting through the window. My steps falter, and for a moment, I forget to breathe. I've never seen her while she paints before.

She's a vision. Wearing paint-splattered overalls, her hair tied up in two messy braided pigtails, she looks completely at ease. The sight makes my heart lurch in a way I wasn't prepared for.

Through the window, I watch as she paints, her movements fluid and rhythmic, like a dancer lost in the music. One hand holds a palette, dabs of color bright against its surface, while the other sweeps the brush over the canvas in gentle, precise strokes. It's mesmerizing. She's mesmerizing.

The intensity on her face, the way her lips purse ever so slightly when she concentrates—it's like she's poured every ounce of herself into the art. I have no idea what she's painting, but whatever it is, it's clear it holds a piece of her heart.

Realizing I'm just standing there staring like some kind of creep, I shake myself and step up to the cabin, knocking lightly on the door.

"Just a minute!" Jenny calls, her voice muffled but warm.

A moment later, she opens the door. Her cheeks are flushed, and there's a streak of paint smeared across one of them. Specks of color dot the backs of her hands, and a stray lock of hair slips from her braid, curling against her temple.

"Oh, hi!" she says, a little breathless. "I wasn't expecting you."

"Were you expecting someone else?" I tease, raising an eyebrow.

She rolls her eyes and swats my arm, the corners of her mouth twitching in a barely restrained smile, before turning back toward her easel.

Yeah, I deserved that.

"I mean," she says with a playful smile, "I wasn't expecting you until later."

"You need a few more minutes before we head to my—I mean our house?"

"I just need a couple minutes to clean up," she says. "Come on in."

I step inside, taking in the organized chaos of her cabin. Canvases lean against the walls, brushes and paint tubes scattered across every surface. The faint smell of turpentine and lavender drifts through the air, oddly comforting.

"I love what you've done with the place," I say, chuckling as I step over a drop cloth.

"Sorry for the mess," Jenny says with a shrug, waving a paint-streaked hand. "Soon it won't matter. I'll be able to turn this whole cabin into a proper studio." Her eyes light up as she speaks, her excitement almost tangible. "You have no idea how much that means to me. I'll finally be able to work on multiple projects at once, have everything set up permanently so I can just dive in whenever inspiration strikes. No more having to tidy up for guests."

"Well, I'm glad it makes you happy," I say, my voice softening. "I like seeing you happy."

As soon as the words leave my mouth, I cringe internally. Smooth, Trent. Real smooth.

"You like making others happy, don't you?" Jenny says, tilting her head, her eyes searching mine.

I nod, swallowing the lump forming in my throat. Safer to keep quiet this time.

"I noticed that about you the first time we met," she continues, a playful glint in her eye.

"You mean when I saved you from becoming a pancake?" I ask, smirking.

Jenny narrows her eyes and points her paintbrush at me, a tiny splatter of blue landing on my shirt. "We don't talk about that day. It was one of my lowest moments, and you know it. But," she adds, her voice softening, "you were a bright spot for me. You turned things around, and I don't know if I ever really thanked you for that."

"Well, speaking of bright spots," I say, gesturing to my paint-splattered shirt, "looks like I've got some of my own now. Does that mean I get to help paint?"

The horrified look on Jenny's face when she notices the splatter is almost too much. I bite my cheek to keep from laughing.

"Oh no! I'm so sorry!" she exclaims, rushing off to grab a washcloth. "It's acrylic paint, so it should wash out. I can treat it tonight."

She dabs at my shirt with the damp cloth, her movements quick but gentle. The warmth of her hand against my chest makes my pulse quicken. I catch her wrist lightly.

"It's fine, really," I say, my voice steady. "This shirt isn't special. Don't worry about it."

Her lips press together. "Are you sure?"

"Yeah," I reply, smiling. "I can just take care of my shirt when I get back to my place."

"Okay, well let me clean up really quick and we can head over there. I am excited to see the place." Jenny wipes her hands on a rag before disappearing to clean up. When she returns, there's still that small streak of paint on her cheek.

"Hold on," I say, stepping closer. I reach out, cupping her face gently in my hand.

"What are you—"

"Just a second," I murmur, dabbing at the paint with the washcloth. Her skin is soft, and the warmth of her cheek beneath my fingertips makes me pause longer than I probably should.

"Did you get it all?" she whispers, her wide eyes meeting mine. The space between us feels charged, her breath warm against my neck. My gaze flickers to her lips, soft and inviting. For a brief second, I wonder what it would be like to kiss her.

What the heck, dude? Get ahold of yourself. You can kiss her when you say "I do."

My thoughts snap back, and I step away, clearing my throat. "Right. Got it all. Let's head to our place then."

I set the washcloth down and turn toward the door, stepping outside to put some distance between us.

No, I tell myself firmly, you have no right to kiss her. Kissing her now isn't what we agreed on. Physical affection only when necessary, and this moment isn't necessary. Even if she is my fiancée.

Chapter 12
Jenny

Did Trent almost kiss me? Why did I want him to so badly? My heart hammers as I grab my keys and phone then follow Trent out the door into the cool evening air. The scent of pine and earth fills my lungs, and I try to keep my thoughts from spiraling.

"I don't think I know where your house is," I say, quickening my steps to catch up to him.

"Not too far. I walk to work, but when I had it built, I set it a little out of the way so people wouldn't come knocking on my door anytime they had a question." His voice is light as he leads the way back toward the marina lodge. The fading light casts long shadows, giving the quiet marina an almost ethereal glow.

"You built it? I thought your parents lived there before and just moved away."

"Nope," he says, shaking his head. "They wanted a little more work-life separation and built a house on the other side of the lake. They'd just drive the boat into work each morning."

"That's cool," I reply. The quiet companionship between us feels natural as we walk past the docks, the marina shop, and the gazebo. The occasional chirp of crickets fills the silence, the lake's water gently lapping in the distance. When we reach a path veiled with a dense tree line, Trent motions to it with a nod.

"I've never noticed this path before," I say, peering into the woods. "How'd you keep it so hidden?"

"I didn't even out the entrance where it meets the woods, but as soon as you pass the tree line, the path is clear. It's not the only way in, though. There's a driveway that leads to the main road, but it's long, and I mostly use it for deliveries."

"So that's why you keep your truck at the marina," I say.

"Yeah, pretty much," he says with a chuckle, stepping out of the way for me to see. "Here it is now."

The path opens to a clearing, and my breath catches at the sight of his home. A covered wraparound porch surrounds an adorable two-story log cabin. The golden light spilling from the windows makes the wood glow. To the right, the faint outline of the lake glimmers in the last vestiges of sunlight. The scene is idyllic, straight out of a postcard.

"Come on," he says, motioning me forward. "I'll give you the tour." I follow him to the porch. The wood creaks faintly underfoot, and I catch a hint of cedar mixed with the earthy scent of the woods.

Inside, I'm floored by the beauty of the space. The downstairs is open-concept, with a massive living room flowing seamlessly into a chef's dream kitchen and a cozy dining area. The downstairs is simply designed. It's definitely got a rustic feel. I make my way around the space, taking in everything. Large windows line the walls, and I'm drawn to one immediately. Outside, the moon's reflection dances on the water, casting silvery light across the lake.

"Of course, your house would overlook the lake," I say, shaking my head with a smile. Glancing down, I spot a fire pit and a dock just visible in the moonlight. Adirondack chairs complete the picturesque scene.

"It's a gorgeous setup," I add.

"Thanks," Trent says, standing a little straighter. He tugs his hat off and runs a hand through his hair, the gesture endearing. "The porch wraps around the whole house. You'll notice exterior doors on three of the walls."

"I bet it's breathtaking in the mornings," I say. "You have a really nice place."

"Uh, thanks," he replies, his ears turning pink. "It's, uh, soon to be yours too. Do whatever you like with the place."

Right. "How about you show me the bedrooms?" I suggest. "Or, I guess, the upstairs?"

"Sure, follow me." As we ascend the staircase, my fingers trail along the smooth, polished wood of the handrail. It's clear he's poured his heart into every detail of this house.

At the top of the stairs, Trent gestures to the open space. "This is the loft. It overlooks the living room." I turn and see the sweeping view below, the glow from the kitchen casting soft light across the rustic space.

"To the left is my room," Trent says, "but we don't need to head that way. At the back is an all-purpose room. Kind of an office-slash-catch-all space. I haven't done much with it yet. We just finished building the place last spring."

"That's pretty recent," I say, following him to the back room. When I step inside, my breath catches. The wall-to-floor windows frame the lake, now bathed in moonlight. The scene is stunning—peaceful yet alive with subtle movement.

"It's beautiful," I whisper, imagining lazy mornings curled up with a book in this very spot.

"Thank you," Trent replies, shrugging. "I kind of like the lake."

His understatement makes me laugh. "Yeah, that wasn't hard to figure out, even before seeing your house."

"Ready for the rest of the tour?" he asks, his blue eyes glinting with amusement.

"Absolutely. This place has three bedrooms?"

"Yeah," he says. "The master bedroom and two guest rooms. You can pick between the two. The smaller one overlooks the lake, and the other faces the woods. The bathroom is in the middle, but it's all yours. Sorry, the rooms don't have their own bathroom."

"Trent, that's more than fine," I assure him. I step into each room. Both have stunning views.

"So, which room would you prefer to sleep in?" Trent says, then quickly adds. "By yourself, I mean. And not that kind of sleeping." His face turns red.

I laugh. "I know what you mean. I liked the forest view. I'll take that one," I say, picturing snow-covered trees in winter or catching sight of an owl at night.

"Good choice," Trent says with a small smile, his gaze distant. He clears his throat. "Make yourself comfortable. I'm going to throw this shirt in the wash and grab a clean one."

"Alright," I reply. After he leaves, I enter the soon-to-be-my room and take a moment to flop onto the bed with a sigh. In three weeks, this kind, sweet man will be my husband. How did my life change so quickly? So much has changed from that first morning we met. I feel like I blinked and now I have a job and am engaged and Grandpa Henry is going to be taken care of.

"So, what do you think?" Trent asks, stepping into the doorway while working on buttoning a clean shirt. My thoughts scatter at the sight of him—his shirt is open, revealing a sculpted chest. I stand and take a step toward him.

"I like you," I blurt, then immediately backtrack. "I mean, I like it. The room. The house. The whole package is great." I drop back onto the bed, groaning inwardly. Why can't the ground swallow me whole?

"I'm glad you like the room. And the house. And . . . I like you too," he says softly.

My heart stutters. "You do?" I ask, half-propped up on my elbows.

"Yeah. I couldn't have asked for a nicer person to go through a mutually beneficial marriage with," he replies, his sincerity making my chest ache.

Right. He likes me as a person. Of course.

"You missed a button," I say, rolling off the bed and stepping close to him. I point to his chest. "Here, let me help. It's my fault you had to change anyway." My fingers work quickly, brushing against his skin. When I feel the rapid thrum of his heartbeat, I freeze.

I glance up, and our eyes lock. The intensity in his gaze sends a jolt through me. His eyes flicker to my lips, a silent question hanging between us.

Screw it, I'm going to marry the guy in three weeks anyway.

I lean in, closing the distance. His lips are soft and still for a moment, and I'm about to pull back in panic when he relaxes, one hand cupping my cheek as the other slides to the small of my back.

His kiss deepens, his touch anchoring me as my arms circle his neck. The warmth of his body, the strength in his hold—it's intoxicating. I press closer, savoring the way he feels against me. For now, in this moment, he's mine.

His lips are soft and delicious against mine. I didn't know how he would react, but he's reacting like he wanted this too, maybe as much as I did. I don't know if it's the charged energy between us with the upcoming wedding or what, but I am all for it. I can feel the muscles under his shirt, and it sends a thrill through me.

This sexy specimen of a man is going to be my husband soon, and I get to kiss him. I am kissing him. I don't know what our relationship will look like when we are married because it's only supposed to be for a short while. But for now, in this moment, he's mine.

When he pulls back, his forehead resting against mine, I'm breathless. "Jenny," he says, "I'm sorry. I shouldn't have . . ."

"I kissed you, remember?" I say, my voice softer than I expected. Stepping back, I tilt my head up to meet Trent's eyes, those beautiful, warm eyes that flicker in the dim light of the room with every shade of blue. "And I don't regret it. Not one bit."

His lips twitch into a smile, equal parts mischief and tenderness. "Is that so?"

"Yes, that's so," I reply, my own lips curving up despite the racing of my heart.

"Well," he murmurs, his voice dropping to a deep, velvety tone that sends a shiver up my spine. "Then I guess it would be okay if I did this . . ."

Before I can process his words, he closes the distance between us, his lips crashing into mine with a fervor that ignites every nerve in my body. This kiss is nothing like the tentative one we shared just moments ago—it's deeper, more deliberate, and brimming with unspoken emotion. The sheer intensity of it makes my knees buckle, but Trent's arms wrap firmly around my waist, holding me steady.

I grip his shoulders, clinging to him as if he's the only solid thing in the universe. His warmth radiates through his shirt, and I can feel the strength in his arms as they pull me closer. It's like he's tethering me to him, and I have no intention of letting go.

The kiss consumes me, drowning out everything else. The faint creak of the floorboards, the chirp of crickets outside, the cool night air seeping through the windows—it all fades until there's nothing but Trent. His lips move against mine with an urgency that sets my pulse racing, and I can't help but melt into him.

This kiss isn't just passion; it's a question, a promise, a fire that burns through every doubt I've ever had. If I could only have this moment, I'd pour everything into it. I wonder if he feels the same, if he's silently carving out a space for me in his heart the way I am for him.

Time seems to blur, and I lose myself in the taste and feel of him. His scent surrounds me—a mix of cedar, lake water, and something uniquely Trent that I know I'll never forget. His hand moves to the small of my back again, pressing me flush against him, while the other tangles in my hair, sending sparks shooting down my spine.

Eventually, Trent pulls back just enough to trail kisses along my cheek, his stubble brushing against my skin. His lips find my neck, and my breath catches as he lingers there, pressing a kiss just below my collarbone. The sensation is electric, and a soft gasp escapes my lips before I can stop it.

If my knees were weak before, now they're jelly. A warm, tingling heat spreads through me, and I grip his shoulders tighter, leaning into him for support.

"I think…" I manage to stammer between breaths, my voice barely above a whisper, "I think I'm going to like this marriage. A lot."

Trent chuckles against my skin, the sound low and rumbling, vibrating through me. "Mmm," he replies, his lips curving into a smile against my neck. "I think I am too."

He pulls back just enough to look at me, his blue eyes searching mine, filled with something I can't quite name—something raw and real that leaves me breathless. His thumb grazes my cheek, and I lean into his touch, my heart pounding so hard it's a wonder he can't hear it.

For a moment, neither of us speaks. We just stand there, caught in this fragile, perfect bubble, our breaths mingling in the space between us.

And for the first time in a long time, I feel completely and utterly seen.

Chapter 13
Trent

The next week flies by in a blur of appointments, decisions, and fleeting glances that linger in my mind long after they've passed. Jenny and I barely have a chance to catch a moment alone together. Every day seems to be packed with meetings, fittings, and checklists, all conspiring to keep us apart. Not to mention fighting off the constant barrage of questions from our friends and family about how long we've been together, how we knew we were the ones for each other, and if we're sure we want to have the wedding so soon.

Luckily, when we met with Holly to finalize the cake, she didn't have any questions about the timing of our relationship. We tasted so many cake flavors that I thought I'd never want sugar again—until I bit into the Sunrise Sin. The rich, tangy sweetness of the orange-cinnamon zest combined with the decadent cream frosting was almost enough to win us over. But then there was the lemon, light and refreshing, with a bright citrus zing that lingered on the tongue. Neither of us could choose, so we didn't. Two tiers, two flavors—it felt like a perfect compromise.

Today, Jenny has been whisked away by Gwen and my mom for dress fittings and bridesmaid appointments. I can picture her now, standing in front of a mirror, the glow of her smile brighter than any spotlight. The thought sends a pang through my chest.

All I can think about is how much I want more time with her. I didn't expect this—falling for my future wife wasn't part of the plan. We agreed this would be simple: a friendly arrangement to solve mutual problems. Get married, stick it out for the agreed time, and part ways amicably. No mess, no heartbreak.

But now, the idea of parting ways feels unbearable. I catch myself imagining forever—her laugh filling the house, her hand slipping into mine, the two of us building a life together. The thought thrills and terrifies me in equal measure.

Is this how it feels in those arranged marriages you read about? Two strangers learning to love each other, except we aren't strangers. We won't be meeting on our wedding day. We set this marriage up ourselves, a modern twist on an ancient tradition. Unorthodox, yes, but maybe it could work.

If only I knew how Jenny felt.

I've been pouring my thoughts into every detail of this wedding. And every time I walk into my empty home, I wish she were living there already. With how busy wedding planning has been, we agreed she'd move her things in the night before the wedding. She's also planning a pre-wedding sleepover with the girls at our house while I crash at Greg's place. The timing of her moving in is a practical arrangement, but it leaves me wondering—will it always feel this temporary?

"What's up, man?" Greg says, pulling me from my thoughts as he steps out of his office across the hall. "You look like you've got the weight of the world on your shoulders."

I glance up from my desk, grabbing my cap and shutting my laptop. "Just wedding stuff."

"Not having second thoughts, are you?" His grin is teasing, but his tone carries a hint of concern. "Not that we could blame you, planning a wedding in three weeks is enough to make anyone run."

"Dude, I'm not even close to thinking about backing out of this wedding."

"I didn't really think you were," Greg says. "But obviously there is something weighing on you."

I hesitate, but I've known Greg long enough to trust him with our secret. He kept his love for Holly under wraps for thirteen years before they finally got together. If anyone can understand complicated feelings, it's him. So, I tell him everything, about my grandfather's contract, Jenny, our agreement, I don't leave out anything.

Greg raises an eyebrow. "Wow, man, that's a lot. So, you and Jenny are kind of not in a relationship?"

"We are in the sense that we're getting married in two weeks."

"But you're not in love with each other?" Greg asks.

I stare at the floor.

"Unless . . ." Greg says. "Are you catching actual feelings for her?"

"Yeah," I admit, leaning back in my chair. "She's amazing. Not just around the marina, but as a person. I don't think I could've picked someone better to marry."

"Then why do you look so glum?"

"Because this wasn't the plan. I'm starting to think that I want this marriage to last longer than a year, but I don't know how Jenny feels about it."

Greg leans against the doorframe, crossing his arms. "Then talk to her. Be honest. You never know—she might feel the same way. Man, I see how she looks at you and how you two are together. I'm on your side and think that you two have what it takes to make this work, as long as you are both open and honest about things."

I shake my head, horrified at the thought of Jenny finding out I spilled everything to Greg. "I can't. Our arrangement was supposed to stay between Jenny and me. I shouldn't have told you any of this."

Greg smirks. "Relax, man. I'm not saying blab to anyone. Just talk to Jenny. You owe it to yourself—and her."

We head out to Greg's car, his words still rattling around in my mind. "That's exactly it, though," I say, sliding into the passenger seat. "What if she only wants to stick to the original plan? What if she's not open to forever?"

"Then wouldn't you rather know now, before you say 'I do'? At least then you can prepare your heart."

I let out a dry laugh. "When did you get so wise? I seem to remember giving you advice not too long ago. How did our roles reverse?"

"That's life," Greg says with a shrug. "Something happens, and it shifts your whole perspective. For better or worse. And I'm willing to bet that in this case, it's for the better."

By the time we arrive at the shop to get fitted for our suits, Gwen, my mom, and Niall are already there, chatting with the attendant.

"There he is!" my mom exclaims, rushing over to pull me into a hug.

"Don't worry, Mrs. Hughes," Greg says with a wink. "I wouldn't let him miss this."

"Hey, mate," Niall says, clapping me on the back. "Ready for the big day? It's coming up fast."

"As ready as I can be," I reply, trying to keep my voice light.

We follow Gwen and the attendant to the fitting area. The tan suits Gwen picked out aren't traditional, but they're sharp—springlike, as she put it. The white shirts add a crisp touch, and by the end of the fitting, I have to admit, we clean up pretty well.

"Don't forget, you and Jenny are coming over tonight for dinner," my mom says for the hundredth time as we're leaving.

"How could I forget, Mom? Six o'clock on the dot, I promise."

I give her another hug, but as we head out, my mind drifts back to Greg's words. Maybe he's right. Maybe it's time to have that conversation with Jenny—before it's too late.

"How did the fitting go?" Jenny asks as I step into the marina shop, the late afternoon light spilling through the large windows and casting golden streaks across the floor. The familiar scent of cedarwood polish and faint gasoline from the dock fills the air. Jenny is behind the counter, her hands busy sorting receipts into neat piles, though her eyes lift to meet mine with a spark of curiosity.

"Good," I say, pulling off my cap and ruffling my hair. "The guys and I got our suits. Gotta say, we look pretty sharp. And my dad and Henry are supposed to go in tomorrow." She grins, the corners of her mouth pulling upward in a way that makes me forget whatever else I was going to say.

"Good, good," she says. "Umm, your mom called. She wanted me to remind you not to forget dinner at their house tonight."

I laugh, a low rumble escaping before I can stop it. Jenny tilts her head. "What's so funny?"

"I just left her, and she reminded me there too. Does she think I'd forget in the fifteen minutes it takes to get from the shop to here?"

Jenny chuckles softly, the sound light and musical. "Well, you have been a bit . . . spaced out lately. Maybe she's worried you'd lose track."

That statement pulls me up short. "I've been spaced out?"

She nods, her smile fading slightly as concern creeps into her expression. "Yeah, probably not noticeable to most people, but I can tell. You haven't seemed like yourself the past few days."

Her words settle like a weight in my chest, and I stare at her dumbfounded. My mind scrambles to replay the last week—had I been so consumed by my own thoughts that I'd been neglecting her? Neglecting my responsibilities?

"Trent," she says softly, her voice like a gentle nudge, "do you not want to go through with this anymore? Are you regretting our decision to get married?"

Her question catches me off guard, and I see the flicker of vulnerability in her eyes. "What?" I say. "No. Why would you think that?"

That's the complete opposite of what I've been thinking.

She hesitates, her hands stilling on the stack of papers. "I don't know," she says softly. "It's just . . . I've been left before, and I don't think I could go through that again. I know this is just an agreement between us that will end, something temporary for a year, and I'm not expecting you to stick around forever. That's not what we agreed to. But the thought of standing up at the altar only to be left again unexpectedly . . . I don't think I could handle that."

I step closer, reaching out to take her hands in mine. Her fingers are cool to the touch, and I squeeze them gently. "Look at me, please."

Her gaze lifts, and the unshed tears lining her blue eyes cut through me.

"I don't regret this—any of this. You've been a bright light in what could have been a really dark situation my granddad put me in. Did I want to have to get married to keep the marina? No, of course not."

She tugs back slightly, but I hold on, desperate for her to understand. "But if I had to pick the perfect person to do this with, I couldn't have imagined, never in my wildest dreams, anyone better than you. You've turned something that could've been awkward and stressful into something . . . amazing. I'm excited to marry you."

Her lips part, surprise softening her features. "Seriously? You're not just saying that?"

I nod, my voice firm. "I'm serious. As serious as the fact that kissing you last week was the highlight of my year so far."

A huge smile spreads across her face.

"And," I say, my voice turning more serious, "I would never ever do what your parents did. I would never leave you, Jenny."

When I pull her into a hug, it feels as natural as breathing. Her tension melts away as she relaxes against me, and the world outside the shop fades to nothing.

After a moment, we pull apart, and she resumes tidying the counter, though her movements are slower, more thoughtful now. "So then, what's been on your mind if it's not the wedding?"

"Oh, the wedding's definitely on my mind," I admit, leaning on the counter as the late sunlight catches the highlights in her hair. "That, and trying to declutter some of my stuff so that you have space when you move in."

She pauses, a hint of teasing in her tone. "I could've helped with that, you know."

Neither of us has had the time to do much more with the house, since we've been so busy with wedding planning. And after our kiss, I don't want to tempt myself with being so near her, but I know that's going to be all for naught when she moves in the night before the wedding. I need to rein in my emotions because I don't want to scare her away. I need her to stick to the agreement not only because otherwise the marina is pretty much gone but also because I'm hoping I can convince her to stay with me past the year we agreed on.

"I know," I say, scratching the back of my neck. "But you shouldn't have to help with my things. Besides, I didn't mind. It's just . . . getting used to this new normal."

Her lips twitch into a small smile, but she doesn't push further. Instead, she changes the subject. "My painting is coming along great, by the way. The views around the lake have been really inspiring. I'm trying something new, but it's not ready for anyone to see yet. Maybe soon, though—if you'd want to see it." She tucks a stray hair behind her ear before making eye contact with me.

I can see the joy and excitement, but also the nervousness in her eyes. I hate whatever put that there, whatever caused her to think she isn't the greatest, most talented person I've ever met.

The vulnerability in her voice stirs something in me. "Of course I want to see it. Maybe you could even paint something for the house, to hang in the bonus room upstairs."

Her eyes widen. "You don't mean that."

"Sure, I do. You're talented."

"How would you even know?" she asks, skepticism tinged with curiosity. "You've only seen a few paintings here and there."

"And just from those, I know you're talented. And . . ." I kick the toe of my shoe against the counter before finally admitting, "when we made our arrangement, I looked you up. I wanted to see your work—to get to know you better. If I was going to marry you, I felt like I should know all of you. You know?"

She's silent for a moment, and I look up to find her watching me, her expression soft and unreadable. "You did that?"

"Yeah. Why wouldn't I? Jenny, I'd be proud to have your art in our home."

Her expression softens further, and a wistful smile tugs at her lips. "My grandma Cora would've loved you. She was the artistic one in the family—she's where I get it from."

"I didn't know that." I lean against the counter as she talks and finishes wiping down her workspace. "I remember your grandma. Every now and then, Henry would bring her to the marina for a picnic, and I got to meet her. She was a very sweet lady."

"She was the best," Jenny agrees, nodding. "I can't believe you met my grandparents before we officially met. I wish I could have asked Grandma Cora what she thought of you."

"She loved me, of course," I say waving at myself like I am Vanna White and just showcased a new letter.

"I do think she would have loved you. Grandma Cora had a love for all things fun in life. She saw the world in a way that others couldn't. It's why she was an artist. She used to say that art could show people the beauty in the world, even when they couldn't see it themselves." Her voice falters slightly, but she continues. "When she got too sick to go out, I'd paint by her bedside. I wanted to bring the world to her, to remind her of all the beauty out there."

"That must've been hard, losing her."

Jenny nods, her smile bittersweet. "It was, but she's with me every time I pick up a paintbrush."

Coming around the counter, she swats my arm playfully. "We'd better hurry or we'll be late. How long does it take to get to your parents' place?" She heads toward the door, and I follow her.

"About forty-five minutes by road," I say, locking the shop door behind us as we step outside, "but only ten if we take the boat."

She grins, the setting sun casting a golden glow across her face.

As we make our way down the path toward the house, the rhythmic sound of our footsteps mingles with the distant whistles of wood ducks. I can't help but think how much I want every journey with her—by land, by boat, by whatever—to last a lifetime.

Chapter 14

Jenny

"Wait," I say, quickening my steps to catch up with Trent, "we're actually taking a boat?" He's nearly at the tree line, his silhouette outlined against the darkening sky, when I finally fall in beside him.

"Of course," he says, glancing at me over his shoulder. "We don't have time to drive—we'd be late, and Mom would hate that."

"Right. You couldn't have told me that sooner?" I scold, trying to keep the breathlessness out of my voice.

He stops abruptly and turns to face me. "Why? Is there something wrong with taking the boat? You can swim, right?"

"Nothing's wrong with taking the boat," I say, crossing my arms against the cool evening air. "It's just a little chilly, and I didn't grab a jacket before we left. And, yes, I can swim, but I don't plan on falling in the lake."

Trent smirks and resumes his trek down the path to his house, his steps crunching softly on the gravel. "It's fine," he calls over his shoulder. "I've got a jacket you can borrow."

I falter slightly, my mind catching on his words. He's going to give me his jacket? The thought makes my heart flutter in a way I'd rather ignore. After we kissed, the idea of being wrapped up in his scent again has been all I can think about.

By the time we reach the dock a few minutes later, I'm cocooned in one of Trent's spare jackets. It's way too big on me, the sleeves hanging over my hands and the hem brushing my thighs, but the warmth—and the subtle hint of his cologne—more than make up for it. It's almost too much to handle.

Standing at the edge of the dock, I watch as Trent moves with practiced ease, checking the boat to make sure everything is in order. The sun has almost completely set, the horizon painted with the last streaks of burnt orange and dusky purple. Overhead, a waning gibbous moon rises, casting a silver glow across the rippling lake.

"Don't worry about it getting dark," Trent says. "I could boat across this lake blindfolded." He holds out a hand to me. "You ready to come aboard?"

I nod, taking his hand carefully as I step onto the boat. His grip is steady and reassuring, and I feel a flicker of warmth in my chest as I settle into the seat.

Once I'm securely seated, Trent unties the boat and pushes us off the dock. The engine hums to life, a low and steady thrum that vibrates beneath my feet as we glide across the water.

The wind is brisk, and I huddle deeper into Trent's jacket, pulling the zipper up to my chin. Despite the chill, there's something calming about the open water at night. The gentle rocking of the boat, the rhythmic lapping of waves against the hull, and the quiet authority with which Trent steers—all of it works together to soothe my nerves. I could get used to this.

Growing up, I spent some time on the lake. My granddad would occasionally take me fishing with one of his buddies, but I've never done this—speeding across the water with the wind whipping through our hair as we navigate from one house to another.

"Boating must be incredible in the summer," I say, breaking the silence. "I can just imagine it—a warm breeze, water splashing up to cool you off, finding the perfect spot to jump in for a swim or tubing."

Trent glances at me, a smile tugging at the corners of his mouth. "You ever go tubing?"

"A few times," I admit. "But not like I'm imagining now."

"Oh, you'd love it," he says, his voice tinged with fondness. "We usually take out a pontoon and a speedboat at least once a month in the summer. It's a full day—tubing, swimming, and grilling out at the marina or my place afterward. It's always a good time."

"That sounds amazing," I say, already picturing the scene.

"We're almost there," he says, nodding toward a light glimmering in the distance. "See that? That's Mom and Dad's dock. We're actually a little early, which should make Mom happy."

He chuckles softly as he slows the boat, maneuvering it skillfully alongside the dock. Once we're secured, he offers his hand again to help me out of the boat.

If I was impressed by Trent's house, his parents' place is on a completely different level. The sprawling mini-Mansion looms in the distance, its windows glowing warmly against the darkening sky. It's elegant yet somehow inviting—a perfect reflection of Mrs. Hughes herself. She dresses like she just walked out of fashion week in Paris and talks as though she is well-to-do, but she is the sweetest person. I'm so lucky to have her as a mother-in-law soon. And I feel proud knowing I am filling some of the same roles at the marina that she did when she ran the place.

Before we make it to the front door, Mrs. Hughes comes bustling out, her arms outstretched. She wraps us both in a hug that's as effervescent as she is. "Oh, look at you two!" she exclaims. "I wasn't sure if you'd come by boat, but I had a feeling. How did you like the ride, dear?"

"I loved it," I say honestly. "It made me imagine what it'd be like when the weather turns warmer."

"Oh, you're going to adore it in the summer!" she gushes. "Trent, you have to take her out as soon as it warms up."

"I already planned on it, Mom," Trent says, pulling her into a hug.

She swats him playfully on the arm. "Come on inside. I've got a wonderful meal planned for you two—and we have a guest tonight."

"You didn't mention any guests, Mom," Trent says, his tone careful.

"Well, they're not really guests," she replies, her voice turning evasive. "It's just one person, and he's family, so I didn't think you'd mind."

Trent stops walking, his expression hardening. "Mom, who is it?"

Mrs. Hughes hesitates, wringing her hands. "Now, don't be upset . . ."

"You're not making it easy not to be upset," Trent says. "Just tell me, please—for Jenny's sake."

She sighs, looking genuinely apologetic. "It's your grandfather."

The air seems to thicken around us. Trent freezes, the muscle in his jaw ticking as he clenches his fist.

"I'll give you two a moment," Mom says, turning into the house.

Reaching out, I gently take his fist in both of my hands, prying his fingers open and lacing mine through his. "Trent," I say softly, trying to meet his eyes, "why are you upset your grandfather is here?"

He exhales sharply, his tension easing slightly under my touch. "It's not that," he says. "I love spending time with my grandfather. It's just that this is the grandfather—the one with the marriage stipulation. I'd be devastated if he somehow found out that I created a kind of loophole to get the marina by arranging a marriage with you. I wish Mom would've let us know he were coming, and then we wouldn't have to walk in here unprepared."

"She doesn't know about our agreement," I remind him. "And this isn't the first time you and I have had to reassure people about our marriage."

"You're right," Trent says. "It's just that he's one of the people I love and respect the most."

"We can handle anything he asks about our relationship. I promise."

Trent studies me for a long moment before nodding. "We can do this."

Smiling, I squeeze his hand. "I know we can."

Together, we head toward the house, the glow from the windows casting long shadows across the manicured lawn. I steel myself for whatever awaits inside.

When Trent and I enter the dining room, an older man is sitting at the head of the table. For a moment, I could swear I am looking at an older version of Trent—same strong jaw-line, same air of quiet confidence. His white-blond hair, softened to the color of sun-bleached straw, frames a face carved with the lines of a life well-lived. A neatly trimmed beard of the same pale shade hugs his jaw, and when his gaze lifts to meet mine, his gray-blue eyes—clear and sharp despite their age—hold me steady. There is a warmth in that look, a kindness that softens the firm set of his shoulders and the roughness of his weathered hands resting on the table's edge. "Samson," Mrs. Hughes says to him warmly, "this is Jenny, Trent's fiancée—the lady I was telling you about. Jenny, this is Trent's grandfather Samson."

Samson's bright eyes sweep over me, his expression warm. "Fiancée, huh?" he says. "Who would've thought Trent would finally find someone. And not a moment too soon either." He gestures toward me, "Come here, then. Let me get a good look at you."

I let go of Trent's hand and step forward, my heartbeat quickening. Samson stands and extends his hand for a formal shake. I wave it off with a smile and pull him into a hug instead. "It's so nice to meet you," I say, keeping my voice light and sincere. "Trent has said only wonderful things about you."

He stiffens in surprise, clearly not expecting the hug. But when we pull back, he has a soft smile on his face. "I like her," he says to everyone in the room. "But I can't help but wonder how this engagement came about a little . . . suddenly."

"Samson," Mrs. Hughes interjects gently, but Samson waves her off with a slight shake of his head.

"It's not every day a man like Trent, not interested in dating, goes from single to engaged in the blink of an eye," Samson continues, his gaze settling back on me. "And call me old-fashioned, but I've seen my fair share of impulsive decisions fall apart under careful scrutiny. I hope the timing of this engagement doesn't have anything to do with the marina."

Trent steps beside me and grabs my hand. "It doesn't," he says. "I know our relationship came about suddenly, but we're happy together."

"When you meet the right person," I say sweetly, squeezing Trent's hand, "you don't second-guess it."

"Of course," Samson says, "if you two are happy, then I'm happy. But how you managed to rein him in in such a short time is perplexing to me."

I glance up at Trent with a soft smile. "Trent didn't need any reining in. He's such a sweet and loving person. And he shows that to me. He has such passion for your marina, too. And I have to say—it's gorgeous. You couldn't have picked a better spot on the lake for the lodge and marina. The views are breathtaking, and the whole place feels so thoughtfully designed. You must have had such a wonderful vision for it. I'd love to pick your brain later—I'm an artist, and I love learning how others see the world."

Samson's brows lift slightly in surprise and we all take our seats at the table.

The meal Mrs. Hughes prepared is as exquisite as it is abundant—each bite more flavorful than the last. The conversation remains polite, but I can feel Samson's watchful gaze on Trent and me, his unspoken questions hanging in the air.

Leaning back slightly, I listen as Mrs. Hughes speaks. "Edmund and I are so excited for Trent to fully take ownership of the marina soon," she says, her voice brimming with pride.

"I can't wait to pass the marina on to Trent either," Samson says, "but he's not married yet. We still have a few days before that happens, right?" Samson laughs.

Beside me, I feel Trent tense, no doubt worrying about the stunt we're pulling with this wedding. Without thinking, I rest a hand lightly on his leg, giving it a gentle squeeze. He glances at me, his shoulders easing ever so slightly.

"The marriage does seem sudden," Trent says, "but I assure you that this engagement isn't some quick decision."

"When Trent and I met," I add, addressing Samson directly, "things seemed to click for us in a way I can't quite explain. Trent is an incredible person, and I'm lucky to have him in my life."

Samson studies us for a moment. "Those are wonderful sentiments, you two," he says, his voice soft. "But words are easy. It's the actions that prove if something is real. A marriage is more than an engagement and a wedding."

"That's very true," Mr. Hughes says.

"Winifred," Samson continues, "my wife of fifty-two years, was the love of my life, the other half of my soul. We built the marina together from the ground up, and she poured more spirit into that place than I ever could. I want to honor her and our legacy by making sure the marina is passed down to a couple who shares the same love we had." Samson gestures to Mr. and Mrs. Hughes. "These two managed the place and brought a love to it for years. Trent, you've done wonderfully too, but it does need a woman's touch. That's something a man can't bring. That marina needs a true partnership to keep it alive. Do you two have that?"

"Did anyone tell you," I say, "about the day Trent and I met?"

All four sets of eyes turn to me. Mrs. Hughes and Mr. Hughes look curious, Samson seems intrigued, and Trent—his gaze steady—looks at me with quiet calmness.

"I actually don't think anyone has," Mrs. Hughes says. "Why don't you tell us, dear?"

I smile and take a deep breath, organizing my thoughts. "Well," I begin, "I'd been having one of the worst days. I'd just gotten some not-so-great news, and the stress of other things going on in my life had consumed me to the point where I wasn't paying attention to the world around me. And I'm not exaggerating—Trent quite literally saved me. I was so distract- ed that I nearly stepped out into traffic, but Trent pulled me back just before I got hit. He took the brunt of the fall himself when I lost my balance. It was such a small moment in the grand scheme of things, but for me, it changed everything, like I was given a second chance at life."

The dining room remains silent for several seconds, the weight of my words settling over the table.

"I mentioned before that I'm an artist," I say, looking at Samson. "At the time, I'd lost all desire to paint. With the pain of losing my grandmother earlier in the year, and the stress of everything else going on during that time, life had just . .

. dulled for me. But after Trent saved me, he made sure I was okay and even took me to For the Love of Sugar for a treat. Wouldn't you know it, while I sat there smelling the savory scent of baked goods, I found myself sketching again. It wasn't much—just a simple sketch—but it reignited something in me. Ever since then, I've had my vision back, my passion for creating."

I pause, letting the memory wash over me before continuing. "So that was the day we met—the day my life took a turn for the better. And since then, I've seen firsthand how much Trent cares about the things and people he loves. He's dedicated, compassionate, and driven. He has a passion for life and cares with all his being about succeeding and making his family proud. If there's anyone who can make the marina thrive, it's him."

A sniffle breaks the silence, and I turn to see Mrs. Hughes dabbing at her eyes with a napkin. "That was so lovely," she says, her voice thick with emotion. "I knew my Trent was a good man."

Mr. Hughes reaches for her hand, pressing a kiss to her knuckles. "We did a good job raising him," he says softly.

Trent, for his part, remains silent beside me. I'm too nervous to look at him directly, afraid he'll see what I'm trying to keep buried—the fact that I might be falling for him, agreement or no agreement.

Samson remains silent, his soft expression thoughtful as he studies me. After a long pause, he clears his throat and says, "What I want to know is what you sketched that day."

"Oh," I say, waving my hand dismissively, "you don't really want to know."

"I really do," Samson says, with a warm smile.

I hesitate, but the gentle encouragement and approval in his eyes remind me of my own grandpa. Taking a deep breath, I glance at Trent and finally confess, "It was a sketch of Trent."

Chapter 15
Trent

Beginning my rounds at the marina, I'm still shaken from dinner last night—keeping the truth from my family and Jenny's revelation about sketching me. The dampness of morning dew clings to the grass, and the faint smell of lake water mingles with the earthy aroma of pine. The sun is still low, casting long shadows across the docks. My footsteps echo faintly on the wooden planks as I walk, each creak a reminder of the countless mornings I've spent here.

I'm hoping to find Henry. With the wedding only two days away, I feel the need to talk to him about Jenny.

Last night, Jenny had no trouble convincing Grandfather that we were together for the right reasons. Grandfather even seemed to genuinely like Jenny. I could have kissed her for how well she handled everything. It was all a relief, really, not just because I think Grandad will pass the marina on to me when we're married, but because it truly felt like Jenny is going to fit into our family. For the first time in a long while, I'll have someone by my side at family dinners.

But on the boat ride home, Jenny was quiet, her usual brightness dimmed. I wanted to say something—anything—to break the silence, but the right words never came.

When we reached the dock, she gave me a quick wave good-bye and headed toward her cabin. By the time I'd fully docked the boat, she was almost to the tree line, her silhouette fading into the shadows. Clearly, something had upset her. I thought about following, but it didn't feel right. So I let her go.

The memory lingers as I walk down the dock where Henry is fishing. I'm greeted by his voice, rich and welcoming. "Look what the cat dragged in. Come sit down, Trent, and talk for a bit."

He's seated on a bench at the edge of the dock, his weathered hands resting on his fishing pole. A thermos of coffee steams beside him, the aroma drifting toward me as I approach.

"I was actually coming to look for you," I say, taking the seat he pats beside him. The wood is rough beneath my hand as I steady myself.

Henry chuckles, his eyes twinkling with mischief. "Didn't do something I shouldn't have, did I?"

"No, you could never," I reply with a small laugh. "It's about Jenny."

His expression shifts, his ears practically perking up. "Is everything okay? Is she okay?"

"She's fine," I reassure him quickly. "In fact, I saw her up at the shop this morning."

He swats me lightly on the arm, a gesture so familiar it makes me grin. Must be where Jenny gets it from. "You can't say something like that and leave me hanging—you trying to give me a heart attack?"

"Sorry. No, definitely not." I shift in my seat, suddenly feeling the weight of what I want to say. "I just . . . it's about the wedding."

Henry studies me for a moment, his gaze sharp but kind. "You're not going to back out, are you?"

"No, no," I say quickly, shaking my head. "I just wanted to talk to you and ask for your blessing to marry Jenny. To let you know that I promise to take care of Jenny. To make sure she never wants for anything and that I'll be a good husband to her."

Henry lets out a hearty laugh, the sound rumbling like distant thunder. "Oh, is that all? Boy, you had me nervous for nothing. Of course, you have my blessing. And I know you will take care of her. Look at what you've already done. You're a good egg, and I know you and Jenny will be very happy together." He leans back in his seat, the wood creaking softly. "Did I ever tell you that her grandmother Cora and I knew each other for about a month and a half before we got engaged? Son, when you know, you know. I couldn't be happier to have you join the family. Did you think I was worried about the timing of all this?"

"Yes . . . no . . . I don't know," I admit, pulling off my cap and running a hand through my hair. "It's just that I never expected to find someone so soon. I always figured I'd want to get married one day, but then Jenny came into my life. Quite literally fell into it. And nothing's been the same since."

Henry nods, his smile softening. "Oh yeah, Jenny told me about the day you met. I never properly thanked you for saving her life. I don't know how I'd go on without my granddaughter. Losing my Cora was the lowest point of my life, and if it wasn't for Jenny . . . I don't know where I'd be. I couldn't be more grateful, son."

His words hit me like a wave, and I feel a lump rising in my throat. Tears prick at the corners of my eyes, and I look down, blinking quickly to hold them back. Even if this marriage started as an agreement, I realize I want Jenny to feel cared for and valued. Maybe, just maybe, the connection that's developing between us doesn't have to end when our agreement does. Maybe we could make it work—like Henry and Cora did—and have a life full of love and happiness.

I rise, placing my cap back on and offering Henry my hand. He takes it firmly, his grip steady and reassuring. "Thank you, Henry, for everything. I won't let you down."

His smile deepens, the kind of smile that carries years of wisdom and unshakable faith. "I know you won't, son. I know you won't."

"Alright," Greg says, flashing a grin as he steps onto the pontoon boat, "let's do this." The wood of the dock creaks beneath his weight, and I catch the faint smell of sunscreen and engine oil as the evening breeze picks up.

Greg, Niall, and I pile into the boat, the aluminum hull wobbling slightly under our shifting feet. It's one of the marina's trusty pontoons—nothing fancy, but perfect for nights like this. We've got a cooler loaded with sodas and snacks, fishing poles leaned up against the railing, and the calm waters of the lake stretching out ahead of us.

The air is fresh, carrying the mingled scents of pine and lake water. Above, the sky is streaked with hues of orange and pink, the last remnants of the sunset casting a golden glow over the rippling surface. It's peaceful out here, the kind of peace I hadn't realized I'd missed until now.

Life has been a whirlwind, and while we don't need an excuse to hang out, tonight's "bachelor party" finally gave us the chance. It feels like forever since we've done this—just the three of us.

The three amigos.

The three musketeers.

There's nothing we can't figure out together, no secrets we can't share.

Which is why, as the boat slows in the middle of the lake, I feel like I have to say it now. The engine's gentle hum fades, leaving only the soft lapping of water against the hull. The lake stretches out around us, dark and endless under a sky now sprinkled with the first stars of night.

"I have to tell you something, Niall," I say, breaking the silence. My voice sounds steadier than I feel.

"Alright, mate," Niall replies, his attention on baiting his hook, "out with it."

I take a deep breath, staring down at my hands. "Jenny and I are only getting married because of some rule my grandfather made about owning the marina."

"What?" Niall stops, his fishing pole forgotten as he turns to face me.

"We're only getting—"

"No," Niall holds up a hand. "What are you talking about? I thought you and Jenny fell in love while she was working at the marina."

"Well, we like each other, that's for sure," I admit. "But it didn't start off that way."

Greg leans back, crossing his arms. "You'd better explain it all to him, starting from the beginning."

I grip the brim of my cap, twisting it nervously. "You know how my grandfather's been on my case about settling down?"

Niall nods.

"There's a reason for that. He's ready to pass on the marina to me, but when he wrote up the stipulations for handing over the marina, he included a rule that the new owner has to be married."

Niall lets out a low whistle. "That's . . . an interesting requirement to run a marina."

"Tell me about it," I mutter, then continue. "Anyway, my extended family knows that my grandfather is itching to pass on ownership. And they know that I'm not married, so they want to know if the marina can go to one of them instead."

"You'd be heartbroken," Niall says, "if you lost the marina. This place is everything to you."

"It is," I say. "So all this has been weighing on me for a while, and Jenny noticed I was acting a bit off, and she asked me about it. I ended up opening up to her about my frustration with the whole situation. And apparently, she'd been thinking about what I'd said. Because not too long after, my mom came into the shop talking to me about finding someone to be in a relationship with, and Jenny told her she and I were engaged."

"She what?!" Niall sits forward, nearly knocking over the cooler.

"Yeah, it threw me too," I admit, letting out a dry laugh. "I eventually wanted to get married, but I'd been so focused on improving things at the marina and lodge that I hadn't taken the time to look for someone. This proclamation from Jenny completely shocked me. Later that day, Jenny and I had a heartfelt conversation and I found out Jenny had her own reasons for wanting to get married. So, we came up with the agreement and decided to, you know, get married."

"So this whole engagement," Niall says, eyebrows raised, "is all fake?"

"Kind of," I say. "It's fake in the sense that we didn't date and then fall in love in the traditional way. But it's real in the sense that we're getting married in two days."

"That's a lot." Niall says.

I place my head in my hands. "Am I making a huge mistake? I feel like I'm dragging Jenny into something she doesn't deserve."

Greg shakes his head slowly. "First off, you're not dragging her into anything."

Niall asks, "She offered to get married first, right?"

"Yeah," I say, "she did."

"So," Niall says, "what's she getting out of it?"

"Job security and a place to live forever," I say.

Niall's brows knit together, his head nodding in understanding, while Greg claps me on the shoulder. The weight of my secret feels lighter now, the tension easing with their silent support.

"And" Greg says, "how are you feeling about the arrangement now?"

"I still want to go forward with it, but there's something else there too." My voice raises as I finish, almost like I'm asking if there is.

"What?" Niall asks.

"I think I'm falling for her."

Niall lets out a laugh. "That's only good news, mate. And for most marriages, what you would expect."

I smile too. "I know. It's a bit ironic." I shift to a more serious tone, "I'm just worried that if I fall for her and she doesn't fall for me, this deal or marriage or whatever you want to call it is going to be a lot harder than I thought."

Niall nods, and Greg says, "You two will figure this out. I know it."

We cast our lines into the water, the quiet punctuated by the occasional splash of fish or creak of the boat.

As the evening wears on, the stars grow brighter, their reflections shimmering on the dark surface of the lake. We laugh, tell stories, and tease each other like old times.

On the way back to the dock, the boat hums softly, the marina lights glowing faintly in the distance. As we pass my house, I glance up and see Jenny's silhouette in the great room window. I hope she and the girls are having just as much fun at their bachelorette party. Her figure is backlit by the warm glow of the lamp inside, and for a moment, the world feels still.

"Oh crap," I mutter, sitting up straight.

"What now, mate?" Niall asks.

"I haven't officially asked her to marry me yet. I mean, we agreed to this whole thing, but I never actually said the words."

Greg bursts into laughter, shaking his head. "You'd better get on that, man. You marry the girl in less than forty hours."

As the boat glides past my house, her silhouette lingers in my vision, her presence calm and steady. I smile to myself.

The guys are right. Jenny and I are going to figure this out. And while I don't know how she feels, I can't deny what's been growing in my own heart.

I'm falling for her.

Chapter 16
Jenny

The late morning sun streams into my room at Trent's house, casting shadows on the floor from the trees outside the windows. After saying goodbye to the girls this morning, I went to work moving my things to Trent's house. Before I'd moved back to Chessie Valley, I'd sold all my furniture, only keeping a few keepsakes and clothes—and of course, my art supplies were staying in the cabin. So when Trent showed up to help me, it didn't take long to finish.

Now, in the midst of cardboard boxes and items to unpack, I get ready for the day and the wedding rehearsal later on this afternoon.

I finish putting in my earrings and turn—only to let out a small, startled gasp, my hand flying to my chest as I try to calm my racing heart. Trent is standing in my doorway. "Where did you come from?" I say, trying to steady my breath. "You scared me half to death."

"Well, we don't want any of that now, do we?" Trent says, his voice soft, almost timid. "May I come in?"

I nod, still a little breathless, as he steps through the doorway. My eyes can't help but linger on him. He looks incredibly handsome dressed up in a button-down shirt and nice slacks, his backward baseball cap still perched on his head. The combination of casual and refined makes him somehow effort-lessly charming and puts a smile on my face.

Just looking at him makes my insides go all fluttery. I remind myself not to become emotionally attached. The wedding that will take place in just over twenty-four hours is just a contract, not a real marriage.

"How do I look?" I ask. "Do you think this is okay for the rehearsal?" Trent reaches out to me, his hand resting gently on my shoulder as I finish a little spin.

"Beautiful," he says, his grin widening. "You look beau-tiful. And how could it not be okay? It's our wedding re-hearsal, so whatever we say goes, right?"

I laugh, swatting him lightly on his arm. "I don't think your mom or Gwen would agree, but thank you all the same."

"I especially like your white cowgirl boots," he says with a playful smile.

"Me too!" I stick my foot out, showcasing the boots proudly. "I love these things but don't get the chance to wear them often. I thought they looked fancy enough with-out being too much, you know? And I don't think I've ever seen you wear that green shirt before."

"Nope, this is for special occasions only."

"Well, it looks great on you," I say, my gaze drifting to how well the shirt fits him. The way his slacks hug his legs and the hint of his form beneath makes my heart skip a beat. I shake my head, trying not to notice how handsome he looks.

"Thanks," he says, and then does a little spin of his own, making me giggle. I don't miss the way his pants hug his butt, a smile creeping up as I try to look away. Damn, he looks good.

I don't know what I'll do when he's all dressed up for the wedding tomorrow.

"Hey," Trent says, "I fixed us up some sandwiches. It's a beautiful day. I want to take you out on the lake."

"The lake? Dressed like this?"

"Yes," Trent says, "you look perfect."

"Okay, but we can't be out too long. I still have some things I need to do to get ready for the rehearsal."

"It won't be too long." He takes my hand, leading me to the front door. "I want to take you to one of my favorite spots on the lake."

When we reach his boat, I make myself comfortable as he preps to go. In a matter of minutes, we're off.

"So, what makes this location so special?" I ask.

He glances over at me, his smile widening, making my heart jump to my throat. "You'll just have to wait and see when we get there."

How is it that this guy is still single? I shake my head in disbelief. Well, I guess he's technically not, but still . . .

I watch him as he steers the boat across the water, waving at other boats as we pass. He's a sweet guy with a big heart who clearly cares deeply about his friends and the people who come to the marina. He helped me out when I was just a random stranger. He's educated, has a great job—and yet, he's still been single.

I shake my head. I just don't get it.

"What's that look on your face for?" Trent asks, his eyes flicking over to me. I hadn't realized he'd been watching me.

"I just don't get how someone hasn't already snagged you by now. How is it that you haven't already been married off to some great gal?"

Trent flinches slightly at my bluntness, but his response comes quickly. "Honestly, I just haven't been looking for anyone. My focus has been on the marina ever since I got back from college. Yeah, I had a few girlfriends here and there, but nothing serious. I also need someone who's okay with this life I've chosen. It's not like I can just uproot the marina and move wherever my wife wants to live, you know?"

"I can understand that," I reply, my thoughts drifting to my own mother, who left me on my grandparents' doorstep because I didn't fit into her life. Trent wouldn't be that kind of person, I'm sure of it.

"It's why I'm so grateful you came up with this marriage arrangement. It ended up solving all my problems."

"And mine too," I add.

"Right," Trent says, "I just hope I can be the kind of man you deserve, even if we're only together for a year."

I nod, but stay quiet. Only a year . . . that's all I get with him. Well, if that's the case, I'm going to make the year worthwhile.

I kick up my feet and settle in as he steers the boat over the water. I still think I am getting the better end of this deal.

We finally slow as we reach our spot. From a distance, it looks like any other part of the lake, but as Trent rounds a bend and stops the boat, I gasp.

The sight is breathtaking. A small, secluded cove with sandy beaches stretches out before us, the water calm and crystal clear. Beyond the shore, thousands of wildflowers bloom, their vibrant colors breaking up the green of the trees that enclose the valley. Even from here, I can see the fluttering of butterfly wings, tiny specks of movement against the stillness. It's like something out of a fairy tale.

"This is beautiful," I say, breathless.

"It really is," Trent agrees, his eyes locked on mine. I smile at him, feeling the warmth of his gaze, and my cheeks flush.

Grinning, he turns back to the view. "I love coming out here this time of year, when the weather is just right. It's peaceful."

We eat our sandwiches in silence, both of us watching the breathtaking scene before us, the sense of calm washing over us as the lake glistens in the afternoon sun. I try to take it all in—the slight lapping of the waves as other boats pass by, the colors of the wildflowers, the movement of the butterflies, the gentle sway of the leaves in the breeze.

I'm going to paint this for Trent. This will be the picture he hangs in his house.

After we arrive back to the dock, Trent says, "I have one more place to take you before we head to the lodge." He holds out his arm like we're a couple in one of my favorite historical novels. "Shall we?"

"We shall," I reply, moving my hand to link my arm through his. Together, we walk down the dock, following the path that leads us to the marina. My hand rests on Trent's arm as he guides us to the lodge, walking toward the gazebo.

The area surrounding the gazebo reminds me of the hidden cove we saw earlier and our special wedding spot all rolled into one. Wildflowers stretch across the grass, the vibrant colors contrasting beautifully with the deep green of the trees. Cherry blossoms are starting to bloom along the path, their petals fluttering gently in the breeze. It's a picturesque little haven. Maybe I should bring my paints out here sometime.

"What are we doing here?" I ask, glancing around, taking in the beauty of the spot. I even glance out toward the lake, watching as it shimmers in the sunlight.

"Well, I realized something," Trent says, his voice quieter now, uncertain. He stops and takes a deep breath, his expression serious. "I need to make it right before tomorrow."

The unsure tone has my stomach tightening as I turn to face him. "What's wrong?"

"Nothing's wrong," he assures me, his smile soft. "I know we have an agreement, but I wanted to do right by you. Jenny, it's been so amazing getting to know you, and you've become a really good friend to me."

Before I know it, Trent drops to one knee, and my hands fly up to my mouth, my heart racing.

Oh. My. Gosh. Oh my gosh.

"Jenny," Trent says, his voice steady but nervous, "would you do me the honor of becoming my wife?"

He pulls out a beautiful diamond ring, the sight of it nearly rendering me speechless. Goosebumps race up my arms, and my knees go weak. This feels almost too real—like something out of a fairy tale—and I'm overcome with gratitude that he wanted to make sure we had all the right moments.

"Oh, Trent, of course I will. This is so sweet. You're so sweet," I whisper, my voice trembling as I lean down to kiss him on the cheek. Then, as I wrap him in a hug, tears sting my eyes.

He stands, and I step back, my hand trembling as he slips the ring onto my finger. The diamond catches the light, making my stomach flip with a mixture of joy and nerves. It feels official now, like this is more than just an arrangement.

"The past few days," Trent says, "something was feeling off. But now it feels right."

"This is what was bothering you?" I ask, my eyes wide with surprise.

He nods. "I didn't realize it until I saw you last night in the window of the cabin. I realized why I'd been feeling so off. We were about to embark on a big moment in our lives— even if it is just for our agreement. But I felt I owed it to you, to both of us, to do this right."

"Has anyone ever told you that you're literally the sweetest man in the whole wide world?" I ask, my voice cracking with emotion.

"I mean, a few times," Trent replies, his smirk returning, "but I won't object to you telling me again."

I swat him lightly on the arm, tears welling up. "You are something else, Trent Hughes."

"One of a kind," he says, his voice gentle.

I can't help but agree with him.

We make our way to the lodge, and before I know it, the rehearsal passes in a whirlwind, the details blurring together as my mind drifts back to the gazebo with Trent down on one knee.

Chapter 17

Trent

"Hey, hey, lover boy," Greg says, bounding into my room with exaggerated cheer and making a ruckus with a kazoo that screeches its way into my still-drowsy consciousness. "Wakey-wakey, it's your wedding day!" He jumps on my bed, bouncing up and down.

"Dude," I groan, propping myself up and rubbing my eyes. "It's too early for all that noise."

"Sorry, mate," Niall says, leaning against the doorframe with two coffee mugs in his hands. "I tried to get him to change his mind, but he insisted the kazoo would add to the celebration."

"I'll forgive you if you tell me one of those cups is for me," I mutter, my voice still rough from sleep.

Niall chuckles softly and steps forward, handing me a mug. I take it gratefully. The hot ceramic warms my palms.

"Thanks," I say, settling back against the headboard with the cup cradled in my hands. "Now this I can handle."

"Aww, come on, man," Greg says with a hopeful grin, "you can't be grumpy today. It's your wedding day."

"You're still going through with it?" Niall asks.

"I'm not grumpy, and I'm not changing my mind. I'm getting married today," I mutter with a sigh, blowing across the surface of my coffee before taking a sip. The bitterness is familiar and comforting. "I just didn't expect to be awoken to your kazoo. Kind of catches you off guard."

"Yeah, yeah, yeah," Greg says, "get up sleepyhead and come eat your breakfast before it gets cold. You'll need your energy up today." With that, Greg leaves the room with a dramatic flourish, and I set the coffee on the nightstand, leaning back against the headboard once more.

"You alright, mate?" Niall asks, watching me with a quiet concern.

"Yeah," I nod. "I just can't believe I'm getting married today."

"Well, believe it, because it's happening. But you still have time to back out. No one would fault you for it," Niall says firmly, giving me a reassuring nod.

"Like I told Greg, I'm not changing my mind. And I'm not backing out. I'm sure about this."

"Alright then, if you're sure." Niall says. "We'll be downstairs if you need us." Then he leaves my room.

I'm getting married today.

Me.

Trent Hughes.

I am getting married.

Somehow that thought doesn't freak me out. I thought it would, but it does the opposite. My stomach twists in anticipation—yes, I'm nervous—but a sense of rightness settles over me.

I'm getting married today. To Jenny.

I take a deep breath, letting the reality sink in. I'm the luckiest man in the world.

The morning rushes by in a blur, each moment slipping past me in a haze of motion and anticipation. Before I know it, I'm standing before the altar, dressed in my tan suit—pants, vest, white shirt, and pink tie neatly in place. Greg and Niall stand by my side.

We wait in silence as the guests file in, the anticipation thick in the air. The location couldn't have been more perfect—cherry blossoms in full bloom, their soft pink petals fluttering gently in the breeze. The white chairs are neatly arranged in rows and adorned with delicate pink and yellow flowers at the ends of each section, adding a touch of elegance.

A wooden arch stands behind me, its beams decorated with the same pink and yellow blooms, creating a stunning backdrop. Through the opening in the trees, the lake stretches out before us, reflecting the crystal clear blue sky, serene and expansive. The gentle lapping of waves serves as a soothing backdrop to the quiet hum of the day.

Soft music fills the air, carried by the breeze and the DJ set up just off to the side. The crowd whispers softly, a quiet lull as they settle into their seats, anticipation humming just beneath the surface.

I take a deep breath, letting it fill my lungs, savoring the stillness. This couldn't have been a more perfect location. The perfect weather.

Our wedding.

Jenny and I are getting married.

Am I really doing this?

The music shifts, signaling the bridesmaids' entrance. Gwen appears first, followed by Holly. My heart races as they take their slow, steady steps, each movement graceful and deliberate. They reach their spots, their faces serene, their smiles soft.

"All rise," the officiant says, his voice clear and steady. The music changes again, and the opening notes of Bruno Mars' "Marry You" begin to play. Now, as the familiar melody fills the air, all my nerves dissolve. A smile spreads across my face, and I let out a quiet laugh, the tension in my chest easing.

Then I see her.

Jenny steps into view, her grandpa Henry by her side, looking dashing in his tan suit. His hand rests gently on her arm, guiding her forward with quiet pride. Jenny's curls fall gracefully over one shoulder, and her dress billows gently as she moves. She looks like a princess from a fairy tale, every step elegant and effortless.

For a moment, I forget to breathe. It isn't until I hear Greg's soft whisper from my side— "You've got this, man" —that I finally exhale, the sound shaky.

I meet Jenny's eyes, and a smile lights up her face. My smile must be dopey, but I can't help it. She is stunning—radiant, glowing in a way that feels otherworldly. My eyes sting with unshed tears, but I ignore them, not wanting to break our eye contact.

The song, with its carefree lyrics about finding something dumb to do, seems laughably misplaced. Because choosing to marry Jenny feels anything but dumb—it feels right.

We are really doing this.

Henry presses a kiss to Jenny's cheek before gently placing her hand in mine. "Be good to her, sonny," he says, his eyes alight with happiness.

"I will," I manage, my voice barely above a whisper, thick with emotion.

Taking her hand in mine, we step forward together up the last few steps toward the arch where the officiant waits. Jenny hands her bouquet to Holly, her fingers brushing mine in a lingering touch before she lets go.

The officiant begins, his voice steady and calm, but his words barely register in my mind. My attention is consumed by Jenny—the way she holds my gaze, the unwavering steadiness of her smile. She's a beacon, a lifeline, grounding me in a moment that feels both surreal and monumental.

"Ladies and gentleman, family and friends," the officiant says, his tone warm and inviting, "we are gathered here today to celebrate and hold witness to one of life's greatest moments—the union of two wonderful people, Trenton Hughes and Jenny Monroe, as they come together in marriage. Marriage is more than just an exchange of rings or a legal contract . . ."

The mention of a contract lands like a stone in my chest. For a brief, sharp moment, the weight of our arrangement presses down on me, threatening to unravel the calm I've carefully maintained.

Jenny's hand tightens around mine, her grip firm yet comforting. The subtle squeeze sends a jolt of reassurance through me, a reminder that I'm not alone in this. We're in this together.

When we reach the vows, the officiant's voice becomes a steady rhythm in the background as I focus entirely on Jenny. I promise to love and honor her, to stand beside her in good times and bad, to support her and remain faithful to her for as long as we both shall live. The words flow effortlessly, as though they've been etched into my heart long before this moment.

Jenny repeats her vows, her voice steady and filled with an unshakable warmth. Her eyes brim with joy, radiating a happiness so genuine that it feels like sunlight breaking through a storm. There isn't a hint of hesitation or regret in her expression, and it strikes me how perfectly she fits this moment—how perfectly we fit together.

We exchange rings, the cool metal sliding over my finger a tangible symbol of everything we're agreeing to. Then, we reach the final, most pivotal part of the ceremony.

Turning to Jenny, I take both of her hands in mine. They're warm, steady—a counterbalance to the pounding of my own heart. I know the words I'm about to say will change everything forever, cementing what began as an idea into something real.

"Do you, Trenton Hughes, take Jenny Monroe to be your lawfully wedded wife, to have and to hold, in sickness and in health, for richer or poorer, in joy and in sorrow, until death do you part?"

The officiant's gaze shifts to me, but my eyes never leave Jenny. Her face is a canvas of light and quiet strength, and in that moment, the answer comes as naturally as breathing.

"I do," I say, my voice firm yet softened by the weight of emotion behind the words.

The officiant nods and turns to Jenny, repeating the same question.

Her focus shifts briefly to him, her expression neutral, unreadable, as he outlines the promises she's about to make. I watch her closely, searching for even the smallest flicker of doubt. But when she turns back to me, her hand tightens around mine once more—a silent declaration of her resolve.

"I do," she says, her voice clear and unwavering, the words carrying an irrefutable strength.

The officiant smiles, his gaze sweeping across the gathered guests. "Then by the power vested in me by the state of Tennessee, I now pronounce you husband and wife."

Cheers erupt around us, a wave of sound that feels distant, almost muted, as I'm pulled deeper into the moment. I barely catch the officiant's next words. "You may now kiss the bride."

Oh, this—this I'm going to enjoy.

Jenny's eyes meet mine, bright and filled with laughter and joy. Her eyes briefly fall to my lips then back to my eyes. My chest tightens, a surge of something I can't name sweeping through me. I release her hands, one moving to brush a stray strand of hair from her face while the other lifts her chin gently.

As our lips meet, I'm tentative at first, mindful of the crowd around us, of the weight of expectations. But before I can pull back, Jenny leans into me, her presence as electric as a lightning strike.

My hands shift instinctively, one cradling the back of her head, the other drawing her closer against me. Her arms wrap around my neck, pulling me in, her kiss deepening with a soft, breathy sigh that sets my senses on fire.

I'm drowning in her—her scent, light and floral, the warmth of her body pressed against mine, the way she moves with a confidence that leaves me completely undone. My heart races as I lose myself in the moment, the rest of the world falling away. I tip her back and deepen the kiss, wanting this moment to last forever.

Then, a subtle clearing of a throat brings reality crashing back in.

I reluctantly ease Jenny back upright, my hands lingering on her waist as I step away just enough to appease our audience. Her cheeks are flushed, her eyes sparkling with mischief and something deeper—something that mirrors the chaos swirling within me.

To anyone who didn't know the truth, we must look like we've been deeply in love for years. To everyone here, there's no hint of the arrangement that brought us together.

But I realize, as I watch her, that the lines between what's real and what's not are blurring.

I think—I might actually be falling in love with her.

"Everyone, for the first time," the DJ announces, "please help me welcome Mr. and Mrs. Hughes!"

We step into the barn-turned-reception hall. The space is transformed, beautifully decorated. Strings of twinkling lights drape across the wooden beams above, casting a soft, warm glow that makes the room feel magical no matter where you look. Each table is adorned with pink and yellow centerpieces, crafted around old-fashioned lanterns that flicker gently. The lights reflect off the polished wood floor, illuminating the room with a cozy, romantic ambiance. In the center, a dance floor gleams under the glow, inviting couples to sway under the stars created by the string lights.

We make our way through the crowd, the sound of applause and cheers echoing around us. The scent of fresh flowers and sweet vanilla from the candles in the lanterns hangs in the air. I help Jenny settle into her seat at the head table, my hand resting on hers for a moment longer than necessary.

"Everything looks so beautiful," Jenny says, glancing around in awe. Her eyes shine.

I turn to take it all in too—the lights, the decorations, the joy on everyone's faces. But nothing is as captivating as the woman standing next to me. "You look beautiful," I reply, leaning in to press a soft kiss to the back of her hand.

She laughs softly and swats my arm playfully, a mischievous twinkle in her eyes. "Oh, you. You've said that at least a dozen times now."

"I can't help it," I say, grinning. "Your beauty has cast a spell on me."

She laughs again, the sound like music in my ears, as the caterers arrive, placing our plates of food before us.

My grandfather Samson makes his way toward us, his expression one of warmth and pride. He reaches out, shaking my hand firmly. "Jenny, you're a sweetheart, and we welcome you into the family." His gaze shifts to me. "Trent, my boy, I never thought I'd live to see this day. Just don't muck it up, and make sure it lasts."

I can only nod, his words sinking in.

"Thank you, Samson," Jenny says softly. "It was a beautiful ceremony, and I'm so happy to be welcomed so graciously into your family."

With that, Samson heads back to his seat beside my mom and dad. Mom is smiling, tears glistening in her eyes. She's been crying nonstop since the rehearsal last night, and I'm surprised she hasn't run out of tears by now.

Since the wedding party was entirely made up of couples, we decided to nix the traditional seating arrangement of brides-maids on one side and groomsmen on the other. Instead, Gwen and Niall sit to Jenny's right, and Greg and Holly to my left.

"Gwen," Jenny says, "you did such a beautiful job. Every-thing about the wedding has been gorgeous."

"It was a group effort, for sure," Gwen replies, picking up her drink. "Trent, your mom had some wonderful ideas. Everything came together beautifully."

"Cheers to that," Niall adds, raising his glass.

"How about a toast?" Greg's voice cuts through the quiet hum of conversation. The DJ hands him a microphone, and everyone falls silent, turning their attention to him.

"To the happy couple," Greg begins, his voice full of warmth and humor. "I never thought I'd see the day when some lucky girl would finally capture Trent's heart. But, Jenny, I couldn't be happier that it's you. You've made Trent so happy, and I hope nothing but the best for the two of you."

A round of applause follows, and Greg raises his glass high, his grin wide.

Holly takes the microphone next, a soft smile on her face as she speaks. "I remember the day I first met you, Jenny. And from that first moment, I could tell you were smitten with our Trent. He's got such a big heart, always looking out for everyone else. I'm so thankful that now he has you to look out for him. We wish you both a lifetime of happiness and love."

Everyone cheers again, glasses clinking together in celebration. Jenny and I exchange a quiet look, both of us aware of the truth beneath the surface. We're fooling everyone—our friends, our family—but we've come this far, and there's not much we can do now except move forward with the plan.

But the way I've been feeling lately—there's a part of me that wonders if maybe, just maybe, something more could come from all this. I already feel myself falling more in love with Jenny with each passing day.

In this moment, as we stand together at the head table, I can't help but notice how natural it feels to hold her hand. How every small touch, every glance feels weighted with something real—something I didn't anticipate. I try to brush it off as the nerves of the day, but deep down, I know it's more than that.

Jenny leans into me, her smile tender, and she squeezes my hand gently. I feel her warmth steadying me in a way I didn't know I needed.

"This," she whispers, her eyes shining with something I can't quite place, "is everything I could have dreamed of for today."

I meet her gaze, my heart thudding a little harder. "And it's everything I didn't know I was missing."

We hold that moment, surrounded by our friends and family, the quiet whispers of happiness weaving through the space. The future may be uncertain, but in this moment, it feels right.

Who knows what will happen in a year? But for now, it's enough to sit here, hand in hand, and imagine the possibilities.

After the festivities finally wind down and enough time has passed for us to leave, we ride back to my house—our house now. The truck hums beneath us, the night outside still and quiet, broken only by the occasional rustle of leaves in the breeze. Jenny is quiet beside me, her gaze fixed out the window and her hands resting loosely on her lap.

When we pull into the driveway, the headlights cut through the darkness, illuminating the familiar porch. I hop out, circle the truck, and help Jenny down. She hesitates as I lift her into my arms.

"Trent, what are you doing? I can walk," she protests, though there's a soft inflection of amusement in her tone.

"It's tradition for a husband to carry his wife across the threshold," I reply matter-of-factly, a grin tugging at the corner of my mouth.

"Fine," she concedes with an exaggerated sigh. "But you can put me down right after that."

I nod solemnly, cradling her securely as I carry her toward the door. The faint scent of her perfume lingers in the cool night air, light and floral, mingling with the earthy aroma of the outdoors. Once inside, I step over the threshold and set her down gently.

"Thank you," she says, brushing a strand of hair behind her ear. "I need to get out of the dress."

I watch her ascend the stairs, each step revealing the subtle sway of her dress, her figure silhouetted against the soft glow of the hall light. At the top, she turns down the hallway toward her room. I stand at the foot of the stairs, hand running absently through my hair. I'm not supposed to follow her up, right? That's not what we agreed on.

The events of the day replay in my mind like a reel of film. I'm a married man now. The marina will be safe. It should feel like a relief, but the weight of it all presses against my chest in a way I hadn't anticipated.

"Umm, Trent," Jenny's voice floats down from upstairs, tinged with an edge of uncertainty that sets my heart racing.

"Yes?" I call back, already bounding up the stairs two at a time. By the time I pause outside her door, I'm slightly breathless. Her door is ajar, a sliver of light spilling into the hallway. "Everything okay?"

"You might as well come in," she replies, the nervous edge now tempered with a hint of exasperation. "I'm not going to be able to get out of this dress without some help. As much as I love it, I definitely don't want to sleep in it."

I swallow hard, my hand hesitating on the doorframe before I slowly push the door open.

Inside, Jenny stands by the bed, the light catching on the intricate fabric of her dress. She turns toward me, her expression both sheepish and determined. "I knew I shouldn't have let your mom talk me into all these buttons. It's impossible to undo by myself." She lets out a huff of frustration.

"She probably didn't think you'd be undressing alone," I say before immediately regretting it. My face flushes as the words hang in the air.

Jenny arches a brow, her lips curving into a knowing smirk. "So . . . do you think you can help me?"

I nod, words failing me as she turns her back to me.

When I remain frozen, she asks, "Are you okay back there?"

I clear my throat, trying to steady my hands. "Yep. Just figuring out where to begin."

"I'd suggest starting at the top," she says.

"Right." Taking a steadying breath, I reach for the first button at the nape of her neck. Her skin is impossibly soft beneath my fingers, a warmth that sends an unexpected shiver through me. As I work my way down the line of buttons, the fabric parts to reveal more of her back, smooth and pale under the light.

Jenny shifts slightly, a subtle shiver running through her as her dress opens further. The air between us feels charged, every quiet rustle of the fabric amplified in the silence.

By the time I reach the final button at the small of her back, I'm acutely aware of how close we are. She steps forward, clutching the dress to her chest, and turns to face me, her cheeks faintly flushed.

"I think I can manage the rest," she says softly, her eyes meeting mine. "Thanks."

"You're welcome," I say, feeling heated. I want to stay with her, but I'm not sure if she feels the same way. And I don't want to put her in that position. I look at the floor, breaking our eye contact. "Sleep well, Jenny," I say, stepping out her door.

Once inside my room, I close the door and lean back against it, exhaling a breath I hadn't realized I was holding. The feel of her skin, the intimacy of the moment—it's overwhelming in a way that I can't quite explain.

"It's just the emotions from the day," I tell myself, trying to rationalize the storm swirling in my chest. "There's no room for emotions in a marriage of convenience."

Jenny agreed to this arrangement on the condition that physical affection would only happen when absolutely necessary. The last thing I want is to burden her with my own tangled feelings. But then I think of our wedding kiss, the warmth of her lips against mine, and my heart rate spikes again.

I can't help it. I run down the hall, stopping at her closed door. My hand hovers over the knob, a battle raging within me. She didn't agree to anything beyond kissing or necessary affection. She probably doesn't feel the same things I'm feeling now.

I drop my hand back to my side, turn, and walk back into my room.

A cold shower and a good night's sleep will do me some good.

Chapter 18
Jenny

The moment Trent leaves my room, my legs feel unsteady, trembling under the rush of adrenaline and the butterflies that have taken permanent residence in my stomach. How is it that his light touch, so careful and reverent as he undid the buttons of my dress, made me feel like I might spontaneously combust right there on the spot?

I let out a shaky breath and step out of the dress, the luxurious fabric sliding effortlessly down my body to pool at my feet. Gathering it up gently, I hang it in my closet with care.

I change into soft pajamas, trying to settle the whirlwind inside me. I exhale deeply and flop onto the bed. What a day.

I'm married now.

To Trent.

We actually did it. His marina is safe. My job and home are secure. On paper, everything went perfectly. Things will be better now for both of us.

If only I could get a handle on my emotions. . .

Ever since I caught that first glimpse of him when I walked down the aisle, my heart hasn't stopped feeling like it might burst out of my chest. Trent's gaze was fixed on me, his expression one of pure joy. His eyes shimmered with something so raw and real. In that moment, it felt like the rest of the world didn't exist.

Trent may not care about me beyond the promises we made, but something is changing for me—this relationship isn't just an agreement anymore.

I close my eyes and think back to the feel of his hands, the way his calloused fingers had hesitated before undoing the first button, like he was afraid to overstep. That same flicker of nervousness had been in his gaze when I had asked him to help with my dress. Sweet, considerate Trent, always so careful of my boundaries.

The memory of his hands grazing my back as he worked his way down the line of buttons sends a shiver through me. It was such an intimate moment, far more so than I'd expected.

Trent had to feel that connection too, didn't he? Is he feeling the same way I am? He must be. I grab my phone from the nightstand, ready to call Trent, to tell him how I feel, that he should come back in this room with me. But I can't seem to push the call button. It's too much. Too soon.

The ceremony was everything I could have hoped for and more—a fairy tale come to life. I want to convince myself that the wedding, the kiss, this life together is all real. That our connection, Trent's care, his love—is all genuine. That this man chose me out of the billions of women in the world to share his life with. That he loves and cares for me.

But it's not real.

We made a deal, and I've committed myself to holding up my end of the bargain. Falling for Trent was never part of the plan.

I hover over the call button for a long moment, my chest tight. I can rein these feelings in. I have to. I can't let my emotions take over. Allowing myself to become emotionally attached, knowing there's an inevitable end, is only setting myself up for more heartache—something I'm not sure I can endure.

I set my phone face down on the bedside table, as if that will keep it from tempting me again. With a flick of the light switch, the room plunges into darkness. Forest shadows stretch out around me, the faint hum of the night settling into a gentle backdrop.

Tomorrow, everything will feel simpler. It has to.

"Good morning," I say, walking down the stairs.

"Good morning, wife," Trent responds.

My heart skips a beat at the word wife, the familiar yet surreal sound causing my hand to pause mid-motion. I'm a wife now. Trent's wife. It still feels like a dream, and the weight of that reality hits me with a mix of wonder and uncertainty.

"I'm all packed up and ready to go," I say, placing my bags by the door. "Though we could just stay here, and no one would be the wiser."

Before the final words leave my mouth, Trent is already shaking his head, a small, amused smile playing on his lips. "No can do, Wifey. After our quick engagement, we can't risk skipping a honeymoon. My grandfather and everyone else expects us to go. Plus, it'll be nice to get away for a bit. Help us get to know each other better, have some fun along the way."

"You always have to keep busy, don't you?" I say, arching an eyebrow as I eye him.

Trent pauses. "You know, I've never really thought about it before. It's just been me at the marina for so long, I guess I got used to being busy. I don't often get the chance to just sit and enjoy the view. Most of the time, I'm rushing to get into the office, prepping boats for the day, or fixing things in the cabins. It's nice when I get to relax for a bit."

"Then that's what we'll do on our 'honeymoon,'" I say, finishing with air quotes. "Instead of running around keeping busy the whole time, let's do things that are more relaxing—just enjoy nature and each other."

"You know what, Wifey?" Trent says, his smile genuine. "I think that's a brilliant plan."

"If you're ready to go, then we can hit the road. It's just under four hours to get to the cabin in Gatlinburg."

We pick up our bags and pile into the truck. The first part of the drive is quiet, the miles stretching out ahead of us. I stare out the window, the landscape blurring into a wash of green and fog. Even though it's only been about twenty minutes, the tension sitting between us is impossible to ignore.

"Okay," I say, shifting in my seat to face him. "Is it just me, or does this feel a little awkward to you too?"

A grin tugs at the corner of his mouth before he answers. "Honestly, I was just thinking that. I don't know why—it's not like we've never spent time with each other before. We're just two people who happen to be married, going on a honeymoon."

I laugh. "Well, when you say it like that, I guess there's no reason we should feel awkward. It's not like we'll be sharing a bed or anything."

My cheeks flush at my own implication.

"Right," Trent responds with mock seriousness, his tone light. "I did make sure to book a cabin that has two rooms."

I adjust the radio, and we settle into a comfortable rhythm—singing along with the music or chatting about nothing in particular.

Honestly, I have no idea why I was so nervous about this trip. Trent has always been kind, always steady. He's never done anything to make me feel uncomfortable. It's my own insecurities. I have to remind myself that I'm no longer the cast-off kid living with her grandparents, hoping that she's good enough for them so they don't cast her out also. But now, with Trent, for the first time in a long time, I feel like I belong. Like I matter to someone, and someone matters to me.

These past few months have been a whirlwind—moving from having no idea how I was going to stay afloat and take care of my grandpa to having a job that allows me to see him every day and have enough time to do my artwork. It just so happens that all that came with a husband that I'm now on a honeymoon with. If you had told me six months ago that I'd be here, I would've laughed in disbelief and called you crazy.

Looking over at Trent, I see the soft morning light catch in his hair beneath his backward baseball cap. There is a quiet calm in his presence, and I feel an unexpected warmth bloom in my chest.

What would my life have become if he hadn't stepped in that day and saved me from stepping into traffic?

I reach for his hand resting on the console, lacing our fingers together. He glances at me, his smile easy and relaxed. He squeezes my hand gently before returning his focus to the road.

Yes, I could get used to a life with Trent—even if it's only temporary.

Chapter 19
Trent

"What do you mean, there was a mix-up with our reservation?" I ask Sheryl, the receptionist at Whispering Falls Cabins. My voice rises slightly as I struggle to process how something like this could have happened. The words come out sharper than intended. I made our reservation weeks ago, meticulously ensuring every detail was in place.

Sheryl's eyes flicker with nervousness, and she adjusts her nametag as if searching for answers. "I'm not sure what happened, but someone else checked into your cabin yesterday."

"It's okay," Jenny says softly, her voice a soothing balm as she places a gentle hand on my arm. The warmth of her touch calms me. "Is there another cabin available by chance that we could have instead?"

Sheryl taps at her keyboard for a few moments, her fingers moving quickly but with a quiet desperation. The click of the keys reverberates in the small office, creating an almost unbearable silence. Finally, she looks up, her expression a mixture of apology and resignation. "We do have one available—it's a bit more secluded, but it's next to a nice trail that leads to a beautiful waterfall. And it has its own firepit."

"Great," Jenny says, her voice steady, though there's a hint of forced cheer. "See, Trent? Everything is good. Sheryl was able to find us another two-bedroom cabin. It's fine that it's not the one we had signed up for, and I love a good waterfall."

Sheryl's gaze flits between us, uncertainty deepening the lines on her face. "Well, it's actually not a two-room cabin."

"All good," Jenny says quickly. "More space is perfectly fine with us."

"No, you misunderstand, Mrs. Hughes," Sheryl continues, her tone quieter now. "It's a one-bedroom cabin."

"It's a what?" Jenny's voice rises, the shock apparent in her wide eyes.

"I'm sorry," Sheryl says, lowering her gaze. "It's the only one we have left."

Now it's my turn to try to ease the tension. "We'll take it," I say, giving Jenny's hand a reassuring squeeze. "We'll make it work," I tell Jenny. "Don't worry."

Jenny's wide-eyed stare remains fixed on me as I finish checking in, her expression a mix of surprise and confusion. Sheryl hands us free tickets to Anakeesta, an outdoor adventure park and nature experience with beautiful views of the Smoky Mountains, as compensation. I thank Sheryl and lead Jenny back to the truck.

"One bedroom," she says, as we drive up the winding road toward our cabin. "I can't believe it."

If I hadn't gotten the hint from last night, or from the checkout desk, I definitely do now. Jenny does not want to share a room with me.

"Not a problem," I reply, keeping my eyes on the road. "I'll sleep on the couch."

After pulling up to the cabin, we gather our things and the groceries we picked up on our way through town. We set down our luggage, then survey the cabin. The living room feels sparse, almost bare, with only two chairs and a fireplace. It is nothing like the cozy cabin I had originally booked. "Well," I say, "this is a fun turn of events."

"Trent, I think your definition of fun and mine are a little different," Jenny replies, sinking into one of the worn chairs. "There is no couch, Trent."

"None," I say. "Nada."

"Zip and zilch," Jenny says. "Now what are we going to do?"

I sit down in the other chair and place my feet on the ottoman. "This isn't uncomfortable. I can just sleep here."

Jenny sits up straighter, her brows furrowing as if she's considering the possibilities. "No. You are not sleeping sitting up all weekend. That will not do."

"I really don't mind sleeping here, Jenny," I say, not wanting her to feel uncomfortable, even if volunteering to sleep here is more for my sake than hers. I don't know what will happen if I end up sharing a bed with her.

She looks at me. "I'm guessing by the way you volunteered to sleep out here, there's no way you'd let me sleep in the chair and you take the bed?"

I shake my head, smiling. "Not a chance."

"Okay, then. That leaves one choice—we'll have to share the bed."

We nod in agreement, though the tension lingers between us. Jenny gets up and puts away the groceries, and I carry our luggage into the bedroom. When I step inside and see the bed, I suck in a tense breath. It's a queen-sized bed, and with my big frame, it will feel more like a double. This is going to be . . . interesting.

"How about we head over to Anakeesta?" Jenny calls out to me.

"Sounds good," I say. "I need some space from this cabin."

Chapter 20

Jenny

Anakeesta ends up being a whirlwind of fun and adventure. If I thought Trent was goofy before, it is nothing compared to the excitement he exudes as we ride the railroad and zipline over the mountain. Trent seems lighter here, carefree and full of energy. It's been nice to relax and enjoy nature and each other's company. I feel closer to Trent than I have the whole time I've been working for him.

The rest of the day passes in a blur, and at dusk, I get truly excited because I cannot wait for the hanging bridges. "This has been so much fun," I tell Trent, my voice filled with excitement.

"Definitely," Trent agrees, his grin out in full force. "I don't know why I've never come here before. Our friends would love this place. It reminds me of the activities we did on the cruise we took last summer for Greg and Holly's wedding."

"I bet that was a fun trip."

"It was," he says, "but I'm betting the hanging bridges are going to be just as great."

"I hope so," I say. "From what I read online it looks really pretty at night."

We head over to the entrance of the hanging bridges, and I squeal in excitement. It's more gorgeous than I could have imagined. The lights create a magical glow, illuminating the path through the trees. The strands of twinkling lights line the wooden bridges and wraparound tree trunks. The soft, golden glow reflects off the leaves and trunks, casting gentle patterns of light and shadow, as lanterns hang at random intervals, adding a rustic, whimsical charm. I glance over at Trent, and his smile is brighter than ever.

"This is awesome," he says, his voice filled with awe.

"It feels so magical. Like we're stepping into a fairy tale of sorts."

We walk along the bridges quietly, taking in our surroundings. I love that Trent and I can be together without any words. Even in the quiet, I feel seen. It feels nice to be seen. For once, everything feels simple and right.

"It reminds me," I say softly, "of our wedding." I pull my arms tighter around myself to help keep some warmth as the night gets chillier.

"How so?" Trent asks, his tone gentle and curious.

"The fairy-tale feeling. On our wedding day, I felt that way too."

Trent steps closer to me and wraps his arms around me, pulling me gently against him. His hands trace soothing patterns up and down my arms.

"I had a similar thought that day too," he says. "And you looked beautiful, like something straight out of a fairy tale."

I lean back into him and enjoy his body heat. It never fails that in his arms, I feel safe, cared for. From that first day he saved me to dancing on our wedding day to now, I feel safe and content with him. In this moment, there is no rushing around, no expectations, just him and me, standing in this quiet, magical, fairy-tale world.

Trent pulls me in tighter, his embrace comforting and strong. After a while, I say, "We should probably head back soon." I reluctantly pull away from him.

Trent nods in agreement. "You're right. But Jenny . . ." He lifts his head, his eyes searching mine. The way he looks at me makes my heart skip a beat.

"What is it?" I step closer to him and take his hand in mine.

His gaze softens, and he shakes his head, his expression turning more serious. "Let's get you out of this cold air."

He starts to turn away, but I still have his hand in mine and, almost as if I'm not in control of my body, I pull him softly back toward me. He turns back in confusion, and I don't think—I just act.

Reaching up with my other hand, I cup his cheek. Our eyes meet, and in that moment, I forget everything except the warmth of his skin under my hands. I pull him the rest of the way toward me. His lips are warm and firm against mine as I kiss him.

It only takes Trent a moment to react, and then I'm being pulled flush against his warm, strong chest. Our kiss deepens as he reaches around and cups the back of my head, pulling me closer to his lips. No warning signs go off, no fear of ruining our friendship, just the passion and care that we have for each other coming out in this kiss. It's filled with longing, with emotions we've both kept hidden.

I let go of his hands and pull his jacket toward me, my fingers trembling as I lose myself in this feeling. Our lips move at a slow pace, nothing rushed about this kiss. A tear slips down my cheek, and I let it fall, overwhelmed by the intensity of this moment. How can this guy be so perfectly perfect?

Fire rages inside me and it's all I can do to hold on and not burst into flames. His kiss is passion come to life. His hands, calloused and rough from days working on boats and cabins, brush against my cheeks and through my hair, making me feel cherished.

It's not until another couple walks by that I remember where we are. I step back, blushing furiously.

"I guess we should probably head back," I say in a whisper. My voice is barely audible over the pounding of my heart.

"Yeah," Trent says, taking his hat off and brushing his hand through his hair before putting it back on his head.

Back to our cabin. Our cabin with one bed. One bed that we will be sharing again tonight. But I don't mind. I'll be awake, replaying that kiss in my mind over and over.

At the cabin, Trent offers me the bathroom first. I quickly change into my pajamas before I step out. "The bathroom's all yours now," I say, my voice quieter than usual. My steps falter a bit as I see him standing there in pajama pants and a T-shirt.

"Thanks. You can pick whichever side of the bed you prefer. I'm not picky," he replies, turning toward the bathroom with a smile.

I quickly get settled into bed. When Trent emerges from the bathroom, the dim light of the room casts soft shadows on his face, only highlighting his handsome features.

He turns out the lights and climbs into bed next to me. Even with the weather cool outside, he rolls the comforter toward my side, keeping just the sheet over him. I happily take the covers, as I'm now shivering slightly from both the cold and the nervous energy coursing through me.

"It's so chilly at night here," I murmur, my teeth practically rattling.

"Here," he says, reaching toward me. "Come here?" He gestures toward his side of the bed.

"What are you doing?" I whisper.

"I'm trying to warm you up," Trent says, his voice soft but firm. "Come on, Jenny, just let me hold you. I don't want you to freeze tonight, and I can help give you some body warmth."

I hesitate for a moment, the cold biting at my skin and my thoughts swirling. Slowly, I inch toward him, his warmth radiating like a lifeline. "Oh, alright," I mumble, relenting. "But only for a moment."

As soon as I'm pressed against him, heat floods my chilled body, the contrast almost startling. I try to ignore the storm of emotions roaring inside me as I give in to the comfort of his warmth. Without thinking, I nuzzle into him, seeking more, and lace my fingers with his. "How the heck are you so warm? You're literally like a miniature heater."

He smirks, the corners of his mouth quirking up with that playful charm I've come to know. "I can assure you there's nothing miniature about me," he says, his voice rich with amusement.

I gasp, the heat in my cheeks growing. "Oh my gosh, I cannot believe you just said that. I'd smack you right now if it didn't mean I'd have to leave these warm sheets." I glance down at our entwined fingers, realizing just how much comfort his touch brings. "I feel warmer already."

He chuckles, the sound deep and warm, wrapping around me like a blanket. "You can stay here as long as you'd like. I'm not going anywhere."

Unable to resist, I press myself closer to him, drawn by an invisible force. When I glance up, his face is less than an inch from mine, his eyes soft and full of something that makes my heart skip a beat.

"Hi," he whispers, his voice barely audible.

"Hi," I echo, breathless, my words caught in the gravity pulling us together.

Our lips meet, and the world fades. The kiss ignites something deep inside me, like a spark catching. It's as though we're picking up right where we left off at the hanging bridges, but this time, it's more. His kisses sear through me, spreading heat from head to toe.

The sensation of sharing a bed with him—feeling his warmth, his closeness—sends a giddy rush through me. Trent, my husband, is kissing me. And it feels like magic.

His hand slides down my body, tracing a path to where my pajama shirt meets the waistband of my pants. His fingers slip beneath the fabric, the contact sending a thrill through me. Goosebumps ripple across my skin as his warm hand settles in at the dip of my waist. The simple touch feels reverent, like I'm something precious.

Time seems to suspend itself as we kiss, exploring each other with hands and mouths, lost in the moment. His lips are soft, his movements gentle, a stark contrast to the strength and firmness of his body.

Eventually, the fire between us ebbs into a quiet intimacy. We hold each other in the stillness of the night, the only sounds the soft rhythm of our breathing. His arms wrap around me, anchoring me in a way that feels safe, secure.

"Good night, Trent," I murmur, my voice barely audible as sleep begins to take me.

"Good night, wifey," he whispers back, his voice low and full of warmth.

Wrapped in his embrace, I let myself drift off, my heart full, and my body cocooned in his quiet strength.

Still not fully awake, I snuggle deeper into my pillow, burying my face into its soft, comforting warmth. The bed is like a cocoon—so warm, so inviting—I never want to leave it. The cool air from the cabin drifts softly across my face, sending a gentle shiver down my spine. I press my cheek further into the pillow, savoring the texture of the soft fabric against my skin. But then—something feels off. The pillow shifts slightly beneath my head.

Wait, what? Pillows don't move. My eyes snap open, my heartbeat quickening as last night comes flooding back. It's not the pillow I'm nuzzling into; it's Trent. My leg is draped over his. My arm is tucked into his side; his arms are still cradling me, just as they were last night.

Oh no, what have I done? Jenny, you stupid, stupid girl. Why did you let your emotions take over? Bad, this is bad bad bad. I shouldn't have kissed Trent at the hanging bridges or last night when we got back to the cabin. This is only going to make things more complicated. We are going to separate in a year. You can't be getting physically and emotionally connected to someone you know is going to leave you in a year. Your heart can't take it again. You need to set up boundaries, starting with physical ones—no more kissing, no more sharing a bed. Without boundaries, you're going to get hurt. And this time, it might not be a hurt you can come back from.

Not wanting to disturb Trent's sleep, I carefully lift my leg from his, placing it back on the bed with deliberate slowness. The weight of his arm around me shifts, his breath warm against my skin. I can feel the slow, steady rhythm of his heartbeat beneath his chest. I don't think I can take this much longer. Being this close to him and knowing it's only causing more pain is too much.

A soft "mmm" escapes from him, and he buries his face in my hair and neck. The sound and movement send a flash of warmth through me, igniting something deep inside. As much as I want to pull away, there's something comforting about being held like this, so close and protected.

"Good morning," he mumbles, his voice husky from sleep. His arms curl instinctively around my waist. "I like waking up next to you," he says. His body adjusts to hold me tighter, pulling me closer to his chest.

"Good morning," I reply, my voice quiet. I want to stay in his warm strong arms, but I can't give in to the emotions. Emotions were not part of the plan. This cannot continue or else I'll lose my heart to him. "If you don't mind, could I . . . ?" I gesture to his limbs entangled with mine.

"What?" Trent says, sounding confused.

"I need to get out of this bed."

"Oh, sorry," Trent says, slowly untangling himself from me, his gaze distant. His fingertips brush against my skin as he moves, sending a shiver down my spine. "I guess I thought . . . well, I don't know what I thought."

"No worries," I say as I slide out of bed, my heart still racing at his nearness. I close the bathroom door behind me and lean back against it. My skin feels flushed. My mind replays the warmth of his embrace, the way his arms held me protectively, naturally. Oh my gosh, it felt so good to be held in his arms. It felt like I belonged there, like it was something meant to be. But it's not. We aren't meant to be together. Our time is counting down.

After showering, I feel like I can face Trent without blushing. I head out of the bathroom. Trent is already in the small kitchen, fixing coffee and breakfast. The aroma of eggs and sausage fills the room.

"What's on the agenda today?" I say, trying to keep things light and wanting to skip any awkward conversation about getting out of bed this morning.

"Well, I was thinking we could drive through Cades Cove and have a picnic before we try out the trail Sheryl told us about," Trent says, his voice calm and easy. No awkwardness lingers between us.

"That sounds nice," I agree, taking a coffee from him as he finishes cooking. "Thank you for making breakfast."

"My pleasure. What kind of husband would I be if I didn't take care of my wife on our honeymoon?" Trent's eyes sparkle, and he flashes an easy smile that always seems to catch me off guard. Ugh, why does he have to be so perfect? Jenny you're going to have to keep your walls up today.

Chapter 21
Trent

The winding, eleven-mile loop of Cades Coves brings us to several historic homesteads and churches. And the trails we hike are breathtaking. The trees are tall, their green canopy creating a lush, almost magical feeling. But though the views are gorgeous, something is off with Jenny. She's much quieter than usual, barely talking. And she seems rigid, as if she's trying not to brush up against me or set her hand too close to mine.

At lunchtime, it's not much better. We stop at a quiet picnic area beside a stream, Jenny and I sit across from each other, sharing a sandwich on a small picnic bench. Still she barely looks at me, and she leaves more than several inches between us on the bench. Hours ago, we were nearly intertwined, and today she's distancing herself from me. What happened between then and now?

Finishing our lunches, we dispose of our trash in the bear-proof trash cans.

Once we return to the cabin, we head around to the woods out back and find the trail Sheryl had mentioned. The air is cool and heavy with the scent of pine and damp earth. The dense forest feels tranquil and untouched, as if we're the only ones here. The path is narrow, winding between towering oaks and tangled rhododendrons. The trees seem to stretch upward, their branches forming a natural canopy above us.

We hike on for a good thirty minutes, taking in the sounds and sights of nature. I tap Jenny on the arm, offering her a water bottle from my backpack. She takes it, her fingers brushing against mine before she quickly pulls away.

"Thank you," she says, drinking from the bottle and then flipping her head upside down to put her hair up. She uses a hair band to pull her hair into a messy bun. The simple gesture leaves me momentarily transfixed. There's something mesmerizing about the way the tendrils of her hair fall away from her neck, the flush on her cheeks from the hike adding to her beauty.

"Sorry," she says, glancing at me as she smooths her hair. "I know I look a mess, but I was getting hot with my hair down and had to throw it up."

I nod mutely, unable to form words. How did I get so lucky? This beautiful woman is my wife. What alternate reality did I fall into?

"Trent, you okay?" Jenny asks, tilting her head as we continue walking.

I clear my throat, taking another sip of water. "Yeah, just thinking. I wonder how much further until we reach the waterfall. We don't want to be out when the sun starts to set."

"Oh, good point," she says, glancing at her watch. "We've gone almost two miles. How about we go one more, and if we don't see the waterfall, at least it was a beautiful hike."

"Sounds good to me."

As we walk, my mind races. How am I supposed to share a bed with someone I'm insanely attracted to? There's no other choice, so I'll have to rein it in and deal with it.

Just before we hit the three-mile mark, the dense canopy overhead suddenly gives way to a clearing. Jenny gasps and halts a few feet ahead of me. Before us, a waterfall cascades down a craggy outcrop, its crystal clear threads tumbling into a pristine lagoon below. The sunlight streams through the gap in the trees, scattering a rainbow of colors across the water's surface. The lagoon, framed by moss-covered rocks and large ferns, shimmers in shades of blue and green. A cool breeze carries the soft roar of the waterfall and the faint calls of hidden birds. It seems a place meant for just us, serenity seemingly untouched by human hands.

"This is just . . . incredible," Jenny breathes, her voice filled with awe.

"Yeah," I agree, feeling a sense of wonder take hold of me. When Sheryl mentioned a "little waterfall," I wasn't prepared for this. It's stunning.

We stand there, taking it all in—the sights, the sounds, the smells—for what feels like longer than it should. I alternate between watching the view and stealing glances at Jenny, her artistic eye seemingly absorbing every detail. I could tell she wants to capture this scene in a painting someday. I'll have to remember this place and bring her back when she has her canvas and paints.

A shift in temperature alerts me that too much time has passed. "Jenny, we should head back. It's going to be dark before we make it back to the cabin."

She looks down at her watch, then back up at me, her expression apologetic. "I'm so sorry, I just got lost in the beauty of this place."

"No need to apologize. I did too."

With one last glance at the waterfall, we turn and make our way back to our one-bedroom cabin.

Back at the cabin, Jenny is all business, making quick work of brushing her teeth and changing into pajamas. She doesn't even meet my gaze as she grabs the extra pillows from the closet and begins lining them down the middle of the bed.

"I think this should suffice," she says, stepping back to admire her handiwork.

"What is this?" I ask, gesturing to the pillows.

"This way we can make sure to stay on our own sides of the bed."

"Um . . . okay?" I say. Something is definitely going on with Jenny. Last night, she was fine with us sleeping close together, embracing actually, and now she's back to not wanting to share a bed. "So you're making a pillow fortress?"

"Exactly," she says, adjusting the pillow again.

"Didn't realize we were preparing for a siege," I quip.

"Better safe than sorry."

I wouldn't mind being a bit sorry. The thought passes through my mind so quickly, the memories of waking up with her in my arms and the kiss we shared blooming warmth within me.

But I won't make her uncomfortable.

"Jenny," I say gently, gesturing to the wall of pillows. "What's really with the fortress?"

She sighs and moves to sit on the edge of the bed, her shoulders slumping slightly. "Last night was . . . great," she says hesitantly, her voice barely above a whisper. "But I can't do this. I'm sorry."

"You don't have to be sorry," I reply, keeping my tone soft and steady. "If a fortress of pillows is what you need, then that's exactly what we'll do."

Her eyes flicker toward mine, relief mingling with something unspoken. "Thank you," she says quietly. "I don't know how to explain it, I just—"

I hold up a hand to stop her, offering her an easy smile. "No need to explain."

I swallow the lump of pride rising in my throat and focus on reassuring her. My smile must do the trick because a small one tugs at her lips in return.

We settle into our respective sides of the bed, the pillow wall an imposing divider between us, forcing us closer to the edges of the mattress than is comfortable.

Jenny seems to fall asleep easily—her breathing evens out, and her occasional sighs break the cabin's quiet stillness. I lay on my back, staring at the wooden beams of the ceiling and listening to the muffled rustle of leaves outside and the faint croak of frogs in the distance. The smell of pine lingers in the air, mingling with the faint lavender scent of her shampoo.

I turn on my side, careful not to disturb the wall of pillows, and study her outline in the faint moonlight filtering through the curtains. Her hair is spilled over her pillow, and her face is relaxed, peaceful in a way I rarely see when she is awake.

The memory of our kisses from yesterday replays in my mind, vivid and electric. Her lips had been soft, tentative at first, but when she leaned into me, her touch grew confident, igniting something I hadn't expected.

Kissing Jenny wasn't just a moment; it felt like a turning point. It reminded me that beneath all the pretense of our arrangement, there was something real there, something worth exploring.

But then there was this wall, both literal and figurative. The pillow fortress is a clear reminder that she isn't ready to blur the lines of our deal. My feelings for her are growing stronger, but the weight of what we are—what we aren't—keeps me awake long after Jenny's drifted off.

Clearly, the closeness from the last few days was too much. Even though I swear she was the one who instigated the kissing both times. What happened? I can only hope that she is starting to feel the way I am. Even if she isn't quite ready to acknowledge those feelings.

In the morning, we pack up quickly, a silence filling the room. Jenny seems lost in thought, and I don't want to push her. As we leave the cabin, I look back at the wall of pillows that had stayed intact all night. Then I close the door, and we leave in my truck.

When we get back to Chessie Valley, the rhythm of daily life picks back up as if we never left. We unload the car, and then Jenny gives me a distracted smile before heading toward the marina shop. "Don't wait for me after work," she says, "I'll be in in my studio. I need some time to paint."

I nod, then add, "Take all the time you need."

A few weeks pass with Jenny and I keeping each other at arm's length. We're both busy at the marina, and in the evenings, she heads to her art cabin. Not wanting to go home to an empty house that reminds me of my empty marriage, I stay late at the marina, finding more to do. Tonight is no exception. I prep cabins for a wave of renters coming tomorrow, fix rudders on two rental boats, and replace slats of wood on the docks. In the evening, I trim back bushes and prep for sunset yoga.

We started the yoga back in the fall. Guests loved the serene setting with the gazebo perched by the lake and framed by wildflowers. I would have to agree, even more so now that I proposed to Jenny there. It makes for a beautiful stage for yoga. And while I don't normally stick around for sunset yoga, tonight I decide that it would do me some good.

The soft hum of music drifts through the air as the yoga instructor adjusts the speaker system. The gazebo lights blink on, casting a warm glow over the water. The scent of freshly cut grass mingles with the floral perfume of the nearby wildflower blooms.

I'm just starting to stretch when a familiar voice catches my attention. "Hey there, hubby," Jenny says.

I turn to see Jenny approaching, yoga mat in hand, her cheeks flushed from the cool evening air. She looks radiant, her yoga attire hugging her in all the right places. Who am I kidding, she'd look radiant in a potato sack.

"I didn't expect to see you here," I say.

"I wasn't sure if I would make it tonight, but sometimes when I get lost in a painting and my mind starts to think too much, I'll do a bit of yoga to settle it. Helps me get back in the right headspace."

"I'm glad you're here," I say.

She smiles back at me.

"Were you wanting some space?" I ask. "I can head out if you were planning on doing yoga alone."

"No," she says, "please, stay."

I unroll my mat and lay it on the grass. "Isn't this the perfect backdrop for an outdoor yoga session?" I say, gesturing to the gazebo and the view behind it.

"I'd have to agree with you there," Jenny says, a smile fluttering across her face. "I have a soft spot for this gazebo."

Damn if my heart doesn't stop short at those words and the sight of her. She's a vision. I thought she looked good in her hiking outfit on our honeymoon, but this yoga look is even better. I turn my face from hers and grab my water, gulping it down right before the instructor starts.

Today's session of yoga is especially difficult. It's not just physically demanding—it is mentally challenging too. My mind keeps drifting, especially with Jenny next to me. It's been so long since we've spent an evening together. Jenny effortlessly flows through each pose. She makes it look easy, her movements graceful and controlled, her breathing steady.

I'm sweaty and exhausted by the time the session is over. I run my hand through my damp hair. I must look like a mess.

I catch Jenny watching me out of the corner of her eye. "Like what you see, wifey?" I tease.

She rolls her eyes, a hint of pink dusting her cheeks. She stays that way for a minute before responding. "I've just never seen you work up such a sweat before, and you've worked on boats and mended cabins. Didn't think yoga would be the thing to take you down."

"Don't let it fool you. This was next-level yoga." I grin, about to give her a retort that she's sweaty too, but looking her over closely, I see that she's serene, barely even glistening. "And how is it that you're not even sweating?"

"Probably because I do yoga just about every day. Plus, none of these poses were especially difficult so it was more like a movement meditation for me."

She does yoga daily? I guess it's not easy to miss that when we're not spending much time together. But you think I would've noticed it at the cabin in Gatlinburg.

"You didn't do yoga on our honeymoon," I say flatly.

She chuckles softly and whispers, "If you recall, that place barely had enough space for two people to walk around. But I did do some sun salutations when you were in the bathroom in the mornings."

"Damn, and I missed it."

"What?" she eyes me curiously.

Oh shit, did I say that out loud? "Oh um, nothing. I'm just going to miss that cabin."

"Right." She full on laughs now, eyes crinkling as she wipes away tears.

Man have I missed that laugh. I lean in close to her. "What? When else will I have the chance to share a bed with my wife?"

Her laughter comes to a screeching halt, and she freezes. For a split second, I think I've gone too far. Maybe she's not ready to joke about our not-honeymoon. But then she shakes her head and swats me on the arm. "You're so bad," she says.

After the session ends, I tuck my rolled mat under my arm and grab Jenny's mat with the other. Then I grab my water bottle and wait for her to gather her things. "Well, wifey, what do you say we head home?"

"I'd say I'm exhausted and that sounds wonderful."

As we walk back to the house, the moon hangs low in the sky, it's soft light illuminating the path ahead. The cool night air carries the faint hum of crickets and the rustle of leaves. Jenny walks beside me, her water bottle in one hand, her other hand occasionally brushing against mine.

"Thanks for coming tonight," I say quietly.

She glances over at me, her smile small but genuine. "Thanks for letting me crash your yoga session, hubby."

Her teasing tone makes me laugh. We arrive at the wrap-around porch quickly. "Welcome home," I say, holding the door open for her. As she steps inside, the warmth of our home wraps around us.

"Thank you." Jenny gives me a quick smile, her eyes flickering with something I can't quite place before she heads up the stairs.

For the first time in a long time, I feel like maybe, just maybe, the wall built up between us isn't as impenetrable as it once seemed.

Chapter 22

Jenny

The next few days fly by in a blur of activity. New people check in to rental cabins, families line up for pontoon boats, and fishing gear flies off the shelves. I find myself constantly restocking the marina store, trying to keep up with the demand. The energy at the marina feels electric, alive with laughter, conversations, and the occasional bark of a dog trotting alongside its owners.

In my spare time, I'm painting and processing everything that I want this relationship between Trent and me to be while balancing it with what I know the relationship is and has to be. Some days are better than others, but both Trent and I are adjusting and finding a rhythm.

I haven't seen Trent much, except in passing, because he's been buried in maintenance work. Whether he's repairing motors, replacing dock boards, or handling some plumbing issue in the cabins, he's always on the move. I honestly don't know how he managed to juggle all this before I came onboard. Greg's marketing efforts have clearly paid off—this place is busier than I ever imagined a marina could be.

"Hey, Greg," I call out one Thursday as he makes his way back into the lodge after his lunch break. The scent of fresh coffee wafts in with him, mingling with the faint tang of sunscreen from customers wandering around the store. "Bring any goodies from Holly?"

Greg pauses mid-step, raising an eyebrow. "How'd you know I was there?"

I lean on the counter, smirking. "I'm not blind, and you're a man of habit. Every Monday, Tuesday, and Thursday you go over to For the Love of Sugar to have lunch with Holly. Don't even try to deny it." My gaze drops to the paper bag in his hand. "But I just know this time you brought me something back in that bag of yours. Am I right?" I could really use one of Holly's sweet treats with how exhausting this week has been so far.

Greg chuckles, shaking his head. "You're scary accurate, you know that? I made one mention to Holly at how slammed we've been this week, and she loaded me up with treats to bring back for everyone."

I beam and reach for the bag. "I could kiss her! Oh my gosh, let me see what she sent."

The bag rustles as I dig through it, immediately pulling out two Sunrise Sin muffins. Their golden-brown tops glisten in the sunlight streaming through the lodge windows, and the smell of cinnamon sweetness makes my mouth water.

"I'm going to take one of these out to Trent," I say. "He should be finishing up an oil change on one of our pontoons. Can you hold down the fort for a bit?"

"Sure thing," Greg replies with a grin. "Trent would never turn down his favorite baked goods."

Outside, the late spring air is warm but not stifling. A gentle breeze dances across the lake, carrying the crisp scent of pine and the occasional splash of water as boats pull in and out. The April sky is a perfect shade of blue, with only a few wisps of clouds scattered like paint strokes. I wave at some boat owners tinkering with their engines as I make my way down the dock.

"There you are!" I call out when I spot Trent wiping grease off his hands with a rag. "If we didn't work together, I'd be worried about you. I haven't seen you all week."

He looks up, his face breaking into a smile that makes my heart skip. "Hey there, wifey. Everything okay?" His gaze shifts to my hand. "Wait—is that a Sunrise Sin muffin, or are my eyes deceiving me? I worked through lunch, and I'm starving!"

"I'd wondered if you'd eaten. I hadn't seen you in the lodge today, so I wasn't sure." I hand him the muffin. He takes it eagerly, tearing into it with the enthusiasm of a kid.

I take a bite of my muffin as well, and the rich, sugary flavor melts on my tongue. Holly is literally the best baker I've ever known. These are to die for.

"Thanks," Trent says around a mouthful of muffin. "That hit the spot." His eyes flicker to my muffin, still mostly intact.

"Eyes off, mister," I warn, holding it out of his reach. "If you want another, Greg has more in the lodge. But you'll have to actually take a break to go get one."

Trent rubs his chin slowly, his eyes clouding over as though he's sifting through the pros and cons of what I just said.

"Is it really that hard to take a quick break?" I ask, tilting my head.

"No, it's not that," he says slowly. "I'm just trying to figure out how long I can afford to step away. There's still so much to do—office work, the boats, the cabins . . ."

"What if I helped with more?" I suggest, crossing my arms.

He raises an eyebrow. "You want to help with more? You already do so much with the shop." Then he shrugs. "But there's no way I can turn down help at this point. How do you feel about office work?"

"I used to work as a secretary for a real estate firm back in Atlanta for a while, so I think I could handle the marina office." I smile before taking a bite of my muffin.

"How about small maintenance work?"

"I had to help out with minor repairs to some of the rental locations when we were short-staffed, so I can help with some of that."

"You really have worked in pretty much anything, haven't you?"

"What can I say? I'm a jack-of-all-trades. Plus, this marina is my home now. I'd do anything to help around here."

Something in his expression shifts as he steps closer. His hand comes up and cups my cheek brushing it lightly. The warmth of his touch sends my heart racing. Although it's been weeks since we last kissed, my heart rate still spikes each time he comes close. I can't help but want to kiss him again.

The world seems to fade—the chatter of boaters, the hum of the marina, even the gentle lapping of waves against the dock. It's just us. His piercing gaze locks into me, and my breath catches as his thumb grazes the corner of my lips. My breath stutters as my lips part slightly. I can feel his warmth even though we are still a few inches apart. Is he going to kiss me again?

A flash of something passes through Trent's eyes and he steps back, his face unreadable as he drops his hands from my face. "Sorry," he mutters, clearing his throat. "You had a crumb just there." He motions to his bottom lip.

My eyes zero in on his movement. I bite back a sigh. Ugh, what I wouldn't give to kiss those lips again. "Thanks, I guess."

Before either of us can say another word, a familiar voice cuts through the moment.

"What are you two doing out here?"

I turn to see Samson, his weathered face lit with curiosity. Trent is a ball of nerves beside me. "Samson!" I greet him, walking over with a smile. "How are you doing?"

"Wonderful, my dear," he says, his eyes crinkling with warmth. He glances at the unfinished muffin in my hand. "Is that from the bakery downtown?"

Man, I should really eat faster.

"Yes, sir. Greg brought some back after his lunch with Holly."

"Well, that Holly sure knows her way around a kitchen," Samson remarks, rubbing his hands together.

He looks between Trent and me, a glimmer of mischief in his eye. "I didn't expect to see you all back so soon. I know it's been a few weeks, but I heard your honeymoon lasted only a day or two. That was mighty short."

"We had some big reservations coming up," says Trent, "so we needed to get back to the marina."

"Yes," I add, "we plan to take a longer trip once we are in the offseason. With the main season just starting, we didn't want to sacrifice our customers just so we could have a longer honeymoon."

Samson nods approvingly. "Smart. Timing is everything. That sounds well-thought-out. Great job, you two. I would have done the same myself had I gotten married right before the busy season, but I planned it right, and the missus and I got married in the offseason so we didn't have to worry about timing."

"Tell me about your wife," I ask, hoping to get the discussion off Trent and my honeymoon.

Samson's gaze softens and a small smile flits across his face. "My Winnie was the sweetest gal. She worked at the ice cream shop in town, and I'd go get a vanilla ice cream every Friday. When I finally got the courage to ask her out, I was surprised she said yes."

"That's so sweet," I say.

"She was the heart of this marina," Samson continues. "Everyone loved my Winnie. She mainly worked the marina shop once we got this place up and running. She was so good with people. She was a free spirit and a friend to everyone. You remind me a little of her."

A lump rises in my throat at his words. To be compared to someone so wonderful makes me proud.

"I know it may seem odd to you young kids," Samson says, "that I would require each successive business owner to be married. But Winnie is the reason I put that clause into my business plan. I truly feel that a marina like this needs a couple at its core. It's the couple that keeps the heart in this place. Both of us working together at the marina not only helped business thrive but also helped bring Winnie and I together over the years. I think it will do you and Trent good as well."

I glance at Trent, his profile thoughtful against the sunlit lake. I feel a small smile light up my face.

Maybe Samson's onto something.

Chapter 23
Trent

"There's supposed to be bad weather tonight," I say, glancing out the lodge's wide front window as heavy gray clouds creep toward the horizon. "So I'm closing up the marina early. I've already let the rentals know to keep an eye out tonight."

"Do you need me to help with anything?" Jenny asks, her voice light but with a tinge of concern.

"No, I've gotten most things done, I just need to do some paperwork, then I'll be heading back to the house."

"Alright, I'll be painting in my cabin if you need me," she says as she slings her bag over her shoulder and makes her way out of the lodge.

I watch her leave, the swing of her bag matching her stride as she crosses the gravel path toward the tree-lined trail. A warm breeze stirs the air, carrying the faint, earthy scent of rain. As she disappears into the woods, a thought strikes me like a bolt of lightning: I should build her a painting cabin closer to the house.

The notion makes me freeze. It's not just a practical idea—it feels like permanence, something I shouldn't be contemplating about Jenny. Not when this arrangement is meant to be temporary.

Shaking off the thought, I head back to my desk stopping first at Greg's office. "Can you add something to the website about our early closure today? Include links to emergency services and the 'what to do in an emergency' FAQs. We've got a few residents in the cabins, and I want them to have all the resources they may need."

"Already on it," Greg replies, his fingers flying over the keyboard. "Just putting some finishing touches, and it will be live. Then I'm going to head on over to the bakery and help Holly wrap things up. Don't stay too late—it's looking nasty out there, like it's going to hit right over us tonight."

"Not looking good," I agree. "I'll be out of here in an hour or so."

Back in my office, I bury myself in the accounts and scheduling for the week ahead. The rhythmic pulsing of the wind against the windows begins softly, building as the storm draws closer. By the time I finish, the trees are swaying as the wind howls. I switch off the lights in the lodge, pin a paper with emergency contacts to the front door, and lock up.

I'll have my cell on all night in case anyone needs me. It's been a long time since we've had a bad storm hit Chessie Valley, and hopefully it will avoid us tonight as well.

I start to head toward the house, but my gut tells me to check on Jenny. I have a feeling that she's still in her painting cabin.

After walking around the lodge and down the walkway, I'm proven right. For a moment, I can't help watching her. Jenny in her paint-splattered overalls, her hair loose and curling slightly from the dampness in the air. Her lips move faintly as if she's humming to herself, completely immersed.

Watching her is like watching a composer creating a musical masterpiece, her emotions on full display in the work she creates. It's mesmerizing, and I don't want the moment to end.

A crack of lightning breaks me out of my trance, and I quickly open the cabin door. "The storm is supposed to hit soon," I say with some urgency.

She jumps slightly, turning to me with wide eyes and then looking out the window. "That doesn't look good," she says. "How long have I been out here? I only meant to paint for an hour." She looks over at her wall clock and her jaw drops. "Oh no, I didn't mean to stay out this long."

"It's okay," I reassure her. "I just finished up at the lodge and thought I'd check to see if you were ready to head back home."

She nods, hastily packing up her paints and brushes. "Thank you for coming to get me."

As we leave the cabin, the first fat raindrops splatter against the earth. We're halfway back to the house, just passing out of the woods, before the skies open up and unleash a downpour of water on us. The rain is icy against my skin, soaking us through in seconds.

We exchange wide-eyed looks and run toward the house. But the wet grass turns treacherous. I slip, landing hard. Jenny turns back to help me.

"Go on!" I shout over the storm. "I'll catch up!"

"No way! I'm not leaving my husband," she yells.

Though the storm is intensifying, I can't help but feel relieved hearing her say those words.

"Here, take my hand," she yells. Lightning flashes, illuminating her determined expression. As I grab her hand, she jolts at a crack of thunder. "I appreciate the lightning better when I'm inside," she says, breathless, her hair plastered to her face.

"Come on," I say, standing. "Let's get inside before we drown out here."

Holding her hand in mine, we make it the rest of the way into our house. Jenny lets out a sigh of relief as we step into the warmth. Even drenched to the bone, she is stunning. This beautiful, smart, kind, sexy woman is my wife.

"Hold on," I say, "I'll get us some towels." I kick off my shoes and head for the bathroom. When I return, I stop short. Jenny's fingers work through the damp strands of her loosened braid, untangling it with practiced ease. Her clothes cling to her, soaked through from the storm, while flashes of lightning spill through the window, illuminating her in short, radiant bursts. The glow frames her figure, ethereal and striking, as if the storm itself conspires to make her look like a goddess.

"Oh, good, a towel," she says, snapping me out of my reverie.

Right, towels. Though my throat is dry, the rest of me is not. I hand a towel to her, then start drying myself off.

She wraps her hair up in the towel and heads toward the stairs. "I'm going to change before I catch a cold."

"Same."

The lights flicker ominously as I swap out my wet clothes for dry ones and come back downstairs. It's going to be a long night.

I light the fireplace and heat water for hot chocolate. Jenny joins me, now dressed in soft loungewear. "Hot chocolate sounds amazing," she says, taking a mug and sitting at the island.

"Want to sit by the fireplace?" I ask. "I don't trust that we will have power all night." The words barely leave my lips before the power cuts out. "Well, that was perfect timing," I say flatly.

Jenny laughs, and I just stare at her, my hands on my hips. "You think that's funny, do you?"

Nodding, she breathes out, "Yes, yes I do."

We sit by the fireplace with our hot chocolates and blankets. The storm rages outside, but the heat from the fire keeps us warm. We talk for hours about everything and nothing. Conversation comes easily, which feels right. My feelings for Jenny only continue to grow deeper.

"I'm going to head to bed," Jenny says. "It doesn't seem like the storm is going to be ending anytime soon." She stretches and gives a soft yawn.

"I think you're right about that," I agree, folding my blanket and laying it over the back of my chair.

"Sleep well, Jenny," I say.

As she stands, I catch the faint scent of her shampoo. "You too, hubby," she says. Then she stands on her toes and presses a kiss to my cheek.

My heart skips a beat as she walks away, leaving me with the storm and the lingering warmth of her touch.

Chapter 24

Jenny

Up in my room, the storm feels alive—louder and more intense than I anticipated. The sharp howling of the wind and the relentless drumbeat of rain against the windows create a symphony of chaos. I stand at the window for a moment, watching the skies, which have turned a deep, menacing blue, almost black.

The trees outside sway wildly, their branches flailing like desperate arms in the storm, making me question if it was the right decision to choose this room. Their swaying feels almost predatory, ominous in the flickering light from the storm.

I close my blinds, trying to shut out the storm's angry flashes, but a particularly bright bolt of lightning sears through the slats, illuminating the room in a harsh white light. A deafening crash of thunder follows, shaking even the foundation of the house.

Crawling into bed, I pull the blanket up to my chin and stare at the ceiling. My heart pounds as I picture the lake's churning waters, waves smashing against the marina's docks. I can only hope the boats will weather the storm unscathed.

The house groans and creaks as if it too is fighting against the tempest. The sound of the wind slipping through the tiniest cracks creates a haunting whistle that seems to come from every direction. I toss and turn for what feels like hours before exhaustion eventually wins out. I drift off into a restless, dreamless sleep.

A sudden, earsplitting bang jolts me awake, and I sit up with a scream. The sound of shattering glass fills the room, sharp and jarring. The wind shrieks through what must be my now broken window. Icy rain slices into the room, pelting my arms and face.

Above the chaos, I hear Trent calling my name. It's faint, but it's enough to spark a flicker of hope. I quickly throw back the covers, ready to go to him, only to be showered with the shards of glass and sticks that covered the blanket.

"Trent!" I scream. Then something heavy crashes into me, sending a sharp pain through my head.

The world tilts and fades. I can barely make out Trent's voice above the storm's ferocious roar as darkness swallows me whole.

Chapter 25
Trent

"Jenny!" I yell.

The sound of the storm is overwhelming, pressing in from all sides like a living force. Sirens wail, fragmented and distant. My chest tightens, adrenaline flooding my veins as I struggle to process what's happening. A tornado. The realization slams into me, and with it, a wave of panic.

"Jenny!" I yell again. "I'm coming!" I run to my bedroom door, ready to throw it open when a deafening roar overpowers me. It sounds like a freight train barreling directly past me, making my ears ring. The books on my nightstand fly across the room, a drawer from my dresser hits the wall above my head, and my bed flips as if it were as light as a feather. I've heard people describe being hit directly by a tornado like this before, but nothing could prepare me for the all-consuming pressure and the primal fear that comes with it.

But as suddenly as the deafening roar began, so does it fade. I hope—pray—that the tornado is moving away, sparing what remains of my home and of the marina. My room is intact, the walls and ceiling holding firm, but the contents of it are strewn across the room.

When I finally pull open my door and step into the hallway, my knees give out as I take in the destruction.

The end of the hallway where Jenny's room once stood is obliterated.

A massive pine tree lies sprawled across the ruins, its splintered branches jutting through what used to be the ceiling, now on the floor of the room and hallway. Rain pours through the gaping hole, carried by gusts of wind that swirl pine needles and debris into a chaotic dance.

My panic threatens to overtake me, but I can't let it.

"Jenny," I whisper, my voice cracking as tears blur my vision. My heart pounds painfully against my ribs.

I claw my way to my feet, weaving through the wreckage. I have to get to her. I have to know if she's okay. Her scream echoes in my mind, an endless loop of terror and helplessness. She has to be okay. She just has to. I can't lose her after I just got her.

Climbing over broken beams and shattered furniture, I finally reach a vantage point where I can see her room—or what's left of it. My stomach twists.

Jenny lies at a weird angle in her bed, a massive tree branch looming over her like a predator over its prey. The jagged edges of the broken branch rest precariously, held aloft by her shattered dresser and the crumbling remains of the hallway wall. The branch hovers only inches above her.

Her face is pale, ghostly against the dim light filtering through the debris. Her eyes are closed, lashes resting delicately against her cheeks. She's so still, too still, and a cold knot of fear twists in my stomach.

I strain to see from where I stand, but the shadows and wreckage block my view. I can't tell if she's breathing but can see blood in her hair. My pulse thunders in my ears along with the storm outside, drowning out all else.

"Jenny!" I scream, my voice hoarse and desperate. I attempt several times to get to her, but with all the wreckage, I know I'm wasting time. Time she may not have. I scramble back through the debris to my room, nearly tripping in my haste. My hands fumble for my phone, but the screen mocks me with the absence of signal bars.

Panic tightens its grip. The marina is so isolated that help won't arrive for hours unless I act. I dig through the mess in my room and finally find the two-way radio—Grandfather's emergency wisdom echoing in my mind. "Better to be always prepared and never need it, then not prepared when you need it most."

I grab it and press the button. "Hello, is anyone there? This is Trent at the marina. We've been hit by a tornado. Over."

Static fills the line for a moment before a familiar voice crackles through, sending a sliver of relief through me. "Trent? This is Niall. What's the status over there?"

"It's Jenny." My voice breaks, and I take a shaky breath. "I can't . . . she's trapped in her room, and there's a tree."

"Don't worry, mate. We're on our way. Can you get to her?"

"No, the tree's massive."

"Hold tight. We'll be there as soon as we can."

"Niall, she has to be okay."

Jenny has to be okay. She just has to. I don't know what I'll do if she isn't. I made a vow to protect her and care for her no matter what, and I intend to do just that.

Ending the call, I force myself into action. First, I make sure the breaker is off—no sense risking electrocution when the power inevitably comes back on. My thoughts briefly flit to the renters in the cabins, but I can't bring myself to leave. Jenny needs me here.

I return to the debris that blocks my way to Jenny, determined to clear what I can before help arrives. My hands ache as I wrestle with splintered wood and branches, but it barely makes a dent. The rain continues to pour, soaking me to the bone as I work.

When the sound of sirens pierces the storm, relief surges through me.

Finally!

I race to the front door as Niall and the rest of the firefighters pull up. Moments later, the wail of an approaching ambulance joins the chaos.

The firefighters assess the damage quickly, their movements efficient despite the storm. They begin cutting the tree into manageable sections, their chainsaws roaring above the wind. Each cut feels like an eternity.

Jenny still hasn't moved.

An EMT, Silvia, places a hand on my arm. "We'll know more once we can reach her. Stay calm, okay? And let's get you checked out."

"I can wait," I choke out. "Please. That's my wife in there. Bring her back to me."

Her eyes soften, but she doesn't waste time with reassurances she can't promise. She just nods and moves toward the clearing path, her flashlight cutting through the darkness of the early morning hours.

A voice from one of the firefighters calls out on Silvia's walkie-talkie, "Silvia, Jon, you're up in just a minute, we've almost gotten through. Be ready."

"On it, Sarge," Silvia calls back through the walkie-talkie at her shoulder. Silvia adjusts her gear and turns back briefly. "We're going in now."

I step aside, fists clenched, as the EMTs disappear into the ruins of Jenny's room. The storm still rages, the early morning sky a murky gray, but I barely notice. My world is reduced to one singular hope: that Jenny will come back to me.

Chapter 26
Jenny

The first thing I notice as I come to are the sounds. They're quieter than before but still loud enough to keep me on edge. Distant voices mix with the low rumble of chainsaws and the patter of rain on shattered wood. It's disorienting, like waking up underwater, every noise muffled yet pressing in on me.

Darkness surrounds me, and a searing pain stretches across my head. Breathing feels like a monumental effort, each shallow inhale burning in my chest. I try to move, but a sharp pain shoots through me, freezing me in place.

Gentle hands touch my neck, and I flinch instinctively. A soft voice speaks close to my ear, soothing and steady. "Shh . . . You're safe. My name is Silvia, and I'm taking your vitals. Try to stay as still as you can. There's a lot of debris and broken glass."

A small beam of light pierces the darkness as she shines a flashlight into my eyes. The brightness stings, and I squint, my eyelids heavy as lead. "Hurts," I manage to say. My voice sounds foreign to me, raspy and weak.

"I know it does," she replies, her tone gentle but firm. "The other firefighters are working to get you out of here. You're doing great—just hang in there."

I try to glance around, but my view is blocked by a chaotic tangle of branches and debris. The air smells of crushed pine and damp earth, a sharp contrast to the fresh, slightly sweet scent of sawdust lingering in the background. My chest tightens as I process the confinement, panic clawing at the edges of my mind.

"Trent," I gasp, my voice improving despite the pain. "Is he okay?"

Silvia's expression softens, and she crouches lower so I can see her face clearly. "He's fine," she reassures me. "He's just outside and very eager to see you. Let us finish in here, and you'll be back with your husband in no time."

The word husband echoes in my mind, grounding me. Trent is okay. Relief washes over me, and I manage a weak smile before my eyes flutter shut again.

"Hey, no sleeping," Silvia says, her voice firmer now. She shakes my shoulder, her touch light but insistent. "I need you to stay awake for me, okay?"

I nod faintly, fighting the pull of exhaustion. My entire body aches, the pain radiating in waves with each movement.

"We're going to put you on a backboard now and get you out of here," Silvia says. "You're doing amazing. Just a few more moments, and we'll have you back out there where you can see your husband." Her voice is calm, but I can hear the urgency beneath it.

A familiar Irish brogue cuts through the noise. "Alright, Silvia, ready to transport?"

"Niall," I whisper, recognizing the firefighter's voice, "is Trent okay?"

"Hi, Jenny," Niall says, leaning into my field of vision. His face is smeared with sawdust, but his eyes are warm. "He'll be loads better once he sees you. Poor lad's been a right mess since he called us."

I muster a small smile, letting Niall's familiar presence soothe my frayed nerves. If Niall says Trent's okay, then Trent is okay. The EMTs lift me onto the backboard with careful precision, strapping me in securely.

"Jenny!" Trent's voice is hoarse and raw, and the sound of it jolts my heart. Tears well up in my eyes as his face appears above me, rain dripping from his hair and down his cheeks.

"Trent," I whisper, my voice breaking. Tears spill from me eyes because he really is okay, even up and moving around. I reach out my fingers to him.

As soon as he's close enough, his hand wraps around mine. His grip is warm and steady, a lifeline in the chaos. "I'm so sorry, Jenny," he says, his words tumbling out. "Everything's going to be okay. The EMTs think it's nothing too serious, but they're taking you to the hospital to be sure. You were unconscious for so long."

"Stay with me," I plead, my fingers curling weakly around his.

"Always," Trent vows, his voice fierce with emotion. "They couldn't pry me away with a crowbar."

A soft chuckle escapes me, but the motion sends a jolt of pain through my head. I wince, sucking in a sharp breath. "Hurts to laugh," I admit, grimacing.

"No more jokes," he promises, his lips twitching into a faint smile. "I'm just so glad you're alright."

"Me too," I murmur, my voice barely audible.

As they carry me out of the house and into the ambulance, Trent stays by my side, never letting go of my hand.

His thumb traces soothing circles against my palm as we pull away from the house. For the first time since waking, I allow myself to believe that we'll make it through this.

Together.

The next twenty-four hours pass in a whirlwind of fluorescent lights, sterile smells, and constant monitoring. Nurses flit in and out of my room like hummingbirds, each bringing a new piece of equipment or a clipboard full of questions. The doctors seem to run an endless string of tests—scans, X-rays, and pokes and prods that leave me tender and tired. Apparently, being knocked out and coming within inches of being crushed by a massive tree raises enough concerns to keep an entire medical team occupied.

By some miracle, all my tests come back clear. No internal bleeding. No fractures. Just some bruising and a soreness that will take time to fade, along with a neat row of stitches tracing across my forehead.

When the last doctor leaves, I turn to Trent, who's slumped awkwardly on the small couch in the corner. His broad frame barely fits, and the dark circles under his eyes tell me he hasn't slept at all.

"Trent," I say softly, my voice still raspy from disuse. "You really didn't have to stay here with me. Have you even left the hospital at all?"

He straightens up, rubbing the back of his neck sheepishly. "Well, one would be a very stupid husband to leave his wife," he says with a faint grin. Then his expression sobers. "But since a giant tree did fall on our house and basically wiped out half the upper floor, I did have to step out for a bit. I've been fixing up a place for us to stay once you're discharged. I couldn't bring you back home to that mess."

"And the renters?" I ask for what feels like the hundredth time. "Are you absolutely sure they're going to be okay?"

"Everyone's fine," he assures me. "You don't need to worry about all that."

"Tell me," I say. "The marina is my home too."

"You're right," Trent says, looking into my eyes with a warmth I haven't seen before. "The marina is ours."

I smile up at him. "So?"

"No one was severely hurt, just shaken up. Most renters decided to cut their stay short," he says, "which is understandable considering the tornado. And honestly, with the cleanup we have ahead, we'll need to clear out the rest of the renters. At least for this week. Most cabins have some exterior damage—broken windows, some shingles blown off. Those will be a quick fix. A few of the cabins have extensive damage that will take some time to repair. We've got a big cleanup project ahead with all the debris the tornado left."

He exhales, rubbing a hand through his hair as his gaze flickers toward the window. "As for the boats, a few of the smaller ones were overturned or knocked against the docks. One pontoon broke loose and ended up along the shoreline, along with one of the docks, but the pontoon boat is mostly intact. The larger boats held up pretty well, though we'll need to inspect them all for damage before anyone takes them out again. Some of the other docks have loose boards and missing planks, but nothing we can't repair."

His tone softens slightly as his eyes meet mine. "Your art cabin's fine. A couple of big branches came down near it, but they missed the roof. There were just a few broken windows from the wind, but that's an easy fix. Honestly, I was worried when I saw how close that one tree came to the back corner, but you got lucky."

He shifts his weight, his shoulders easing slightly. "Mom and Dad's place had some debris hit the side, but nothing major. We all dodged a bullet this time. All in all, we got lucky."

He reaches across the small hospital table to take my hand, his grip warm and reassuring. "I know I did," he adds, his voice quieter.

I squeeze his hand, trying to will him to believe that I really am okay. "I'm ready to go home as soon as they give me the all clear," I say, a determined edge creeping into my voice. "I need to see it, Trent. I need to see how close I was to . . ." I swallow hard, pushing back the surge of emotion that threatens to overwhelm me.

Trent's eyes darken with concern. "You don't need to see that."

"Yes, I do," I insist, my tone firmer now. "I need to see the aftermath. My memory is so vague—it was dark, and everything happened so fast. I need to understand, to process it."

He hesitates, then nods reluctantly.

Before long, the doctors return with my discharge papers, running through a list of things to watch for, like dizziness, nausea, and shortness of breath, and how to care for the stitches. Trent listens intently, his brow furrowed as he absorbs every word.

When the nurse brings a wheelchair, I say it isn't necessary but allow her to help me into it. Trent walks beside us, his hand never leaving my shoulder.

At the truck, he surprises me by scooping me up effortlessly and setting me in the passenger seat. "You didn't have to do that," I say, half amused, half embarrassed, and a little grateful. "I could've climbed in myself."

"You're my wife," he replies simply, brushing a strand of hair from my face. "I'll take care of you."

As he shuts the door and walks around to the driver's side, I catch him muttering something under his breath. "What was that?" I ask, studying him. His face is a flood of emotions—guilt, frustration, something I can't quite name. "Trent," I lay my hand on his leg and his face softens. "Tell me."

He exhales sharply, gripping the steering wheel before meeting my gaze. "You should've been with me," he says finally.

"What do you mean?" I ask, waving my hands between us. "You never left my side."

He smiles humorlessly. "No, Jenny," he says, his voice tight with emotion. "You shouldn't have even been in that room. You're my wife. You should've been in my room. Our room. With me."

"But our agreement—"

"To hell with the agreement." He runs his hands through his hair in frustration. "That stupid agreement we made—it's what got you hurt in the first place."

"Trent," I say gently, "you don't mean that."

"I do," he says, his voice breaking slightly. "If that tree had landed at a different angle, if that dresser hadn't been there, or if the wall hadn't broken the tree's fall . . ." He looks at the ground, his eyes misting with tears. "You could've been killed, Jenny."

"But I wasn't," I counter, reaching out to place my hand on his leg. "It wasn't the agreement that almost killed me—it was a tornado. Unless you've somehow gained the ability to control the weather, I'm not blaming you."

His lips twitch into a reluctant smile, and some of the tension leaves his shoulders. "It scared me," he says quietly. "I know you're my wife because of our agreement, but I care for you. More than I thought I could."

"I was scared too," I reply, my voice soft. "But we're okay now. We'll rebuild our home, clean up the marina, and everything will go back to normal."

He nods, his grip on the steering wheel loosening. "That sounds like a good plan."

"It is," I say, a teasing smile tugging at my lips. "I'm good at plans. Remember? I'm the one who came up with our whole engagement."

He chuckles, shaking his head. "Oh, I'll never forget that."

For the first time in days, the weight between us eases, and I finally allow myself to relax. Trent's care and concern remind me that this marriage—this partnership—is turning into something real.

And that's something I may be ready for.

Chapter 27
Trent

Now, as we pull up to the remains of our home, Jenny's voice catches in her throat. Her eyes fix on the shattered shell of what used to be our sanctuary, and for a moment, she says nothing.

"It looks a lot worse than it seems," I offer gently, trying to lessen the shock. "I met with Niall and the structural engineer to assess the damage this morning. They said it'll need significant repairs, but it's not a lost cause."

Jenny's gaze stays locked on the wreckage; her lips press tightly together as tears brim in her eyes. "Our beautiful home . . . It's destroyed." Her voice trembles, barely a whisper.

"But you weren't," I reply, turning toward her. Without thinking, I pull her into my arms, holding her as tightly as I dare. "That's all that matters to me."

After a beat, I lean back, brushing a tear from her cheek with my thumb. "Actually," I say, trying to lighten the mood, "I'd love to have your insight on how best to redo the upstairs."

Her eyes widen slightly, the hint of a smile breaking through her sadness. "You do? But, Trent, I'll only be here for less than a year."

"It doesn't matter," I say, my voice firm but kind. "It's our home."

The weight of those words seems to settle between us, tangible and real.

Back in the truck, we make our way over to the marina lodge. After we park, I hop out and circle around to Jenny's side, opening her door before she can protest.

"Trent," she says as I scoop her into my arms, "you don't have to carry me."

"I insist," I reply with a grin. "Plus, it's only right for a husband to carry his wife over the threshold."

Jenny folds her arms with a mock huff. "That's only on the wedding day."

"Well," I counter, feigning seriousness, "I think it should apply anytime said husband and wife get a new place to live."

Her skeptical look gives way to curiosity as I carry her into the lodge. "We're living here?" she asks, glancing around the space.

"Yes and no," I reply, heading toward the back of the building. "There's one place I haven't shown you yet." I stop in front of a plain wooden door in the corner of the shop. "Would you mind turning the knob?"

Jenny raises an eyebrow but complies. "Doesn't this just go to the attic? We're not living in the attic, are we?"

I chuckle. "Sort of. It's more than an attic—there is also a studio apartment up there. It's where I stayed while I was building the house. I swung by yesterday to clean it up and grab a few things from home."

We climb the narrow staircase, Jenny insisting on walking despite my protests. I'd been enjoying the feel of her in my arms. At the top, she stops short, taking in the sight of the modest space.

The apartment is simple but serviceable: a small kitchenette with mismatched cabinets, a sitting area with a loveseat and an old armchair, and a bathroom off to the side. The centerpiece is a single king-sized bed, its navy comforter neatly smoothed out.

"There's only one bed, Trent," Jenny points out, her tone a mix of amusement and apprehension.

"Yes," I reply, leaning casually against the doorframe. "But it's a king, so there's plenty of room for your pillow fortress."

She swats my arm playfully, then moves to inspect the space. Her fingers trail over the countertops, and she opens a few cabinets before stepping into the bathroom for a quick glance.

A voice from downstairs interrupts the quiet.

"Who's that?" Jenny asks, peering back toward the stairs.

"That must be Margot," I reply, heading toward the noise. "Holly's younger sister. She works for the Tennessee Pacers, and she said she'd bring some of the guys from the team to help clean up the marina."

Jenny's face lights up. "That's so thoughtful! Let's go greet them."

"Jenny, the doctors said you need to rest," I caution, though I already know I've lost this battle.

She waves me off with a playful swat. "You're worse than a mother hen. I won't do any heavy lifting—I just want to say thank you."

With a resigned sigh, I follow her down to the marina yard, where Margot stands with a group of towering athletes.

"Hi, Trent," Margot calls, hurrying over to give me a hug. Her smile falters as she notices the stitches on Jenny's forehead.

"Jenny, I'm so sorry to hear about what happened. Are you feeling better?"

Jenny nods graciously. "A little bruised, and these," she says, gesturing to her stitches, "but nothing I can't heal from. Thank you so much for coming out to help—it means a lot to us."

"It's no problem at all," Margot says, her tone earnest. "When I told the team owner about the damage, he was more than happy to have the guys pitch in. I only asked for a few volunteers, but over half the team wanted to help. Especially since they knew it was for friends of mine."

"We're always happy to help out Boss Lady here," says one of the players, his deep voice tinged with warmth.

"Welcome to the marina," Jenny says warmly, her smile genuine as she looks between Margot and the players who came with her.

"We're so thankful for your assistance," I add, extending a hand to each of them in turn. "It would take us ages to clean up this place without your help."

"Happy to pitch in," Margot says. "I was sorry to hear y'all got hit pretty bad."

"Yeah, the storm wasn't kind," I reply, glancing toward the scattered debris and leaning docks.

After a few moments of small talk, I address the group, raising my voice slightly so everyone can hear. "Alright, here's the plan. There are some key things we'll need to tackle today. I've already walked the grounds and noted the damage—secured any loose boats too—but there's a lot of cleanup to do. We'll need to clear both small and large debris: wood, metal scraps, loose items from the docks and walkways. The tree removal crew is working on hazardous trees, but we need to gather the rest. For now, let's make organized piles. Later today, a truck will bring in a large dumpster, and we'll transfer everything then."

The group listens intently, nodding in understanding.

"We might also need to do some small repairs on the docks," I continue. "Replacing broken planks, securing benches. If anyone has handyman skills, I could use the help there."

Margot doesn't miss a beat, directing some players here and others there.

"This will be a huge help," I say, tipping my baseball cap back and running a hand through my hair. "Honestly, without you all, I'd be working on this cleanup for weeks by myself."

"You're not alone," Margot says, placing a hand on my shoulder. "We've got this."

I glance at Jenny, who's been quietly observing the interaction. "You doing okay?" I ask softly, leaning toward her.

She exhales, her shoulders sagging slightly. "Yeah. I just wish I could help with something."

I study her for a moment, gauging her energy. "Well," I say finally, "if you're determined to pitch in, you could grab some waters and pass them out to the volunteers. It's going to be a long day, and I'm sure everyone will appreciate it."

Jenny's face brightens, and she gives a small nod. "I can do that."

I watch her walk toward the lodge, her steps a little slower than usual but still purposeful.

The way she holds herself, even now, fills me with a quiet awe. This woman—my wife—is the kind of person who can't help but focus on others.

Turning back to the group, I clap my hands together. "Alright, let's get to it."

Chapter 28
Jenny

After the volunteers get their directions from Margot and Trent, they spring into action. The energy on the marina grounds is bustling yet focused, with voices calling out instructions and the rhythmic sounds of debris being cleared. I make my way around, handing water bottles out to the players.

"Thanks, ma'am," one of them says, his forehead glistening with sweat as he pauses to take the bottle. The genuine gratitude in his voice catches me off guard. I'm the one genuinely grateful for their help.

As I move from one group to the next, offering a smile or quick words of thanks, I can't help but be in awe at how much is being accomplished. They really do work well as a team. I'd love to see them in action on the football field one day.

Trent hangs up his phone and walks over to me. "Just got off the phone with Mr. Newman. He's checking on his boat again. I feel like my phones been ringing off the hook since the tornado—boat owners making sure their boats survived. Thankfully, Mr. Newman's one of the lucky ones."

"That's good," I say, my voice heavy with exhaustion.

Trent steps closer, his hands gently gripping my arms. "How are you holding up? You look worn out. Why don't you head up to the studio apartment and rest for a bit?"

I nod, glancing around at the volunteers still hard at work. "That actually sounds like a good plan." I make my way up to the small studio apartment that Trent and I will be calling home for the foreseeable future. I can't imagine it will be a short timeframe to get the house relivable, considering how long it took Trent to build it in the first place. As I close the door behind me, the sounds of the cleanup fade to a dull hum.

The space is modest but cozy—just enough for the essentials. Trent brought over a few of my surviving belongings and added some of his own, blending our lives into this temporary shared space. I lay down on our bed, my head throbbing. I'm amazed that passing out water bottles has drained me this much. I close my eyes and drift into sleep.

I wake up to a soft knocking at the door. I slowly get out of bed and open the door.

"Jenny!" My grandpa's voice is thick with emotion. "I was so worried about you!" He glances up at my stitches. "Are you alright?"

"I'm okay, Grandpa," I say, giving him a small hug. "Come on in."

"Trent told me where to find you," Henry says as he takes a seat by the table. "I wanted to check on you, but I won't stay long. You need your rest."

I pull up a chair next to him. "I'm doing fine, Grandpa. Really. The marina took a hit, but we're already making good progress on repairs. We have a great group of volunteers help-ing us out."

"I haven't been worried about the marina," he says, taking one of my hands. "I've been worried sick about you. You've been on my mind every second since the tornado. Trent's been giving me updates, but it's not the same as hearing your voice, sweat pea."

"I know, Grandpa. But now you know you don't have to worry about me," I reassure him, trying to keep the exhaustion out of my voice. "Trent has been so wonderful. I don't know how he's been managing everything, but he's been organizing, making calls, keeping everyone calm. And he's been making sure I don't overdo things now that I'm out of the hospital. He's . . . amazing."

Henry lets out a soft sigh, the kind that says he doesn't have to worry quite as much. "I always knew he was a good egg. Sounds like he's proving me right."

"He is," I say, my voice soft. "And how are you? I was worried about you too."

"Now, don't you be worrying about me," he says, squeezing my hand. "I'm an old man, you know. This isn't my first tor-nado."

I grin and squeeze his hand back. "I'll always worry about you, Grandpa. No matter how old you get."

Henry laughs at that. "I love you, sweet pea."

"I love you too."

We talk for only a few minutes longer before he stands, readying to leave. "Now that I've seen you with my own two eyes and know Trent is taking care of you, I feel much better." He kisses me on the cheek. "Now, get some rest."

"I will," I say.

When he leaves, I sink into the armchair by the window, exhaustion pressing into my bones. And then, without warning, the tears come.

They're a steady stream down my cheeks as I let the weight of the past few days wash over me. I am thankful—so deeply thankful—to have walked away from the tornado with nothing more than bruises and some stitches. One look at the wreckage of our home, and it was clear how much worse it could have been. I've never been one to look a gift horse in the mouth, but the relief I feel at being able to walk away from that is overwhelming.

And then there is Trent. Sweet, steadfast Trent. He worried for me, cared for me, protected me in ways I hadn't expected. This marriage was supposed to be a convenient arrangement—a yearlong solution to two separate problems. But in the short time we've been together, something deeper has taken root.

I wipe my eyes and inhale a shaky breath. I need to talk to someone about this. And I know just who can help me sort this out.

The familiar scent of sugar and baked goods greets me the moment I step into Holly's bakery.

"Jenny!" Holly calls, rushing out from behind the counter. Her arms wrap around me.

"Hi, Holly," I say, laughing lightly as I return the hug, though I wince at the pressure against my bruises.

"Oh, sorry!" she says, pulling back quickly, her eyes scanning me for any sign of distress. "What are you doing here? You should be resting. Are you feeling okay? How are your stitches?"

"I'm okay," I assure her, though my voice wavers. "Just tired and sore. Honestly, the emotional part has been the hardest."

Holly's expression softens. "I can't imagine. When Greg told me what happened, I couldn't stop thinking about you. But you're here now, and that's all that matters. Come sit down. I'll get you something to eat."

I sit at one of the tables, and Holly joins me, passing me a slice of hummingbird cake and cold water in a glass. "Thank you," I say.

"How's the marina holding up?" Holly asks. "Greg says there's a lot to do over there."

I glance around the cozy bakery and swallow some water. "There is a lot to do. But Margot brought some of the football players to help with the marina cleanup. They are making light work of a big job. Trent and I are so grateful. I thought they deserved some sort of treat for all their hard work. I can't do much physically, doctor's orders, but I figured this was one way I could contribute."

"Say no more!" Holly says, already bustling back behind the counter. She calls out to her assistant, Paige, who hurries over with a bright smile.

"What are you thinking?" Holly asks, her hands already reaching for containers.

"Maybe a little of everything?" I say. "I wasn't sure what exactly you might have available today. There are just over thirty guys, not counting Trent and Margot."

Holly's eyebrows shoot up. "Most of the team came out? That's amazing."

"It is," I agree, smiling at the thought. "Margot may be smaller than the players, but she is mighty. She's got them going every which way, working on just about everything. All the players seem to have a deep respect for her."

"As they should," Holly says, her tone firm but proud as she carefully arranges pastries.

While Holly gathers the treats, my thoughts wander to Trent—to the day we'd first met, him bringing me here, and how far we've come since.

"You okay?" Holly asks, her voice cutting gently through my reverie.

I nod, then hesitate. "Can I tell you something? And you promise not to tell anyone?"

Holly sets down the container she is filling, pulls out a chair, and turns toward me, her expression open and kind. "Of course. What is it?"

And so I tell her. About the real reason Trent and I got married so fast, Samson's contract stipulations, and me wanting to have a permanent job and a place to live that was close to my grandpa. And finally, about the emotions I can't quite suppress.

Holly nods knowingly. "Oh, Jenny, I've known about the marriage of convenience for a while now."

I gasp. "How did you know?"

"Well, Trent told Greg and Niall, and, of course, Greg couldn't keep it from me." She gives me a small understanding smile. "I just wanted to give you and Trent some time to figure it out before saying anything."

"I should have figured," I say. "I know you and Greg are inseparable."

Holly smiles. "He's the love of my life. But tell me more about you and Trent."

"Holly," I say, my voice barely above a whisper, "I think I'm falling in love with my husband."

Holly's eyes glisten as she reaches across the table to squeeze my hand. "That's wonderful news, Jenny. Trent deserves to be loved by someone as kind and genuine as you. Someone to look out for him while he's looking out for everyone else."

"But isn't me falling in love with him a problem?" I say. "Our marriage, it's only temporary. We've only been married a month or so now, but if I'm already feeling this way about him . . ." My heart clenches at my next thought. "How am I supposed to let him go in a year?"

Holly looks me in the eyes. "Tell Trent how you feel," she says gently. "Odds are he's feeling the same way you are. I've seen the way he looks at you, Jenny. That's not just for show. I've known Trent for a long time, and he's not that great of an actor."

I smile. No, no he's not. In the short time I've known him, it's clear that he wears his emotions on his sleeve.

Her words hang in the air, a glimmer of hope that I can't quite grasp yet. Could it be possible that Trent might be falling for me too? The way he kisses me sure makes me think so, but neither of us has said anything specific. I know he is coming to care for me more than as a friend. But could it be love?

Holly stands, her energy brisk once more as she packs up the last of the treats. "These are on the house," she says firmly.

"Oh, but I couldn't possibly—"

Holly cuts off my protests with a wave of her hand. "Nonsense," she says, "I offered. Now go pass those out and win those guys' hearts. I put an extra Sunrise Sin muffin in this bag for Trent." She winks at me.

I smile and give her as tight of a hug as I can stand. I'm so lucky to have a friend in Holly. I feel like a weight has been lifted off my shoulders now that I've shared my thoughts and fears with her.

I leave the bakery with arms full of sweets and a heart full of peace. Telling Trent how I feel might take time—and maybe a few more Sunrise Sin muffins—but for now, this is a start.

Chapter 29
Trent

The next few days fly by in a blur of activity. Thanks to Margot and the football team, the marina reopens far sooner than I had dared hope. The volunteers had been gracious and endlessly grateful for the treats Jenny had handed out. Their enthusiasm and heartfelt thanks had brought a smile to her face—a smile I couldn't help but admire every time I saw it. And while Jenny is taking time to recuperate, Mom and Dad have stepped in to keep the marina running smoothly.

By now, Jenny is nearly healed, though I'm keeping a close eye on her. She's even feeling up to painting again, her energy and creativity returning like flowers in the springtime after a long, brutal winter.

Living in the studio apartment together has been effortless, like we were meant to share our lives more closely like this from the beginning. And waking up every morning with her in bed next to me brings me a sense of peace I can't describe.

This morning is no exception. I wake up early, Jenny sleeping softly beside me. The familiar urge to fish tugs at me. For me, fishing isn't about the catch—it is about the stillness, the chance to think without distractions from the hustle and bustle of life getting in the way. And after the last few weeks, I could use the calm. Besides, it has been far too long since I've joined Henry for one of our quiet mornings by the water. With the marina open again, I know he'll be there. I quietly slip out of bed and tiptoe down the stairs.

When I spot Henry seated at the dock, his tackle box open and his weathered fishing rod in hand, I can't help but grin.

"Good morning, Trent, my boy," Henry greets me with a wave, his face lighting up.

"Good morning, Henry," I reply, holding up my fishing rod and tackle box. "Thought I'd join you today."

Henry pats the bench beside him, and I settle in with a contented sigh. These benches were one of my better ideas back when I first took over the marina. I'd noticed older fishermen struggling to sit on the docks or bring their own chairs, so I'd had sturdy benches installed. Seeing them in use always gives me a small sense of satisfaction.

The lake stretches out before Henry and me, it's surface glittering under the early morning sunlight. The air is crisp, carrying the faint scent of fish and the earthy scent of damp wood. Nearby, the soft rustling of reeds and the occasional splash of a jumping fish break the silence, blending seamlessly with the gentle lapping of the water against the shore.

We sit in comfortable silence, casting our lines and watching the ripples on the water. The quiet is calming, a reprieve from the chaos of the last few weeks. "How've you been since the tornado?" Henry asks, his voice breaking the quiet as he reels in and recasts his line.

"Fine," I say, adjusting my grip on my rod. "The help we got made a huge difference. The marina's getting busier again now that it's back open, and Jenny's pretty much back to normal. She's even painting now that she's no longer in pain."

Henry nods, a soft smile tugging at his lips. "Good. I was so worried about her. I don't think I ever thanked you for taking care of her. It means the world to me, knowing she has someone like you to love and care for her."

"I'm relieved she's okay too," I admit, my chest tightening at the memory of Jenny after the tornado.

Henry glances at me, his eyes twinkling with mischief. "So, do you have plans to move back into your house soon? Or are you still staying above the marina shop?"

"Who knows when the repairs on the house will be done," I say. "We'll be in the studio apartment until then, but it works for us."

Henry waggles his eyebrows. "Nothing like close quarters for newlyweds, eh?"

My face heats, and I remove my cap, running a hand through my hair. Henry has a knack for saying things as he sees them, consequences be damned.

Before I can respond, Jenny's voice carries across the grass. "Hi, Grandpa!" she calls, walking toward us with a warm smile.

"Hi, sweet pea! How's my favorite granddaughter?" Henry replies, his grin widening.

"I'm your only granddaughter," Jenny says, leaning down to kiss his forehead.

"Doesn't mean you can't also be my favorite," he quips.

Jenny rolls her eyes but gives him a hug.

We settle into a comfortable rhythm, the three of us enjoying the quiet morning, surrounded by the sights and sounds of the lake. We talk about the marina, the plans we have for our house, and Henry's fun-filled schedule at the care center. I could have stayed there for hours, but my phone buzzes in my pocket.

"Here, Jenny, take this for a minute?" I say, handing her my fishing pole.

She nods, taking my pole as I pull out my phone. Seeing my mom's name on the screen, I quickly answer.

"Hi, Mom." I say.

"Oh, Trenton," she says, her voice trembling with emotion.

My stomach drops. "Mom, what's wrong?" Jenny and Henry both turn and look at me.

"It's your grandfather," she says, her words catching on a sob. "He's in the hospital. He had a heart attack, Trent."

I grip the phone tightly, my heart pounding. "Is he. . . is he okay?"

"We're on our way there now," she says. "The doctor called us. They're doing some tests now."

"I'll be there as soon as I can," I say, hanging up.

"Trent," Jenny says, her voice gentle, "what is it?"

"It's my grandfather," I say, my throat tight. "He had a heart attack."

Jenny immediately sets the fishing pole aside and comes to me, wrapping her arms around me. I stand there, numb, as my thoughts spiral. My grandfather is one of the toughest men I know, and the thought of losing him is unimaginable.

"I need to get to the hospital," I say, my voice barely above a whisper. "Mom and Dad are already on their way."

"Of course," Jenny says, her voice calm and reassuring. "Do you want me to come with you?"

"No," I say, shaking my head. "Someone needs to cover the marina. I don't think Greg will be in for another few hours."

Jenny nods, then reaches up on tiptoe to kiss my cheek.

"Will you be alright?" I ask her. "I just need to see him, see what the doctors say, make sure he's alright."

"I'll be fine," she says. "Go. And text me as soon as you know more."

I give her a brief nod, wave goodbye to Henry, and head to my truck. As I drive toward the hospital, my mind races. The thought of losing Grandfather feels like the ground shifting beneath me.

Chapter 30
Jenny

After Trent leaves, I sit back down next to Grandpa, wrapping him in a big hug. The familiar scent of his aftershave and the faint scent of his favorite peppermint candy cling to him. At this moment, I am so thankful that he is here with me.

"There, there, Jenny," he says softly, smoothing my hair down with his weathered hand, just like he used to do when I was a little girl. "Everything is going to be alright." His touch is steady, his love a constant I can always count on.

"I know," I whisper, blinking back tears. "I just feel so bad for Trent and his family. First the tornado and the marina, and now this."

"Don't forget, that's your family too, sweet pea."

I look up at him and nod, my chest tightening. He's right. They are my family now too. A sense of determination wells up inside me—I'm going to go above and beyond at the marina today while I wait for Trent to update me.

"I need to get back up to the shop," I say, straightening and brushing off the hem of my jeans. "We have renters coming in today, and I need to get everything prepared so Trent doesn't worry about anything while he's at the hospital."

"Alright. See you later."

"Bye, Grandpa."

When I get to the office, I fill Greg in on Trent's phone call. "Well," I say, gesturing toward the clipboard on the counter, "we have quite a few boat rentals today. Everything's ready except giving the normal rental rundowns. Greg, if you want to handle those, I can manage the cabin renters."

"Sounds like a plan," Greg says with a firm nod, rolling up his sleeves. Despite only working at the marina for just over a year, he moves with the confidence of someone who knows the marina inside and out. It's clear this place means as much to him as it does to Trent.

The hours blur as we both set out to do our best to cover for Trent while he's out. It's a steady rhythm of tasks—answering calls, checking inventory, and organizing keys. Renters come and go, filling the marina with a constant hum of activity.

The air smells of lake water and sun-warmed wood, mingling with the faint scent of sunscreen. Laughter rings out from the docks, where families eagerly load their gear into boats. It's a reminder that life moves on, even in the midst of uncertainty and chaos.

By three o'clock, I finally have a chance to catch my breath. I pull out my phone and find a text from Trent, sent about an hour ago.

> Trent: Grandfather is doing ok. They're giving him a pacemaker, but he should be fine and able to go home tomorrow if everything goes well.

Relief floods me as I quickly reply:

> Jenny: I'm glad to hear he's doing better and that he'll be able to come home so soon. Everything at the marina is good. Greg has been helping me cover today, and we just got done with the last of the rentals.

Three dots appear on the screen, then vanish. My heart beats a little faster as I wait.

> Trent: Thank you. I appreciate you more than you know.

> Jenny: **Heart emoji**

A smile tugs at my lips, and the knot of worry in my chest begins to loosen. Grandpa Samson is going to be okay. I look around for Greg, eager to share the good news.

I step outside and spot him coming up from one of the docks, a clipboard tucked under his arm. "Hey, Greg," I call out, waving as I approach.

"Hi, Jenny," he says, stopping beside me. "Everything okay?"

"Yes," I say, unable to keep the smile from my face. "I just heard from Trent. They're giving Samson a pacemaker, and he should be able to head home tomorrow if everything goes well tonight."

"That's great news," Greg says, his expression softening. "I bet Trent is so relieved. He's likely driving everyone crazy trying to take care of his mom and dad and seeing to his grand-father."

"Yes, he is definitely relieved," I say. "And you're probably right about driving everyone crazy. When I got back from the hospital, he was checking on me constantly."

"Well, you gave us all quite a scare that night," Greg says, shaking his head at the memory. "I've never seen Trent so upset and worried in my life."

"I didn't mean to worry everyone," I say softly, glancing down at my hands.

"I know you didn't," he replies gently. "But we're so happy to have you here. Trent is the happiest he's ever been—and that's saying something."

"Thank you," I say, my throat tight with emotion. "That means so much to me."

"I'm not saying it to be kind," he says, his voice firm and sincere. "You're just what Trent needs. Now, with everything done here, I'm going to head into the office to work on a few things before I leave. Call for me if you need anything, okay?"

I nod, his words leaving me speechless. As he walks away, a lump forms in my throat. The love and acceptance I've found in this friend group feels overwhelming, filling a void I hadn't even realized was still there.

I have to talk to Trent about how I feel. Unless someone dragged me kicking and screaming, there's no way I can walk away from this life—from Trent.

Today is the day Samson heads home. I know Trent is helping Mrs. Hughes bring him back to their house, but the hours drag like molasses.

Every time the chime over the marina shop door sounds, I glance up, hoping it will be my Trent.

My Trent? Yes, he is, isn't he?

The thought fills me with warmth, even as a nervous flutter stirs in my chest. It hasn't been the same sleeping in our little studio apartment without him. I know it's only been one night, but it feels longer—achingly longer.

I want to tell Trent how I feel, but I'm scared. Will it scare him away? He hadn't wanted to get married to me when we started this relationship. It was all my idea. Circumstances forced his hand, his love for the marina outweighing everything else.

But could his heart belong to me too? Mine certainly belongs to him.

I don't want things to end. I've fallen in love with my husband, and now I have to summon the courage to ask if he might stay married to me—not just for now, but for the long haul. For forever.

The shrill ring of my phone breaks my thoughts, making me jump. I hurry to pick it up, my heart thudding against my ribs.

"Hi," I blurt, not even giving the caller a chance to speak, "is everything okay?"

A warm chuckle comes from the other end of the line. "Yes, dear," Mrs. Hughes says, "everything is fine. We just wanted to thank you again for letting Trent stay at the hospital with us. Grandfather was happy to see him there too. And Trent has felt so relieved not having to worry about the marina, knowing it was in such capable hands. Edmund is also so impressed with how you've been with managing everything in Trent's absence."

"Oh, thank you," I say shyly, heat rising to my cheeks. "It was nothing, really."

"It was most certainly not nothing, dear. It was everything," she replies, her tone both gentle and emphatic.

Mr. Hughes voice crackles through the line. "Jenny, I want you to know—there's no way I could have picked a better girl for my son in a million years. You're just what this family needed."

"Thank you," I manage to squeak, barely finding my voice.

"I also wanted to call and tell you Trent is on his way back," Mrs. Hughes says. "It's going to take him a bit to make his way around the lake, but he's heading your way."

My heart skips a beat knowing Trent is heading home, my cheeks warming again as my pulse quickens.

"That's good to hear," I manage. "So that means Samson has settled in at your place?"

"Yes, he has," she says, then hesitates, her voice soft and heavy with emotion. "I also wanted to say . . ."

"Yes?" I prompt gently, sensing something important.

There's a pause before she continues, her voice thick with feeling. "I'm just so thankful that Trent has you in his life. I've never seen my boy so happy and at peace. You've lifted a burden off his shoulders—and mine as well. Plus, now I finally have the daughter I've always wanted. We weren't blessed to have more than one child, and while I love my son dearly, I'd always hoped for a daughter too."

Tears prick my eyes at her heartfelt words. "You're welcome, Mrs. Hughes. You all have been so welcoming. I appreciate you all so much."

"Maureen, dear. Please call me Maureen."

When we hang up, the tears spill over, sliding down my cheeks. Maureen and Edmund's kindness is overwhelming. How much more of this can I take, knowing there's an expiration date hanging over Trent and me?

After closing up the shop, I race upstairs to our little apartment, my mind buzzing with nervous energy. I hurriedly tidy up, straightening cushions and wiping down the counters before throwing on an apron.

In the kitchen, I chop, stir, and season, determined to put something special on the table. I'm not the most skilled cook, but I can manage a few decent dishes, and tonight feels important—like it should be just right.

The apartment smells warm and inviting. Dinner is ready, the little kitchen table is set, and two candles flicker softly in the dim light. And then Trent steps through the door.

Chapter 31
Trent

"What's all this?" I ask, stepping into our cozy place above the lodge.

Jenny is standing by the small kitchen table, a soft blush creeping up her cheeks. The flickering light from the candle casts a warm glow over her face, and she nervously wrings her hands on her apron.

"I thought you might like a dinner with real food after eating at the hospital for the last two days," she says shyly, her voice barely above a whisper.

The scent of buttery rolls and baked chicken fills the room, wrapping around me like a comforting hug. My stomach growls in response, and I take a step closer to her.

I gently reach for her hands, freeing them from the grip of her apron, and hold them in mine. "Thank you. This is so thoughtful. And you're right. I'm definitely in need of some real food." I wrap my arms around Jenny's waist, lift her off the ground, and spin her in a circle. I love the feel of her in my arms.

Her laughter fills the room, light and magical, like the sound of wind chimes on a breezy summer day. It's a sound I could listen to forever, one that makes my heart feel too full for my chest to contain. When I set her down, I place a soft kiss on her forehead and pull out her chair.

"My lady," I say, gesturing for her to sit.

Jenny giggles, her cheeks glowing pink. "Thank you, sir."

We settle across from each other at the table. I take in the meal she's prepared—golden baked chicken, vibrant green beans, fluffy mashed potatoes, and glistening rolls. It's a feast, and my stomach growls again in anticipation.

Jenny watches me carefully, her eyes searching mine. "I hope you like it. It's all things that I've noticed are your favorites."

"They are. It looks amazing." I grab a plate and start piling it high with food. Jenny follows suit, carefully spooning mashed potatoes onto her plate.

The quiet hum of togetherness fills the space between words. When we finish eating and Jenny gets up to clear the plates, I beat her to it, quickly gathering them and placing them into the sink. Together, we fall into an easy rhythm—her storing leftovers while I wash dishes. The domestic act of the whole thing feels intimate.

As I dry my hands on a towel, I glance at her wiping down the counters. Something stirs in my chest, a mix of love and determination.

"I want to show you something," I say, taking her hand. She follows me out of our little apartment and into the open space of the attic.

She looks at me quizzically. "You didn't even let me take off my apron. What do you need to show me all of a sudden? And why are we in the attic?"

I hesitate, my nerves threatening to get the better of me. Clearing my throat, I press on. "I was thinking . . . maybe we could turn this into an art gallery for you, a space to show-case and sell your work. And in the shop, we could display your marina-inspired pieces. Visitors could take a little bit of Chessie Valley Lake home with them."

The thought had come to me on my drive back to the lodge from my parents' place. As soon as it came to me, I knew I had to act on it. The passion Jenny has for her artwork is mesmerizing, and if I want her to see a life with me long-term, I know I have to show her that I am making space for her life with mine.

"This space has the bones for an art gallery, don't you think?" I ask. "And once we are out of the little apartment, we could turn that into an office and lounge for you."

Her eyes widen, but she stays silent, so I keep going.

I pull out my phone and show her architectural plans. "And here, I have plans for your own art studio that we'll build next to the cabin. I figured we might as well have this built while we're working on our house. This way your art studio will be a little closer to home. But you can always keep your painting cabin too, if you want."

I ramble, gesturing around the attic and at the architec-ture plans, until I realize she hasn't said a word. When I turn to her, her face is unreadable, emotions flickering in her eyes. Is it happiness, sadness, nervousness?

"Jenny, is it too much?" I take a step closer to her, my heart pounding. "Are you okay?" I wish I knew what was going on in that beautiful brain of hers.

She startles slightly, as if pulled from deep thoughts. With-out warning, she closes the space between us, her arms wrapping around my neck as her lips meet mine. All thought leaves me as I'm fully engulfed in the feel of Jenny.

The kiss is intense, full of emotions I can't name but feel to my core. Her lips are soft, warm, and insistent, and I'm powerless to resist her. My arms pull her closer, her body fitting perfectly against mine. Damn, I've missed kissing her. I've missed the feel of her in my arms.

Our kiss is intense. I still have no clue what Jenny is thinking or feeling, but right in this moment, I'm hoping a little bit of love is being expressed. Her lips are soft and warm against mine. The fluttering of her eyelashes tickles my cheeks.

When a needy moan escapes her, it stirs a desire that has been brewing inside me, igniting a fire. Without thinking, I slide my hands down her back to just below her butt and pull her up against me. She wraps her legs around me and clings to me tighter, her hands roving through my hair, sending glorious chills throughout my body.

I carry her back to our little apartment and shut the door behind us, the dusty attic space forgotten.

Inside, she clings to me, her whispered plea sending a bolt of desire through me. "Please, Trent," she whispers against my neck. "I need you."

That's all I need. Rational thought fades, replaced by pure, unbridled love.

I walk us over to the bed and set her down. Her hands immediately start tugging at my shirt, untucking it from my pants and then bringing it up and over my head. Her hands explore and move all over my chest and abs.

I undo the apron and unbutton her shirt. The glorious sight in front of me causes my blood to heat. This goddess of a woman is my wife. Mine.

That's the last rational thought that goes through my head before we both are fully undressed and everything else is forgotten. I look down at Jenny, her hair splayed out behind her on the bed. Her eyes are intense with want.

I have never felt so in love with someone in all my life.

Tonight, I'll show her just how much she means to me.

Chapter 32

Jenny

Last night felt like a dream come true. Trent was intense yet tender, a contradiction that left me breathless. I had never made love like that before—had never been with someone who made me feel so utterly cherished. With Trent, I felt worshipped, elevated to a realm I didn't even know existed. He made me feel like a goddess, and he . . . Well, there are no words to accurately describe it.

The morning light filters through the curtains, painting the room in soft, golden hues. I wake up entwined with him, just as I had on that first morning in the cabin on our honeymoon. His arms around me feel like the safest place in the world, as though nothing could ever hurt us, hurt me, when we are together. I lay there, listening to his steady breathing, feeling the rise and fall of his chest against my cheek. The rhythm of his heartbeat is a soft melody to my ears.

Eventually, Trent stirs, planting a sweet, lingering kiss on my lips that sends a pleasant warmth cascading through me. "Good morning," he says, his voice still husky from sleep. Then he gets up, ruffles his hair, and grins at me before heading off to prepare for the day.

I stay in bed, clutching his pillow and inhaling the faint scent of him—woodsy with a hint of his cologne. I don't want to move, don't want to let go of this perfect, fleeting moment. The night before has changed something in me, and I'm not ready to face what comes next.

Talking to Holly had helped; her words were a balm to my troubled mind. But I need more. I need to confide in someone who has always been my safe harbor—my grandpa Henry. His wisdom and advice are what I need in order to muster the courage to tell Trent the truth: that I love him, deeply and irrevocably.

The walk to the lake is peaceful, the morning air crisp and tinged with the earthy scent of damp grass. Grandpa Henry sits on his usual bench, his fishing line arcing lazily into the still water. His hat shades his face, but I can see the peaceful expression he wears as he watches the ripples dance across the surface of the water.

"Hi, Grandpa," I call softly, wrapping my arms around him in a tight hug that smells of lake water and his old cologne.

"Well, that's quite the hug there, sweet pea," he says, chuckling. "You joining your old grandpa for some fishing today?"

I laugh, settling next to him on the bench. "You're not old, Grandpa."

He tilts his hat back and gives me a wry smile. "You're right. I'm not. Only as old as I feel, and today, I don't feel a day over fifty."

I laugh again, shaking my head at his ever-present charm. The soft creak of the bench beneath us and the gentle lapping of the water create a serene backdrop.

"You didn't bring a pole today?" he asks, gesturing toward my empty hands.

"No," I admit. "I was hoping I could talk to you about something."

"What is it?" Grandpa Henry asks, his voice gentle but steady, like the rhythm of the water lapping against the dock.

I hesitate, twisting my hands together in my lap. The words felt heavy on my tongue, weighted by weeks of secrecy. "Well, I haven't been completely truthful with you about something, and it's been weighing on me."

Grandpa Henry turns to face me, his eyes crinkling at the corners as the morning sunlight softens his features. "Go on, then. Let's hear it," he says, his tone encouraging, patient.

I take a deep breath, feeling the cool breeze tickle the stray hairs that have escaped my ponytail. "Trent and I . . . we didn't get married for love. The marriage was actually a scheme we concocted so he could keep his marina."

Henry doesn't react, doesn't flinch or furrow his brows. He simply nods, waiting for me to explain.

"You see," I continue, my voice trembling slightly, "his grandfather Samson had this clause in his marina contract. To fully take over the business, Trent had to be married. His grandparents, Samson and Winnie, wanted to ensure the marina stayed a family-owned, family-run business. Trent's parents were retiring, and without a wife, Trent was at risk of losing the marina. He confided in me about it and then one day, I overheard him talking to his mom about it and . . . well . . . I pretended I was his fiancée."

I pause, looking down at my hands. The confession leaves me feeling exposed, like the world has been stripped away.

Henry tilts his head, the corners of his mouth twitching as though he is holding back a smile. "And then what?"

"So, Trent and I talked it over and came up with a plan." My words tumble out now. "We agreed to get married and stay that way for a year. Then after the year was up, we'd . . . you know . . . go our separate ways."

Henry hums thoughtfully. "I see. And what was in it for you?"

I wince. I had hoped to avoid this part but pressed on. "Trent had already been so generous, hiring me and letting me stay rent-free in one of the marina cabins," I say. "Marrying him was kind of a way to so say thank you but also a way to guarantee I could keep the job and a place to live for at least a year, potentially longer. And the fact that they were both so close to you was perfect."

Henry leans back on the bench, exhaling deeply as his gaze drifts across the water. "And why are you telling me all this now?" he asks, his voice calm and steady. "Why say anything at all?"

My shoulders sag, and a tear slips down my cheek before I can stop it. "Because I'm in love with my husband," I whisper, my voice breaking on the last word. "I don't want our marriage to end, Grandpa. I don't know what to do. I thought . . . I thought you might know. That you could tell me what to do."

To my astonishment, Grandpa Henry throws his head back and laughs. Not a chuckle or a polite laugh, but a deep, full-bodied roar that echoes across the lake.

"Grandpa!" I protest, gaping at him. "It's not funny!"

"Oh, but it is, child," he says between guffaws, wiping his eyes. "Mighty funny indeed."

"Why?" I demand, crossing my arms.

Henry composes himself, though his grin remains. "Because it's as clear as day. You're both madly in love with each other! You'd have thought one of you would've spoken up by now. Hell, I saw it on your wedding day, whether you realized it then or not. You two were already head over heels for each other. It's the sort of thing your grandma Cora would've loved to see happen for you. I'd almost think she had a hand in it."

I sit there staring at him, stunned. This was the last reaction I had expected. Grandpa Henry gives my hand a gentle pat, his tone softening. "And that Trent . . . he's a sly one, that boy."

My head snaps up. "What do you mean by that?"

"Well, sweet pea," he says, his eyes twinkling, "that boy's been secretly paying off my medical bills and helping with retirement home costs since he met me."

I blink, dumbfounded. "He what?"

Henry chuckles. "Oh, yes. Even before you two knew each other. I noticed the changes right away—discounts on medical bills, sudden donations covering a month of fees here and there. That boy didn't think I'd put two and two together after I mentioned my granddaughter struggling to make ends meet?"

"He really did that?" I ask, my voice barely above a whisper.

"As sure as I'm here fishing," Henry replies, casting his line out again with a practiced flick of his wrist. "That boy has a heart of gold for sure."

The knowledge settles over me like a warm blanket. Trent has been helping Grandpa long before our agreement, his kindness extending far beyond any obligation. My heart swells, the weight of my love for him almost overwhelming. I am the luckiest person in the world to be married to a kind, generous man like him.

I won't let this chance slip by. Like Trent said before, to hell with the agreement. I agree—wholeheartedly. I love the marina, this family I've been given, and, more than anything, Trent. I can't lose any of them. Now, I just need to find the right moment to tell Trent that I love him, and I won't be giving him up.

Chapter 33
Trent

After spending the entire day catching up on boat and cabin maintenance and prepping the rentals for the weekend, my body feels like it's been put through the wringer. My shoulders ache, my hands are covered in a fine layer of grime, and the damp scent of lake water clings to my clothes. I'm halfway up the steps to the lodge, ready to collapse into a chair and watch the last rays of the sun slip beneath the horizon, when my phone buzzes in my pocket.

"Hi, Mom," I answer, slightly out of breath. "What's up?"

Her voice is calm but with that unmistakable edge of purpose. "Hi, honey. Your grandfather asked me to relay a message. He'd like to speak with you this evening."

I pause, wiping the sweat from my forehead. "Is everything okay? Something wrong with the pacemaker?"

"No, nothing like that," Mom says. "I think it has to do with the marina."

My stomach tightens at her words. What does this mean? Is there some way he found out about my marriage agreement? I already feel so guilty about not truly fulfilling the clause that's so important to him. And if he knew, I don't know what I would do. "Okay," I say, "I'll let Jenny know, and we'll head over after I clean up."

"No, sweetheart. He wants to talk to just you this time," she says. "I'll come by and have dinner with Jenny so she isn't alone. Besides, I've been meaning to catch up with her."

My stomach twists even more. How am I going to face my grandfather alone? "Alright. I'll tell Jenny about the change in plans, and I'll head over in a bit."

As I hang up, the sky shifts into hues of soft lavender and orange, a stark contrast to the nervousness settling over me. I pull the shop door open, and the tinkling bell announces my arrival. Jenny is behind the counter, her hands gently folding a receipt for a customer. Even in the dim glow of the shop, she's radiant—her long lashes casting soft shadows against her cheeks. The sight of her causes my heart to beat faster. We haven't talked since the events of last night, and I was hoping she and I could talk over dinner. Now with Grandfather's summons, that's not going to happen.

She glances up, and when our eyes meet, a faint blush dusts her cheeks. Her lips curve into a shy smile that makes my heart thud against my ribs. "Hi," she says, stepping around the counter as the last customer leaves.

"Hi," I reply, my throat suddenly dry.

She tilts her head, her gaze searching my face. "Everything okay?"

I nod, though my stomach twists. "Yes . . . and no. My grandfather has asked to see me."

"Oh?" she asks. "What about?"

"I'm not sure, but I think it has to do with the marina."

"Okay," Jenny says, "well, we've gotten through a similar conversation with him before—"

"Actually, he just wants to talk to me—alone."

Jenny nods. Her brows furrow briefly, but then her face softens into a smile. "I'm sure everything will be fine."

"Yeah," I say, but I'm not sure. "Mom's coming here to have dinner with you so you're not alone. I hope that's okay?"

"That's fine. I love Maureen—she's been so sweet to me."

"Maureen, huh?" I tease, raising an eyebrow.

Jenny swats my arm lightly, her laugh like a burst of sunlight. "Yes. She told me to stop calling her Mrs. Hughes now that we're married, but it still feels a little strange."

"I get it, and if you're okay with the plan, I should probably wash up and head out soon. Hopefully, it won't take too long, and when I get back . . ." I nervously shuffle my shoe against the wooden floor. "Maybe we can talk? That is if you are up for it."

Her gaze softens. "I'd love to."

Before I lose my nerve, I lean down and press a soft kiss to her lips. Her whisper of "See you later" follows me out, and it takes everything in me not to turn back.

The marina is quiet as I step onto my boat, the gentle lapping of water against the dock soothing my restless mind. The cool evening breeze carries the scent of pine and the faint scent of gasoline from the boats. The engine hums to life, and I steer toward the open water, passing the cove that hides our little house. Through the shadows of twilight, I can see the contractors' trucks and scaffolding. The sight is bittersweet—it's progress, but it reminds me how far we still have to go.

The lake stretches before me, its surface rippling with the faintest reflection of fading sunlight. The cool air brushes against my face, easing the tension in my shoulders. By the time I pull up to my parents' dock, I feel a little more centered. As long as this conversation with Grandfather goes as smoothly as the last one, I have nothing to worry about.

Dad is waiting on the deck, his hands tucked into the pockets of his jeans. "Hey, son," he says, his voice gruff but warm. "Your mom just left, but she sends her love. You hungry?"

As if on cue, my stomach growls loudly, and we both laugh. "I guess that's a yes," I say.

Dinner is a quiet affair. My father, never one for small talk, doesn't add much to the conversation. Grandfather stays uncharacteristically silent. The weight of the unspoken lingers in the air, but every time I bring up his summons, he brushes it off with a wave of his hand. "Let's just enjoy dinner."

So I update them on the marina. I fill them in on how well the rentals are going and how we are almost done getting the stumps for the clearing Jenny and I got married in, now named Cherry Blossom Grove. I also explain how we've done some minor renovations on the barn to allow for better wedding receptions and parties.

Dad and Grandfather are intrigued by the idea. Both of them want to see Cherry Blossom Grove once we get the set up complete.

After dinner, Dad excuses himself, mumbling something about catching the game on television. That leaves Grandfather and me. We retreat to a parlor room, its wide windows framing a beautiful view of the backyard sloping gently toward the lake. The room is still warm from the day's sun, and the faint scent of jasmine wafts in through the open sliding door.

I glance at my watch. It is getting late.

"I know you're itching to get back to that sweet Jenny," Grandfather says, his gravelly voice tinged with warmth. "But I'm thankful you came tonight."

"Of course, Grandfather." I try to focus on the lake, its surface now a deep indigo, reflecting the last streaks of fading light. The familiar scene usually comforts me, but tonight I feel restless. I know these waters like the back of my hand. But no amount of certainty out there could prepare me for what Grandfather says next.

"Son," Grandfather begins, his tone unusually soft. "I want to apologize to you."

The words hit me like a gust of wind off the lake, sharp and unexpected. I turn to face him, studying his expression. Grandfather isn't a man who apologizes often—or at all, really. So why is he starting now?

"I should never have forced you to get married in order to inherit the marina," he says, his voice thick with regret.

For a moment, I forget to breathe. The weight of his admission, so out of character, settles heavily in the air between us.

After a pause, I manage to say, "You didn't force me exactly, Grandfather." My voice falters slightly. "Jenny and I love each other."

"Codswallop," he says, shaking his head. "We both know the marina was your life, and if that clause hadn't been hanging over you, the thought of marriage wouldn't have crossed your mind."

I stare at him, unsure how to respond. This is not the conversation I'd envisioned when Mom relayed his summons earlier. Did he know Jenny and my marriage was only a ploy to ensure I got the marina?

"I was blinded by my love for my Winnie," Grandfather continues, his voice trembling slightly. "I just wanted you, or whoever took over the marina, to have what we had. But I see now I might've done more harm than good. And you've done a remarkable job running the marina. I know that married or not, you would give your heart to that place." His eyes glisten with unshed tears as he looks at me. "Can you forgive an old man, son?"

I swallow hard, my throat tight. "Of course, Grandfather. I know you didn't write in that clause out of malice. And . . . it means everything to me to hear you think I'm doing a good job with the marina. I've always wanted to make you proud. But there's something I need to apologize for too."

Grandfather looks at me, surprise on his face.

"You may have gathered this already," I say, "but I need to tell you anyway. You're right. Jenny and I did get married just so I could be eligible to take ownership of the marina."

"Oh, Trent," Grandfather says, his voice breaking. "I'm so sorry I forced you into a marriage you didn't want."

"I'm sorry I went behind your back," I say. "I should have just talked to you about how much the marina meant to me." I look at my grandfather, a big smile on my face. "But I think you including the marriage clause worked out for the best."

Grandfather looks up at me more perplexed than I have ever seen him before.

"The marina might've been my heart and soul once," I say, my voice steady despite the storm of emotions brewing inside. "But ever since I met Jenny, my entire heart and soul belong to her." I hesitate, then add, "Our relationship may have started as a marriage of convenience, a way to keep the marina. But it's not anymore. I love her. I love her with all that I am."

Grandfather doesn't try to hide his tears now. They slide freely down his weathered face. "I know you do, my boy."

"You do?"

He nods. "Anyone can see that you two love each other as clear as day."

"You can?"

"Yes," he says confidently. "I dare say it's a love like Winnie and mine."

My heart warms at the thought because I think it is too.

"Jenny is a mighty fine young woman," he says, "to be so willing to work at the marina and to step in like she has—she's incredible."

"She really is," I agree.

"I'm so happy you have found your very own Winnie. I hope you treasure her and every day you get to spend with her." Grandfather pauses, his eyes glinting with the sheen of unshed tears. "You'll never know when it will be your last, and that, my boy, is the scariest thing of all. I thought I would have more time with my Winnie, but she was taken from me too soon. Treasure that Jenny of yours, you hear me?"

"Yes, sir," I say, my throat tightening.

"Your grandmother Winnie would be so proud of you. So proud of both of you. And so am I."

"Thank you," I say, my voice thick with emotion. "That means the world to me."

He pats my shoulder with a trembling hand. "You've been here too long. Why don't you head on back to your lovely wife. And bring her around for dinner on Sunday, alright?"

"Yes, sir," I say, my heart leaping at the thought of Jenny.

As I say my goodbyes and head down to the dock, I think about what Samson said to me, to treasure Jenny because I'll never know when it will be my last day with her.

Unfortunately, due to our agreement, I do know when my last day with her will be. But I'm going to change that. I hurry my steps and get the boat ready to leave, excited to get back home to Jenny.

I grip the wheel tighter, my knuckles whitening as a surge of frustration washes over me. I want to be with her already. I want to tell her how I feel, and I hope she feels the same way. Because if she doesn't, there is no one else for me. Jenny is it. I want to stay married to her forever.

In this moment, I realize I'm irrevocably, madly in love with my wife.

When I walk into our apartment, the place is empty. No Jenny. My heart dips for a moment, but then I realize I know exactly where she is.

The marina feels almost otherworldly as I walk to her painting cabin. The sun has mellowed, casting long golden rays that glimmer on the water. A heron stands statuesque by the shore, its reflection rippling gently below it. The faint hum of distant cicadas blends with the occasional plop of fish breaking the surface.

When I reach her cabin, music spills faintly through the closed door—soft, lilting. I knock softly before stepping inside.

The world tilts.

Her artwork surrounds me, and I freeze in the doorway, my breath caught somewhere between wonder and disbelief.

A massive canvas dominates the room, it's presence almost magnetic. It feels like stepping into a dream. The scene is achingly familiar. It pulls me in with quiet reverence. It's the hanging bridges at Anakeesta.

Suspended in twilight, dark green trees stretch toward the sky, their vast canopies broken only by winding wooden bridges lined with twinkling lights. The entire painting glows as if holding its own breath, waiting. Off to the side, a couple stands in a loving embrace, gazing into each other's eyes, lost in their own world. My chest tightens. It brings me right back to that night. That kiss.

Then I see a sketch—of me—pinned delicately on the wall. The memory rushes back. The day we first met, when I took her to For the Love of Sugar after saving her from stepping onto the street.

Next to it, a larger watercolor painting—our picnic at Cades Cove. The colors bleed and blend in soft dreamy strokes, capturing the way the golden sunlight filtered through the trees, casting the warmth over that morning. It doesn't just depict the moment. It breathes it.

To my other side, a smaller canvas catches my eye. A bride and groom surrounded by cherry blossom trees, frozen in a dip as their love spills from the brushstrokes. Their expressions—pure, weightless joy—pull at something deep inside me.

And then—another. It's the little waterfall from our honeymoon, painted with such vivid intensity that I almost hear the roar of the water crashing into the lagoon below. The painting glows, the greens of the overhead canopy pierced by streaks of golden sunlight. Tiny details—the rough texture of the rocks, the way the light catches on the spray—bring it to life. In the foreground, two shadowy figures stand side by side, their closeness as palpable as the warmth of the memory it brings on. It feels as though I am right back there with her on that hike.

I turn, and my gaze lands on a painting of our cabin. Two people sitting in rocking chairs, side by side, staring out at the lake as the first rays of dawn stretch across the water. A quiet moment. A lifetime held in this single frame.

But it's what hangs beside it that undoes me.

The gazebo overlooking the lake. The place where everything became real. Sunlight spills over sandy shores as crystal clear water laps gently against the land. Wildflowers of every color bloom in the grass, their petals trembling as butterflies flit from one to the next. A wall of cherry blossom trees cradles the scene, their leaves whispering secrets into the breeze. Light filters through the branches, casting warmth across the place where I knelt before Jenny, where I asked her to be mine.

Tears blur my vision. The weight of it all—the love embedded in every brushstroke, the way she has captured not just moments but the very essence of us—presses against my ribs.

My heart cannot take the sheer depth of feeling spilling from the artwork that covers the cabin.

She has painted our love story. And it is the most beautiful thing I've ever seen.

"Jenny . . ." Her name falls from my lips, barely a whisper.

She turns, startled, a paintbrush still clutched in her hand. Her hair is pulled up in a messy bun, stray wisps curling around her face. She looks beautiful, radiant in her element.

"You found me," she says, her voice a mix of surprise and delight.

"This is . . ." I struggle for words, gesturing at the paintings. "Jenny, this is stunning. No—that's not the right word. It's breathtaking. It's like being there, everywhere, all over again. How, how did you do this?"

A soft blush spreads across her cheeks. She sets the paintbrush down carefully, as if the moment requires all her attention. "It was supposed to be a surprise," she says.

"Well, you've succeeded in surprising me," I say, my voice warm with awe. "Can we take these back to the house?"

Her eyes soften, but there's a flicker of something vulnerable in them. "You'd really want them at the house?"

"Of course I would."

"Hopefully," Jenny says quietly, "they'll be up there for a long time—longer than a year."

I look over at her and my soul screams with joy. This woman has to love me, she just has to. Why else would she say something like that? Why else would she paint such vivid and poignant moments of us?

I take a step closer to her, unable to resist. "Jenny, there's nothing I'd want more."

Her breath catches, and I feel the shift in the air between us. The room, the painting, the marina—all of it falls away, leaving only her. I hold out a hand. "Come on, let's go for a walk."

"Okay," she says.

As she slips her hand into mine, her fingers fit perfectly. The warmth of her touch ignites something deep in my chest.

We wander toward our gazebo, the late evening sun bathing everything in a golden glow. The blossoms sway gently in the breeze, their soft fragrance mingling with the pine scent of the forest floor.

I can't hold it in any longer. "Jenny, there's something I've been meaning to tell you. For a while now actually."

As we step into the gazebo, the sunlight filters through the blossoms, painting the ground in soft patches of light and shadow. I guide her to the bench near the entrance and sit beside her, my heart pounding.

"Jenny," I begin, my voice trembling slightly, "I've fallen in love with you. Completely, hopelessly, head over heels, scream it from the rooftops in love. I don't want our marriage to be about an agreement anymore. I want it to be real. Forever."

A soft breeze blows loose strands of hair across her face. I reach over, unable to help myself, and brush the strands back behind her ear.

Her eyes widen, tears spilling over her cheeks. "Trent," Her voice is thick with emotion. "Each day that passes is one day closer to the end of our agreement, and I've dreaded the end of each day because I want nothing more than to be with you forever. I fell for you a long time ago, and the thought of losing this—of losing you—has been unbearable. Because I am madly, utterly, crazy in love with you."

The weight of her words crashes over me, filling every crack in my heart. I pretend to tear up a sheet of paper and blow the pieces into the wind. "There, the agreement's done, gone, vanished into thin air, no more."

I kneel down and take her hands in mine. "Jenny, my beautiful, sweet, wonderful wife, I know you already married me. But I ask you now here in the spot where I first asked you to marry me, will you marry me again, today, marry me tomorrow, every day for the rest of our life?"

Yes," she breathes, her voice breaking into a smile. "Yes, Trent. Forever."

"Then I vow here and now to be the best real husband, with no end date, to you that you will ever have," I say.

"And I vow also here and now to be the best real wife, with no end date, to you that you will ever have," Jenny says.

"Then by the power vested in us, since this gazebo and marina is ours, I hereby declare us real husband and wife, with no end date."

"We may now kiss each other," Jenny says.

When I kiss her, the world stops, leaving only the two of us in the warm embrace of the gazebo. The future stretches before us, infinite and filled with promise. With this kiss I let all my love and devotion to her shine through, letting her know that she is and will always be loved to the end of our days and beyond.

Epilogue: Jenny

The last five months have been the best of my life. Trent and I have worked tirelessly to rebuild our home, pouring ourselves into every detail. We were able to create the perfect balance—keeping the original feel of the home while carving out a space that is wholly and truly ours.

We expanded the master bedroom and relocated it so it now overlooks the gorgeous expanse of the lake. The loft space still gives the cabin an open, airy feel, and now that I am most definitely not occupying a guest room, the spare rooms are ready to welcome our family and friends once more.

And now, standing here, surrounded by those same loved ones, it all feels so real. So complete.

Our home.

The cabin is filled with warmth—both from the crackling fire in the stone fireplace and the laughter of family and friends gathered throughout the space. The scent of cedar and pine lingers in the air, mingling with the aroma of Maureen's mouthwatering apple pie, fresh out of the oven. The lake outside glows under the moonlight, a soft breeze drifting through the open windows.

"This place is incredible," Niall says, whistling as he glances around. "You two really outdid yourselves."

"Seriously," Gwen agrees, sipping from her wine glass. "It's cozy but still open, warm but not cluttered. I'm impressed."

"It helped," Trent says, "that we had a vision of what we wanted the place to feel like." He wraps an arm around my waist. "And that we refused to stop until we made it happen."

"And don't forget the art studio," Holly adds, nudging me. "That's what I can't wait to see."

My heart swells at the mention of it. "They just finished it Tuesday," I say, barely containing my excitement. "It's a little one-room cabin, tucked just far enough away to give me space to create. It's got a big sink for all my brushes, lots of storage space for my supplies, and shelves for my paintings."

"And it's all yours," Holly murmurs, a knowing smile on her face. "I love that for you."

Greg grins. "I don't know, Trent. First, you set up an art gallery for her, then you built her an entire studio, and now you've got this perfect lake house. You're setting the bar a little high for the rest of us, man."

Trent chuckles. "I figure if I make her happy, she might just keep me around."

I roll my eyes, but my smile gives me away. Being married to Trent—without any looming agreements or end dates—has been liberating. We both finally feel free to express our love to each other in any way we see fit. We kiss more often, hold hands without second-guessing, and share little touches throughout the day. The nights of forced isolation behind the fortress of pillows are long gone, replaced by quiet, intimate moments that fill the space between us with warmth.

The conversation of the evening flows effortlessly, shifting between talk of the finished renovations, family, and upcoming plans. The atmosphere is light and joyous. But beneath it all, a quiet anticipation hums in my chest.

Grandpa Henry gives me a calculating look. I just smile before glancing at Trent. He catches my eye, as if reading my thoughts, and gives me a small nod.

I take a deep breath, then clear my throat. "Trent and I have some news to share," I announce, my voice steady despite the butterflies in my stomach.

Niall leans forward. "Don't tell me Trent is building you something else," he teases.

"No," I say, smiling, "but you could say I'm building him something."

I turn toward Maureen, unable to hold back my grin any longer.

"Are you saying what I think you're saying?" she says.

"We're pregnant!" Trent says, then he wraps his arms tighter around me and plants a kiss on my cheek.

For a heartbeat, the room is silent. Then, it erupts into cheers, laughter, and happy tears. Maureen lets out a small gasp before covering her mouth with her hands, her eyes welling with emotion. Trent and I are smothered in hugs and congratulatory words.

"Your grandmother would be so proud of you and happy for you both," Grandfather Samson says, pulling Trent into a hug. "And so am I."

"Wow," Gwen exclaims, "you all didn't waste any time at all—but in the best way!" She raises her glass with a bright smile. "I'm so excited to be an aunt!"

"Oh, Jenny," Holly says, pulling me into another tight hug, "I'm so happy for you."

I squeeze her back, but when I pull away, I notice her blinking rapidly, her emotions spilling over. "Holly, are you okay?" I ask softly.

She sniffles, waving a hand in front of her face. "Everything's fine, I swear. It's just . . . all these hormones."

I blink, processing her words. "Wait . . . what?" I whisper.

Greg places a hand on Holly's waist, his grin giving away the secret before she even speaks.

"We're pregnant too," she says, her voice thick with emotion. "Surprise!"

Laughter bubbles out of me as tears blur my vision. "Oh my gosh, Holly! We're going to have babies the same age. This is like a dream come true!"

"I'm going to be a double aunt!" Gwen cheers, her laughter ringing through the room as the others catch on, her face glowing with pure joy.

More congratulations and hugs follow, the room bursting with joy. I look around at this group—friends, yes, but more than that, family. This sense of belonging, of being loved, has always been something I longed for.

I place my hand on my stomach, where our little Hughes baby is growing—still barely noticeable beneath loose clothing, but there nonetheless.

Our baby.

This child will grow up in this beautiful, loud, and wild family. They will never know the harsh reality that I faced in my childhood, the ache of feeling unwanted. They will only know love and kindness and family.

Trent steps beside me, placing his hand over mine. I meet his gaze, tears in my eyes.

"I love you," I mouth to him.

His goofy grin spreads wide, his happiness reflecting in my own.

"I love you too," he mouths back.

It may have been an agreement that got us here, but it is love that will keep us together. For that, I will always and forever be thankful.

Your Reviews Matter.

No matter which version of this book you've read, leaving a review will help other amazing readers like you discover my work. If you enjoyed—or even just liked—Marry Me Tomorrow, I'd be incredibly grateful if you could take a moment to leave a review.

Amazon

Goodreads

Thank you so much for supporting this series, giving my story a chance, and helping to spread the word about my novels. Your reviews mean the world to me!

Acknowledgments

I'm not going to lie, writing this book was difficult. From the start of the Unlucky in Love series, Trent has been my favorite character, and maybe that's because he reminds me of my husband—a lovable, goofy guy with a heart of gold who would do anything for those he loves. Truly capturing Trent's essence on the page was easier some days than others, but I hope I did him and my husband justice.

With three novels under my belt now, I'm excited to see what this next year brings. I have, of course, the fourth and final book in this series to write, and also some other projects that I'm eager to share more about soon. Every day that I get to sit down and write at my computer and every positive review I read feels like a dream come true.

To the Bookish Babes—April, Bella, Courtney, Katelynne, Mallory, and Sara—you've been the brightest light on this indie journey. Navigating this indie author world isn't easy, but your encouragement and friendship make the challenges feel lighter. I'm so grateful for each of you—you truly are the best!

A heartfelt thank you to my incredibly talented cover designer, Melody Jeffries. Your creativity never ceases to amaze me, and the way you bring my characters to life is nothing short of magical. I have to say—this might just be my favorite cover of the series yet!

Another special thank you to my amazing team of editors at Ever Editing. Thank you for guiding me through the editing process and making this task feel manageable. A heartfelt thanks to Breanna for helping me bring this story to life and for being so accommodating when life got in the way and I had to keep pushing my start dates.

To my husband and kids, thank you for giving me the time to write and edit my stories, for listening to me go on and on about characters that only live in my head, and for giving me feedback on everything from random lines to (no one's favorite) the blurb. Your enthusiasm for my dream fills my heart with joy.

Finally, thank you to all my readers and those of you who follow me on social media. Without your support and willingness to take a chance on an indie author, my books would never have found their way into the amazing world of romance readers. You are making my dreams come true!

Jess Jefferies

Jess currently lives in Tennessee with her husband, three kids, and their dogs. She has a bubbly personality and can almost always be found with a smile on her face.

While reading has always been a passion of hers, she has also dabbled in writing short stories and poems since she was a little girl. *Thirteen Year Crush* is her debut novel, a romcom that released in March 2023.

When Jess is not writing, you can find her swimming with her kids, playing board games, or snuggling up with a book and comfy blanket.

Follow her on Instagram and TikTok:
@jessjefferieswrites
www.jessjefferieswrites.com